PRAISE

"This deft new novel imagines the aftermath of an actual event held in Canada during the 1930s. In *The Great Stork Derby*, Ann S. Epstein illuminates with laser-like precision a family torn apart by obsession, and the choices that reassemble it."
MICHAEL ANDREONI, AUTHOR, *THE WINDOW IS A MIRROR*

"The story of seventy-five-year-old widower Emm Benbow, who as a young husband pressured his wife to compete, now turning to each of his remaining children for a place to live, will break your heart even as it leaves you in awe of the resiliency of family."
DANIEL MUELLER, AUTHOR, *HOW ANIMALS MATE* AND *NIGHTS I DREAMED OF HUBERT HUMPHREY*

"Ann S. Epstein has created an engaging tale of family roles, secrets hidden in plain sight, an exploration of how perceptions can change depending on which family member is heard, and whether they conformed or rebelled against the role placed on them as children. Widower Emm Benbow's journey makes him question his values, discover some home truths about his children's view of their relationships as siblings and with their parents and grandparents, and ultimately whether keeping his eyes on the potential prize fatally damaged his chances to reconnect. There are plenty of moments of laughter and love as serious issues are explored and assumptions challenged."
EMMA LEE, FORMER REVIEWS EDITOR, *THE BLUE NIB*

ABOUT THE AUTHOR

Ann S. Epstein writes novels, short stories, memoir, and essays. Her awards include a Pushcart Prize nomination for creative nonfiction, Walter Sullivan prize in fiction, and Editors' Choice selection by *Historical Novel Review*. Her other novels are *On the Shore*, *Tazia and Gemma*, and *A Brain. A Heart. The Nerve.* Her work also appears in *North American Review*, *Sewanee Review*, *PRISM International*, *Ascent*, *The Long Story*, *The Minnesota Review*, and elsewhere. In addition to writing, she has a PhD in developmental psychology and MFA in textiles, which shape the content and imagery of her work.

Her website is: *asewovenwords.com*

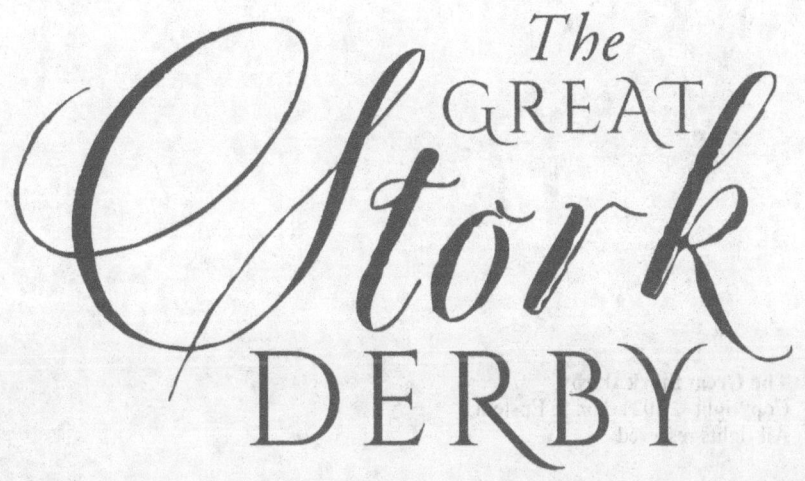

Ann S. Epstein

www.vineleavespress.com

Print Edition
ISBN: 978-1-925965-67-4
Published by Vine Leaves Press 2021

This is a work of fiction. Any similarity between the characters and situations within its pages and places or persons, living or dead, is unintentional and coincidental.

Cover design by Jessica Bell
Interior design by Amie McCracken

A catalogue record for this book is available from the National Library of Australia

To those who prove it's never too late to learn.

PART ONE:
EMM
MARCH 1976

CHAPTER I

Emm Benbow lay on the floor of his house for two days after falling for the third time in as many months. He was frightened, thirsty, and humiliated to be soaking in a pool of his own filth. Yelling "Help!" was pointless because he was upstairs in the bedroom and no one outside could hear. The phone rang once during that time, conceivably one of his children, although their calls were infrequent and Emm couldn't remember the last time he'd seen any of them. Another remote possibility was an old friend from his work days, eager to chronicle the betrayals of his own body. Most likely, it was the pharmacy calling to say that his blood pressure prescription was ready. Whoever it was, Emm couldn't move to get to the receiver. Fortunately, a neighbor spotted two copies of the *Toronto Star* in the driveway and knowing how punctual Emm was about retrieving the paper by seven each morning, rang the bell, banged on the door, and finally, after getting no answer, called for help. Emm passed out in the ambulance.

Now, his right flank bruised, he lay on his other side in a hospital bed.

"Mr. Benbow," said Dr. Sawyer, a brusque man half Emm's age with no bedside manner. Emm missed Dr. Marsh, his late wife Izora's childhood doctor, who'd also delivered and tended to their children. Back then, before national health, men like Dr. Marsh made house calls. Right to your own bed. This new fellow waved a piece of paper and said in an accusatory tone, "The blood test shows you took an extra dose of medication, which made your pressure drop too low. That's why you got dizzy and fell. You're lucky you didn't break anything this time, but a seventy-five-year-old man in your condition simply cannot live alone anymore."

Emm bristled. He couldn't imagine living anywhere else. The old house was where he'd grown up and returned to raise his own family. Granted, he'd gotten lax about its upkeep, but the foundation was solid. If only the same could be said of him. He'd done pretty well the last few years, especially since he'd switched from drinking whiskey to brewing tea, but if his hands were steadier than ever, his feet were not.

The doctor listened to Emm's lungs and scowled. "Why not move in with one of your children? Lord knows, you've got enough of them."

"They're busy with their own lives," Emm said, "and haven't the time or room to take in their old man." Even if they did, he had no desire to concern himself with their problems, or for that matter, to muster the energy to celebrate their successes. They had continually disappointed him with their shortcomings or expected inordinate praise for their minor achievements. Down or up, the house was in perpetual turmoil, a state that persisted until the last one finally moved out. After the hullabaloo of those years, all Emm wanted was to live out the rest of his days in peace and quiet. True, any offspring who were now living in cramped quarters might welcome the chance to move into the big old place with him. But none had suggested it, and Emm wasn't about to issue an invitation. Living alone suited him.

"You never know how your kids will react to the idea of your living with them," Dr. Sawyer said. "They might appreciate supplementing their income with your monthly government pension. In fact, I'm thinking of taking in my wife's mother, along with *her* check, if it means I can retire early." He attempted a chuckle, further proof that the man inside the white coat was tactless.

"They can manage on their own," said Emm. He'd paid the bills while they were growing up, except at the height of the Depression, when, six months shy of his thirtieth birthday, he'd lost his job. But he found work again once the war began, and supported the whole brood thereafter, if not in the grand style he'd once dreamed of, then good enough for most of them to find their way after high school. Having done his part then, he saw no reason to share his hard-earned benefits with them now. Nonetheless, Dr. Sawyer was right. Even if Emm could stay on his feet financially, it wasn't clear how he was going to do the same physically. The next fall could spell the end, and if he'd begun to decompose before he was found, it would be an inglorious one.

"Well, there's always the old age home, Mr. Benbow." The doctor scribbled a note at the bottom of Emm's chart. "A social worker will stop by to go over your options. I can't discharge you until you have a plan other than returning to your house." He walked to the opposite side of the bed, behind Emm, and headed for the door.

Emm tried rolling over to look at him, but the pain along his right side made him wince. So, he called as loudly as his bruised ribs permitted, "I'm not going to sell the place."

"What you do with your house is your business. My concern is your health, and you have two choices: your children or an old age home. See me at my office in two weeks or as soon as you're able to get around with a walker." The doctor's rubber soles squished down the corridor.

Through the window, Emm watched the wind batter a lone leaf from last fall still clinging to a maple tree on the hospital's front lawn. He considered whether he wanted to spend the time he had left alone or living with a member of his family. The doctor was right about Emm having plenty of children to choose from. When he and Izora had gotten married, they'd wanted to have several. At some point, however, things had gotten out of hand. Emm closed his eyes and thought back.

CHAPTER 2

Nearly fifty years ago, on a day as bleak as this one, Emm had raced into the kitchen of their tiny apartment. Izora, eight months pregnant with their first child, was resting her swollen belly against the pitted, grimy counter. He slowly waved the *Toronto Daily Star* in front of her pinched face so she could see the headline: "Rich Eccentric's Will Promises Fortune to Woman Having Most Babies in Ten Years." Izora turned off the water and listened as he read her the article.

> *The estate of Charles Vance Millar will pay a grand prize to the woman who gives birth in Toronto to the greatest number of children, as registered under the Vital Statistics Act, in the decade following his death on October 31, 1926. Mr. Millar, who has no heirs, described his will as "necessarily uncommon and capricious" and "proof of my folly in gathering and retaining more than I required in my lifetime." The prize, now worth $100,000, is to be invested, with the actual award based on its value at the time the winner is declared. In the event of a tie, the prize will be equally divided. Ladies (and the gentlemen who service them), on your marks, get set, the Great Stork Derby has begun.*

The rest of the article described how Millar, an oddball real estate investor and barrister, delighted in exposing greed. A favorite prank was to leave dollar bills on the sidewalk and watch passersby furtively pocket them. His will also awarded shares in the Ontario Jockey Club to pillars of the community who railed against gambling, and deeded joint ownership of a house in Jamaica to three fellow lawyers who detested each other, provided they lived in it together.

"Goodness," Izora laughed. "I can't tell if Mr. Millar was meaner, crazier, or simply had a weirder sense of humor than average."

"Whichever, he was certainly richer." Emm wrapped his arms around his wife, just barely. "Honey, what if we went after the prize and got rich too? With our first due next month, we've got a head start."

The baby kicked, and Izora moved Emm's hands so he could feel that restlessness too. They smiled at the moving bump in her belly. "I don't know, Emm. We both want a family, but shouldn't we take it slower? If we lose, we'll be stuck with more mouths to feed than we can afford. Or than we want." Izora had only one brother, whereas Emm had three brothers and two sisters. Izora pictured them having something in between.

"My parents weren't rich, but we managed. Besides, it was fun growing up in a madhouse with six kids. Always someone to play with. Or fight with. Or drive my folks crazy with." Emm pressed his hands against his wife's stomach, but the baby had settled down. He watched Izora stare past the doorway—to two bedrooms and a sitting room—then back to the eat-in kitchen. "Just think about everything we'll be able to give our children when we win the prize money."

She frowned. "IF we win. Even supposing we do, where would we raise them all in the meantime?"

"By the time our second child is born, I'll buy us a place of our own." Izora often accused Emm of talking big, but it was also one of the things that attracted her to him. He played on that magnetism now. "I was going to wait until we were snuggled in bed to tell you, but I'll spill the beans early to convince you I can take care of things." Emm spread a fistful of dollars on the table. "Mr. Withers did the books this afternoon and promoted me to foreman. Toaster sales are up twenty percent and exports could triple next year."

"Oh, Emm. That's wonderful." Izora clapped. The baby wriggled again.

"Now we can start to save money every month." Emm thrust out his stomach and waddled, anticipating the smile his wife usually bestowed when he imitated her condition.

Instead, Izora eased into a chair and kneaded her lower back. "It sounds exciting, but I'm worried. We could end up jinxing this baby before it's even born by planning the next one."

"And the next, and the next!" Emm tried to pull his wife into a standing position so he could dance her around the table. When she resisted, he shimmied across the kitchen by himself. "Where's the spunky girl I married?" He and Izora grinned at each other. They both knew she'd never been spunky. Determined, yes, but cautious in contrast to his devil-may-care spirit.

"Ask me again in a month, Emm, after we're sure our first baby is born healthy."

Emm gave her a thumbs up and turned to the paper's racing page. "Mr. Millar had a good head for business. Maybe I should invest our savings in the Ontario Jockey Club."

CHAPTER 3

Today Emm wished he had made that investment. The Club outgrew Ontario and went national three years ago, honored by the Queen of England herself. Its august membership was certainly in better shape than he was. Better yet, Emm wished he'd bought the land under which the Windsor-Detroit Tunnel was later built. That long-shot investment had increased Millar's estate tenfold by the time the Derby ended. Of course, if he'd done either, Emm would have a third option now. He could stay in his old house and hire a private nurse to take care of him. Heck, he could also pay for a butler and a valet, not to mention a cook, who could make the dishes Izora used to feed their family: maple-cured bacon casserole and butter tarts. Then again, if Emm could afford round-the-clock help, he'd be living in a mansion with servants to attend to him the very moment he fell.

Over the next few days, confined to his stale hospital bed, Emm brooded on these missed opportunities. He also found himself unexpectedly lonely. He called his two oldest children, more from a sense of obligation to tell them what had happened than any expectation that they'd visit. When neither answered, he didn't try again. He'd have enjoyed seeing one of his former work pals, but his phone book with their numbers was back at the house. Emm was forced to admit that no one, family or friend, would be checking up on him there and asking neighbors his whereabouts. He had only himself for company.

Emm's grievances mounted. The following week, the exercises with which the physical therapist tortured his body gave him another excuse for self-pity. By the end of each twice-daily session, his throbbing limbs didn't care where or with whom he ended up, as long as he got out of the rehabilitation ward and away from her cheery nagging. "Two more steps. Atta boy!" the young woman sang as if he'd gone a furlong instead of a mere foot. Emm had never cajoled his own children as much as she babied him. Or wheedled them into thinking pain was beneficial. He trusted they hadn't raised his grandchildren to believe such rubbish either.

Nonetheless, indignation at the assault on his body and dignity proved a good motivator. Two weeks after beginning therapy, Emm was capable, if not yet nimble, with his walker. One evening, as he eased himself into bed after a particularly arduous session, he heard a knock on his door. He was used to hospital personnel barging in, so the knock was unexpected.

"May I come in? I'm your case worker." The woman actually waited for him to say "yes" before entering. Mrs. Eudora Cray was a stocky, middle-aged lady with short gray hair and matching gray eyes. She pulled up a chair and asked if Emm needed anything: fresh water, a snack, his pillows plumped? Too stunned by her politeness to speak, he shook his head no. Mrs. Cray took a clipboard with an inch of papers from her briefcase. "I've set up an overnight visit at the Kingsbridge Home for the Elderly, Mr. Benbow. An orderly will take you in the hospital van tomorrow and bring you back the next day. After that, you'll have twenty-four hours to decide whether to move in there or be released to the care of one of your children. Please sign here, and initial here and here, and I'll make the final arrangements." She held out the clipboard and a pen.

"Suppose I don't like Kingsbridge? Surely there's more than one place where I can go."

Mrs. Cray flipped through her papers. "I'm sorry. None with a vacancy. At least, that you can afford on your pension. There is one nicer facility, Woodmere, but they only admit pensioners if our agency sends them a letter pleading extenuating circumstances." She smiled sympathetically. "I have several clients at Kingsbridge. It has a good reputation, within its price range."

Emm signed the forms. He was agreeing to a visit, he told himself, nothing more.

***

Early the next morning, before being allowed to finish breakfast, Emm maneuvered his walker down the hospital corridor and out to the van's mechanical lift, enjoying his first breath of fresh air in more than a fortnight. The driver and orderly didn't talk on the ride, which was fine with him. He smiled at the crocuses poking up through the frost-crusted ground, but soon relapsed into brooding. It seemed as though every week the *Star* had an exposé about nursing home abuses: chemical and physical restraints, people lying in their own excrement, aides slapping and cursing at residents. Still, that nice Mrs. Cray had reassured him this place wasn't like that.

A new sign at the bottom of the driveway said, "Kingsbridge Home for the Elderly." The fresh paint raised Emm's hopes, but they dimmed when the van reached the dingy, two-story, sprawling red brick compound. Parked at a loading dock on the right was a line of battered laundry and food delivery trucks. On the left was what passed for a garden: one flower bed, a spindly tree, and two rusting benches. Walkers, not to mention wheelchairs, could never navigate its narrow path. As the orderly lowered him to the ground, Emm saw carved in stone above the massive doorway, "Kingsbridge Home for the Aged and Infirm—Established 1895." He wondered how recently the facility had been renamed, and whether the building would ever be as spruced up as the new sign at the driveway entrance.

The pale, harried manager who came out to greet him needed some sprucing up too, but he smiled and waited patiently for Emm to lead the way inside. A faint odor of urine overlaid with a heavy dose of disinfectant hit his nose. Blue, green, or red lines painted on the faded linoleum floors marked the way to the residents' rooms, dining hall, or infirmary, the manager explained before leaving Emm alone briefly to fetch his paperwork. Emm's eyes followed the green stripe down a hallway ending in closed double doors. On either side sat old men and women, either resting their weight on canes or walkers or with their heads tipped back against the wall, snoring. Emm stopped a man pushing a cart piled with bed linens to ask what they were waiting for.

The attendant shrugged. "The next meal. They come out of the dining hall after breakfast and sit there until the doors open for lunch. Same thing until dinner. Don't get up unless it's to go to the bathroom." He snorted. "Which is actually pretty often for some of these folks. It's the only exercise they get all day." He pushed on, making a left turn when he reached the red line.

The manager returned with a small suitcase and Emm's file. He led him along a series of blue stripes until they got to the room where Emm would be spending the night. It held two beds, each with a red call button hanging on a tangled cord, and a nightstand with a lamp. On top of one, presumably his roommate's, was a radio, wind-up clock, and photo. Each person also had a two-drawer dresser with a mirror, so cloudy and scratched it barely showed any reflection. Emm didn't care; he had no desire to see what his once robust frame had shrunk to. Nor did he mind that there was only one shared closet; he had few clothes and wore those as many days as he could, it being difficult to go to the basement laundry room. Only when his diminishing sense of smell told him to change did he venture down the creaky stairs. Emm was not pleased, however, to see that the bathroom was also shared. It often took a while for him to do his business in the morning, and it would be even harder if someone was waiting outside the door asking how soon he'd be done. "Any private rooms in your establishment?" he asked.

"We had a couple, but none of our residents could afford the extra fee." The manager handed Emm the small bag, which contained starched pajamas, a toothbrush, and a towel. "So, we knocked down the walls and turned them into the men's common room. You'll see it after lunch."

"Men only?" wondered Emm.

At last, some color came to the manager's face. "We discourage mingling. It's led to some unfortunate ... incidents."

Emm could have assured the man that he posed no risk. He'd lost interest in canoodling after Izora died. More accurately, she'd lost interest following the birth of their last child. Emm couldn't blame her. Whatever interested these old folks, he couldn't imagine the ones he'd seen lolling in the hallway sneaking off to one another's rooms.

"We *do* like men and women to sit together in the dining hall, though," the manager added. "Ladies at the table makes for a more civilized mealtime." He cleared his throat and set Emm's loaner pajamas on the pillow. They were covered in a childish pattern of drums and horns. Emm wondered how many people, now dead, had worn them before him.

Emm signed another sheaf of forms and was left alone to "settle in." The manager told him to find his way back to the dining hall in an hour. Apparently, the home was testing him to see if he was fit and sane enough to live there, as much as he was checking them out to see if he wanted to.

Lunch was a sandwich of nameless meat on white bread with the crusts trimmed, a bowl of peeled and chopped fruit, and vanilla pudding. There were eight to a table and, Emm quickly calculated, at least twenty tables. Two places down, a man turned over his fruit. "Cake!" he cried. "Tuesday lunch we're supposed to have cake!" The man next to him took up the chant, pounding his fist. A few stopped to stare at them. The others continued to scoop the food into their mouths.

An aide hurried over. "Calm down, Mr. McCreedy. Cake is only served at dinnertime." The second man ceased chanting, but Mr. McCreedy continued to protest. "This is the third time in a week, Mr. McCreedy. I'm warning you, if you don't stop, you'll be sent upstairs. For good."

The dining hall grew quiet. So did Mr. McCreedy. He spooned spilled fruit back into his bowl and a peach sliver between his chapped lips. A collective sigh rose as those who'd stopped eating started again. Emm regarded their blank faces. What were their lives like before they ended up here? Did the men have jobs in sales or manufacturing? Were some professionals? Were the women mothers and grandmothers? Why weren't any of them living with their children?

When the meal ended, residents once again lined up in chairs along the hallway. Emm followed the handful of men who moved toward the common room. The women turned in the opposite direction. There were more of them, and Emm was curious to tag along, but the manager stood outside the dining hall, checking to see how Emm was fitting into the routine. Emm gave a polite nod but did not return the man's smile.

Unlike the pale green hallways, the common room was painted bright yellow. There were card tables with jigsaw puzzles, dominoes, and checkers, even a chess set, although the board wasn't set up. The only games Emm saw, however, were for children— Candy Land and Clue—and it wasn't clear if these were for the residents or the grandchildren who visited them. A child's drawing was taped to the wall, but the paper was so faded, it could have been done when Emm's own children were young enough to have made it. An activity schedule posted next to it, listing paint-by-numbers and yarn crafts, was three months out of date.

One solitaire player aside, the others sat at the far end of the room, watching *The Price is Right* on television. The volume was turned way up, which Emm supposed was for the hard-of-hearing. He was glad that was one infirmity that didn't yet plague him, but the blasting pained his ears. The man closest to the set changed the channel to *Let's Make a Deal*. Chaos ensued. One person swung his cane at the man's head, three pounded their walkers on the floor, and another threatened to smash his fist through the television screen if it wasn't switched back in time to see what was behind door number three. The channel-changer planted his feet and crossed his arms.

A burly aide strode into the room, sized up the situation, and confronted him. "Okay, Mr. Jackson. Upstairs with you. I'm telling the manager to call your son."

Mr. Jackson stood his ground for a few more seconds. Then, arms trembling, he switched the channel back (too late to see what lay behind the third door) and returned to his chair. Tears rolled down his stubbled cheeks.

"Don't call Donald," he pleaded. "I promise it won't happen again." Emm wondered which of his children the home would call if he turned obstinate, and whether any of them would come to his defense.

The attendant stood next to the television another five minutes, saying nothing, but staring at the men as they fixed their eyes on the screen. "Upstairs," one of them whispered. Those beside him nodded solemnly. Emm could swear the yellow walls shook, and not from the blare of the set.

***

Emm didn't stay to see who won that game show or those that followed. He headed to his room, got lost, and asked directions from an orderly mopping the floor. The man didn't answer. Either he had trouble hearing too or didn't speak English. Finally, after getting his walker stuck in a doorway and making several more wrong turns, Emm found his room and collapsed on his bed.

The rest of the afternoon he napped, waking once with a dry throat. He rang the call bell to ask for juice, waited ten minutes, and rang again. When no one came, he ventured into the bathroom. There was a glass beside the sink, holding a set of dentures, but nothing else to drink from. Emm used his hands to cup water from the faucet and rinsed the clipped hairs in the sink down the drain. He stumbled back to bed until roused by the home's dinner bell. Throwing water on his face and combing his thinning hair with his fingers, Emm set off for his next meal.

He could no longer keep track of where each corridor led, but he chanced on one with a green line, which he knew went to the dining hall. He was surprised not to see other residents walking that way too. He passed the entrance to a stairwell and paused to listen. At first there was silence, then a series of moans followed by shrieks. Emm heard hurrying footsteps, the sound of scuffling, then unintelligible yelling which he somehow knew was an attendant cursing a resident. An "upstairs" resident—immobile, incontinent, insane, or merely uncooperative. Emm stood frozen until a vibration nearly knocked him off balance. A disheveled man, in a hospital gown that hung open behind him, thudded down the stairs. In close pursuit was an orderly, who locked the escapee's arms behind his back, glared at Emm, and shoved the old man back up the stairs. Emm pivoted and raced down the green stripe faster than his walker had ever moved before.

He skipped the common room after dinner, foregoing hot chocolate and graham crackers. Child's fare, he thought, but probably laced with something to put old men to sleep. His instincts helped him avoid the corridor with the stairwell on the way back to his room. Soon after he'd crawled into bed, his roommate appeared. They introduced themselves. The man was friendly, but too hard of hearing to sustain a conversation. He kept calling Emm, "Mr.

Bendo." Emm didn't bother correcting him. He just listened as his roommate identified the people in the photo on the nightstand, turned on his radio at full volume, and went to sleep. When the man's snoring was steady, Emm turned the radio off and tried to sleep too, but the ticking clock kept him awake. It was near dawn when he finally drifted off.

In the morning, Emm declined breakfast and was waiting in the lobby before the van pulled up. As soon as they arrived back at the hospital, he went straight to bed, waking only when the lunch trays were brought around. He asked the aide to fetch the social worker. Right away.

"Good afternoon, Mr. Benbow." Mrs. Cray looked at Emm's full tray; even his cupcake was untouched. "Have you decided already? You have until tomorrow, you know. Unless you're anxious to sign the forms before the vacancy at Kingsbridge is filled by someone else?"

"No. I've decided I'd rather live with one of my children."

"I'm delighted that will work out for you. I have such a close relationship with my parents. When the time comes, they know they're welcome to move in with me."

"Can *I* live with you in the meantime?" Emm turned a schoolboy's eager face toward her, but he was half serious. She was kinder to him than he expected any of his children to be.

Mrs. Cray blushed. "I'm afraid it's against regulations for clients to live with their case workers, although I'm sure you'd make a fine house guest. Provided I could get you to eat." Emm obediently ate a spoonful of peas and licked the frosting off his cupcake. "I'll need your son or daughter to sign the release form and take responsibility for you before you can leave. After that, they'll need to notify my office of any change of address, to make sure you get your pension checks. And I'll visit with you every quarter, just to see how things are going." She took yet another set of forms out of her bottomless briefcase. "Whose name shall I enter under guardian?"

The word made Emm cringe, as if he were one of the "upstairs" residents. "The thing is, I haven't made up my mind. Or actually called any of my children yet."

Mrs. Cray's face registered surprise, then confusion. She flipped through her papers. "But according to our records, you have ..."

"Several to choose from." Emm finished her thought. "It's a difficult choice." He hesitated. "Before I make the call, can you arrange one more trip for me?" Mrs. Cray cocked an eyebrow but nodded for Emm to go on. "I'd like to visit the cemetery where my family members are buried."

"To talk to your late wife? I understand. I often speak to my Robert when I have an important decision to make. I'll reserve the van and schedule an attendant to go with you."

"I'd rather you come," Emm said. He gave her a mournful smile. "I'm bound to get teary-eyed, and I'd prefer a sympathetic soul like you along to prop me up."

"It's highly unusual." Mrs. Cray put away the forms. Still sounding uncertain, she said, "On the other hand, the exercise will do us both good and there's no regulation that forbids it."

"You might even say that comforting a lonely old man is part of your job description." Emm flashed his winsome salesman's grin.

Mrs. Cray laughed. "Is three o'clock satisfactory?"

"I'll be ready. Washed, shaved, and wearing clean clothes." A scruffier look might better prove that Emm qualified for "extenuating circumstances," but he'd learned as a car salesman that he was more likely to close a deal by hinting at his eagerness than by appearing too needy. At the cemetery, he would subtly persuade Mrs. Cray that a man who had worked so hard and given so much to his family deserved to live in a nicer place than Kingsbridge. Then she'd write the letter that would get him admitted to Woodmere. He pictured a sprawling one-story building around a central courtyard, with a well-tended garden in the middle. Admittedly, the odds of convincing Mrs. Cray weren't high, but Emm had sold a lot of cars.

PART TWO:
ARVIL AND IZORA
MARCH 1976

Emm stood next to Izora as she awoke from the anesthesia, the sound of voices singing "Away in a Manger" drifting in from the hospital corridor. Beside her lay a perfect baby boy with long lashes, creamy cheeks, and wet, brown curls. His eyes fluttered open long enough for Emm to glimpse dark blue before his son turned his head and immediately latched onto Izora's breast.

"A Christmas baby, Mr. And Mrs. Benbow," said Dr. Marsh. "You are blessed." Emm felt his face glow as brightly as the holiday lights festooning the ward. He'd insisted that Izora give birth in the hospital, not at home with a midwife, after reading in the newspaper that both babies and mothers were less likely to die. Emm trusted his mother's old-fashioned child-rearing methods—he and his siblings were ample proof that they worked—but at the same time, he kept up with the latest information. After all, if he weren't an avid newspaper reader, Emm might have missed the announcement of Mr. Millar's grand reward.

Izora didn't think going to the hospital was necessary. "Dr. Marsh said my body was made for having babies. Besides, York General costs money that we need for the baby."

"First, we need to guarantee the baby is healthy." Emm had lifted his chin and stared down his nose, the stern look that typically ended

any disagreement. However, to reassure his very pregnant and anxious wife, he'd added that they could afford the hospital fees. "Business at the factory is so good that Mr. Withers is doubling my Christmas bonus. Let's get child number one off to a good start, and make sure you're fit enough to get right back in the race."

Izora didn't argue after that. Emm wasn't sure whether she believed what he'd said about hospitals being safer or was simply relieved that his mother wouldn't be able to meddle during a home birth. Mrs. Benbow meant well, Izora conceded, but she'd complained to Emm that his mother could be pushy. She hadn't added "Like you," but Emm sensed the accusation. He didn't like to take no for an answer either. Izora, by contrast, took after her own mother, a meek and compliant woman, who never crossed their threshold unless she'd been invited.

"What shall we call him?" Emm asked, as the infant's perfect mouth dropped open and he began to snore. Before his wife could answer, he suggested the name begin with the letter A. "If we name our children alphabetically, it will help us remember the order they were born in."

"As long as we don't use up all twenty-six letters," Izora groaned. "How about Albert?"

"I like Arvil," Emm countered.

"What kind of name is that?" Izora cradled the baby protectively. "I want our children to have ordinary names. I hate being the only Izora, and, frankly, no one but you is named Emm."

"That name got me noticed by the boss and promoted to foreman. And yours made me notice you. Unusual names will land our sons good jobs and our daughters good husbands."

Izora sighed and sank into the pillows. Emm promised her he'd teach his son to protect himself from any teasing on account of his name. Izora said she knew he'd be a good father. They smiled at each other as the lights dimmed and carolers, holding candles, surrounded the bed. Nurses followed and then, joined by other new parents on the ward, sang "O Holy Night" to celebrate the arrival of the Benbow's Christmas child. It was a good start to life, indeed.

CHAPTER 4

Emm stood in front of his eldest child's grave. Frankly, Arvil was the only child he could fancy himself living with. Not because he planned to join him in his grave, of course, but because he remembered how wonderful he'd been as a boy and pictured the sort of man he would be now. Smart, strong, and successful. Admired by the community and adored by his family.

Mrs. Cray, likely assuming he'd come to seek his late wife's advice, had walked ahead to Izora's grave, on Arvil's left. She pivoted back when she saw Emm stop at his son's headstone, then read the words below the large cross: Arvil Denner Benbow, Private, 3rd Canadian Infantry Division, Born December 25, 1926, Died June 6, 1944, Beloved Son and Brother, Taken Too Young Fighting for Freedom. "I was twenty-five when the war ended," she said. "I only have a younger sister, so my family didn't lose any sons in the war, but many of my classmates perished. Five alone on D-Day, like Arvil. It must have been a terrible blow. He was your first-born?"

Emm leaned over to trace the long inscription, his tear-stained finger darkening the letters' grooves. "I would have had a quarry's worth of stones carved for Arvil if I could have afforded it. As it was, it took me ten years to pay off the engraver, even with the discount he gave to families of veterans. If I'd saved and invested that money three decades ago, I could afford to live at Woodmere today." Emm glanced up at Mrs. Cray before bowing his head and wiping his eyes.

She helped him straighten up and balance his walker on the soft spring earth. "I'm sure many other parents made the same financial sacrifice, but the words must have brought a lifetime of comfort. I'm sorry I didn't think to buy flowers before I fetched you at the hospital."

"It's kind enough that you brought me here. I wish I could come more often, but I'm dependent on my children to take me and visiting graves isn't on their list of things to do." Except for one child, who often visited a grave in another part of the cemetery, where Emm had never been. He did not mention this to Mrs. Cray. Nor had he ever spoken of it to anyone else.

"What was Arvil like?" Mrs. Cray settled her wide body in a comfortable stance and fixed her gray eyes on Emm. She appeared ready to listen.

Although he often thought of his son, it had been years since anyone had asked Emm about him. He took a minute to collect his memories, but once he started talking, the words poured out. "Arvil was the pride of the family. A real go-getter, like me. When he was ten, the paper had a contest to see which delivery boy could sign up the most new customers. Other kids knocked on a few doors after school when housewives were distracted cooking dinner. Arvil got up early every day for two weeks to catch their husbands when they left for work. He signed up five times as many houses as the second-place winner." The prize had been a new bicycle, to deliver the additional papers. "Izora wasn't happy about it. She wanted Arvil home more."

"Most mothers are like that. They worry about their children when they aren't close by."

"I think Izora got the notion from her father, actually. Lewis stayed home a lot. My father-in-law never pushed himself to work hard. He settled for being a clerk at a haberdashery." Emm grinned. "The man did wear spiffy hats, but they looked out of place with his bargain rack suits. If clothes make the man, then Lewis was a fedora with little mora." Mrs. Cray smiled at the rhyme.

"The one good thing Arvil got from Izora's side of the family was his sweet nature. He helped her a lot with the younger children. I wager my son changed more diapers than me."

"Robert and I never had children, but my little sister was a hellion. I love her dearly now, but Jorgie made my life miserable growing up. She broke my toys, helped herself to my clothes. It was hard on my parents too. She often got into trouble at school for mouthing off."

"Not Arvil. He was always respectful. Not that my boy was a goody two-shoes. He raided his friend's parents' liquor cabinet and got caught stealing cigarettes. But he was smart and very well-liked. A versatile young man who played football as well as French horn. Good dancer too."

Emm tried to shuffle his feet, but the soggy ground trapped his heels. "Arvil wanted to teach me and Izora to jitterbug. She was pregnant, I forget who with, so he demonstrated with me as his partner. We did fine until the step where the man throws the woman out and reels her back in?" Mrs. Cray nodded; she knew the move. "I was caught off guard and flew across the room into a pail of soaking diapers. I'm afraid that forever put the kibosh on pop doing the lindy hop."

Mrs. Cray's laugh was a tonic to Emm. Warm blood rushed through him the way it had in the old days, right after he'd swallowed that first shot of whiskey. He still missed it, especially when he was feeling down in the dumps, like after his recent fall. On the other hand, Emm was sure he would have been down on the floor a lot more the last ten years if he hadn't given it up.

"Goodness gracious, Mr. Benbow. Arvil sounds like a delightful child. No wonder you and your wife were proud of him. I'm sure his grandparents were too."

"As far as my folks were concerned, nothing was too good for that boy. They came to every ball game and concert too." Emm shook his head. "I can't say the same for Izora's parents. They couldn't afford to give him as much as mine, but they didn't even compensate by spending more time with him. Or the others. Lewis claimed he was too tired from working." Emm snorted. "And we'd practically beg her mother, Clara, to visit. I don't know if she was more frightened by the kids raising a ruckus, or by my mother, who was pretty strict about keeping them in check." Emm shrugged. "Izora could be a little lax that way."

"You said Arvil got good grades."

"Math was his favorite subject. He'd have made a fine accountant. He helped me figure out the family budget when I got laid off during the Depression. Then, instead of complaining when there wasn't money for the movies, he got a job as a ticket-taker and watched for free."

Mrs. Cray sighed. "I wish I had your son's head for numbers. I'm generally patient, but when the checkbook won't balance, I fly into a rage. Or as close to one as a person like me gets."

Emm couldn't imagine someone as gentle as Mrs. Cray getting angry, let alone throwing conniptions. "Arvil liked chemistry too," he continued. "He won the sixth-grade science fair for a project about the Toronto doctors who discovered insulin."

"They won a Nobel prize. Perhaps someday he would have too."

"The only prize I needed was for him to return home from the war."

Mrs. Cray looked again at the headstone. "Arvil. It's an unusual name, like Jorgie. My sister got teased a lot for hers. She likes it now, but I'm convinced it's what turned her into a troublemaker. It was her way of getting back at my parents for giving it to her."

"I taught Arvil to defend himself in case he got teased, but it wasn't necessary. He had this aura that deflected criticism. It did the opposite; kids were drawn to him." Emm grinned. "Girls especially. Halfway through high school though, he only had eyes for Jane. They planned to marry once he'd saved a little money. Then he got called up by the Army. Jane came with us to see him off at the station." Emm swayed. "He was killed on the first day of the Battle of Normandy."

Mrs. Cray helped him to a nearby bench and held his elbow as he lowered himself onto the seat. "Arvil sounds like a born leader. If he'd survived, he would have been more than a private by the war's end."

"He'd have gone farther than his old man, for certain, but not left me behind. Arvil would have taken care of me, either in his own home or at the best place in town. I wouldn't be in this situation if I hadn't sacrificed my son to my country." Emm waited for a reaction. Getting none, he continued. "Arvil would have shown his father gratitude. I can't say as much for the others."

"Perhaps you underestimate them. You don't know what they'll say when you call."

"To tell you the truth, Eudora. May I call you that? I'm having trouble deciding which child to ring up because Arvil is the only one I can imagine living with. Him and his wife, Jane." Emm studied the mud on his soles. "We lost touch with her after the funeral."

Mrs. Cray nodded. "The young get on with their lives. The old should too. I had to, after Robert died. We can't get stuck in the past or live in the pretend world of what might have been."

Emm gripped the arms of his walker.

"I'm sorry, Mr. Benbow. I hope I haven't offended you."

"No. You're probably right. He who treads water, no doubt, gets stuck when the tide rolls out." Emm beamed in response to Mrs. Cray's smile. "Besides, I'm only guessing what Arvil would have been like as an adult. Especially after the war. I imagine him as resilient, the same way I recovered from the Depression, gradually working my way up at the munitions factory. But many of the men I worked with said their sons returned from battle embittered. Especially those who saw comrades killed in front of their eyes."

"It's hard to see those you care about go down," said Mrs. Cray.

"It's hard to see yourself go down." Emm stood and walked the ten steps to Izora's grave.

Izora would not accept the Western Union telegram, so the boy handed it to Emm. He dug in his pocket for a tip, but the boy refused and retreated hastily down the front walk. Emm waited until the messenger had turned the corner before leading his wife to the couch and breaking the seal. "We deeply regret to inform you ..." He didn't need to read any further.

A week later, a letter arrived from Chaplain Richard K. Morgan. "It is with real sorrow that I write following the death of your son, Arvil. Private Benbow played a gallant part in our fight against the Germans, helping comrades who had been hit get to a place of safety before being mortally wounded himself. There is no one here who does not feel his death as a personal blow. Arvil was unfailingly cheerful, an excellent soldier, and a fine example to us all." The Chaplain's letter went on to describe the importance of the sacrifice made by Canada's youth, and their families, and assured the Benbows that their son was following in God's footsteps, paying a worthy price for the world's salvation.

Emm was the one who shed tears, copiously, throughout a beautiful summer that seemed as bleak as winter. To his surprise, Izora remained dry-eyed. At first, he thought she was being stoic for the sake of the other children, who ranged in age from seven to sixteen. But watching her listlessly smear fake margarine on toast, he concluded that she was numb. Gradually, what little energy she had disappeared altogether. She lost interest in taking care of her family. The house was a worse shambles than usual. Emm called on his mother for help, and advice.

Mrs. Benbow took charge. She cooked large pots of "Wartime Stew" (leftover bits of meat with cabbage and onions) for Emm and the children. Declaring that her daughter-in-law suffered from "weak blood," she plied her with Lydia Pinkham's tonic. After Izora left an open bottle on her nightstand and one of the younger children drank it all (Dr. Marsh had to be called in), Mrs. Benbow next advised her son to feed his wife iron-rich foods like beetroot and spinach. With vegetables being rationed, when they were available at all, Emm resorted to buying them from the black-market dealers who hung around the munitions plant at lunch time. Izora left the vegetables on the kitchen counter to rot until the flies outnumbered the children by a hundred to one.

Eighteen months after Arvil died, Emm buried Izora. The cause cited on his wife's death certificate was a fatal combination of diabetes and anemia. Mrs. Benbow took the latter as confirmation that she'd been correct in diagnosing Izora's ailment. Dr. Marsh declared, in plainer language, that his long-time patient was simply worn out. Emm, in a rare instance of disagreement with his mother, believed that his wife had died of a broken heart.

CHAPTER 5

The headstone on the grave to the right of Arvil's read: Izora Meara Oxmoor Benbow, Born February 27, 1904, Died December 4, 1945, Beloved Wife and Mother. To her right was the plot reserved for Emm Landis Benbow, Born August 08, 1901. Emm wondered what the date of death, now blank, would say. Ditto the inscription, which was up to his children to write.

Mrs. Cray stood aside to let Emm talk with Izora in private, but he beckoned her over. He was no more used to being alone with her in death than he'd been in life once the children started coming. "A much shorter inscription for your wife than for your son," she said. "Odd when you think that her life was more than twice as long as his. But perhaps those few words say it best."

"Yes," Emm replied. "A wife and mother was all Izora ever wanted to be."

"Then I hope she died satisfied, despite Arvil's tragic ending. Maybe her death came as a relief. As a young case worker, I counseled parents who lost children in the war. Many expressed a desire to join them in death. Of course, my job was to encourage them to live, but in hindsight, some might have been better off having that reunion sooner rather than later."

"Perhaps that's how Izora felt as well. Faith mattered to her. Before she got too busy with the children, she went to church most Sundays. I didn't, nor did I share her faith, but I suppose it provides solace, when tragedy strikes, if you believe that God's will is for the best."

Mrs. Cray admitted she wasn't a believer either, so they agreed to spare each other any more religious platitudes. Instead, she asked Emm to tell her what drew him and Izora together.

"She liked that I was ambitious, and I liked that she was quiet and undemanding. Other girls expected a date to include dinner, a movie or dancing, and an ice cream sundae. Izora was happy with a walk in the park and a root beer float. You know that song, 'Who could ask for anything more?' That was my Izora. They say opposites attract. I was the opposite of her father, and she was the opposite of my mother. Was that true for you and Robert?"

"Not at all. We were very much alike. Both kind and friendly, but basically homebodies. We enjoyed reading in the evenings and listening to music together. Mozart. And opera."

Emm grinned. "Bizet is okay, but Verdi is wordy."

"And Puccini?" Eudora Cray asked.

Emm thought a minute. "Obsceni." She grinned back. He said he and Izora liked popular music, the same singers but different songs. "She loved sentimental numbers, Al Jolson's 'April Showers' and Bill Murray's 'That Old Gang of Mine.' I went for the bouncy ones, like Jolson's 'Toot, Toot Tootsie' and Murray's 'Yes! We Have No Bananas.' Except, after she died, I found myself playing those old, sentimental records. 'What'll I Do?' and 'Tell Me You'll Forgive Me.'" He was glad Mrs. Cray didn't ask what he wanted to be forgiven for. Instead, she asked how Emm and Izora got along with each other's families. She said it was often a sore spot with her clients.

"I never had much to do with the Oxmoors. They seemed happy to have Izora off their hands, financially speaking. Her brother, who was a couple of years older, was too busy with his own life to care about me. And vice versa." Emm's lips curled. "Reggie was lazy, like his father. Content to just be a stock boy. He married eventually, but goodness knows how he managed to support his family. I haven't spoken to the man in years. Decades, actually."

Mrs. Cray wondered how Izora got along with Emm's family.

"I was the fourth of six. My brothers and sisters accepted her as one of the crowd. She got a kick out of our shenanigans, even if she was too shy to join in." Emm guffawed. "One Christmas we exchanged gag gifts, like exploding cigars and whoopee cushions. The children rolled on the floor, mimicking the gassy sounds. My mother told them to stop, but the more upset she got, the more the rest of us, especially me and my brothers, egged them on."

"Did your father step in?"

"It's the only time he goaded us to turn against my mother too." Emm was surprised when Mrs. Cray expressed sympathy for his poor ganged-up on mother. "Boys will be boys. Men can't resist potty humor." Her pursed lips told Emm that now wasn't the time to recite a fart rhyme. He smiled conspiratorially. "Even Izora laughed. Louder than I'd ever heard her before."

Mrs. Cray raised her eyebrows. Emm sat back satisfied. "I gather, apart from that incident, it was rare for Izora to go against your mother?" Emm nodded yes. "When your wife did, though, whose side did you take?"

Emm squirmed. "The fact is, even though my mother could be hard to take, she was usually right. So, I took her side or stayed quiet and let my mother have her way." He closed his eyes and, when an image of his haggard wife filled his mind, forced himself to picture a youthful Izora. "Except once, early on, when I agreed with Izora. Over clothes." Mrs. Cray nodded for him to go on. "When we began dating, in the early twenties, women started to wear their skirts shorter and looser, the flapper look. They also wore—was it called a chemise?—underneath. My mother was the old-style corset type, dresses just above the ankle, *not* an inch below the knee. The second time Izora came to our house for dinner, in a short, pleated skirt, my mother tut-tutted that the new fashions set a bad example for future wives and mothers."

Mrs. Cray took a deep breath and asked if Emm had disagreed. "I didn't have the nerve to do it to her face, but after Izora bobbed her hair, I bought her a cloche hat and asked my mother if she didn't agree that Izora looked lovely in it. The subject of her clothes never came up again." Seeing Mrs. Cray's nod of approval, Emm didn't confess that he also thought a fashionable wife would help him get ahead. She asked about their engagement.

"Are you old enough to recall the Listerine ad, 'Always a bridesmaid, never a bride'? Izora was twenty, but girls in their teens, including my sisters, began fretting about finding husbands."

Mrs. Cray, who'd come of age in the Depression, allowed that women got married much later then.

"I would have been happier waiting until I was more established too," said Emm, "but I didn't want Izora to worry. Or go off with someone else. So, after we'd been dating a couple of years, I proposed." He smiled at the memory. "It was the same year Pep-O-Mint Life Savers added Lime, Lemon, and Orange. Izora loved them."

"I remember when they added cherry and pineapple," Mrs. Cray said. "Cherry was the big prize, but my favorite flavor was pineapple."

"To propose, I bought a dozen packs, undid them, and picked out the citrus ones. Then I re-rolled them, hiding an engagement ring in the middle. The ring was small—that's all I could afford—but I knew it would stand out on Izora's slender hands."

"How romantic. What did she say?"

"Nothing. She slipped the ring on her finger, and popped three Life Savers, one of each flavor, in her mouth. Then she held out the pack to me. I also put three in my mouth, and we kissed, a sort of drooling smooch, and laughed and hugged." Emm's eyes teared.

Mrs. Cray handed him a tissue and fished a roll of Life Savers from her purse. When Emm expressed surprise, she laughed and said she picked up the habit of keeping a roll handy from her mother, who used to dole them out to her and her sister. "I often give them to clients to put them at ease." She offered Emm cherry and chose pineapple for herself. Then she asked about the wedding. "It's traditional for the bride's family to pay, but you said Izora's family didn't have much money."

"We kept it to our immediate families—of course, mine was much bigger—and two friends apiece. Izora only asked one, her maid of honor, so I invited a third, Mr. Withers, my boss at the toaster factory. It was a good business move." A cloud passed overhead at the same time a frown crossed Emm's face. "There was a dust-up over the cake. Back then, it was customary for the mother of the bride to bake it. Ordering one from a bakery was unusual. But store-bought was the only luxury the Oxmoors could afford, and Izora had her heart set on a tiered wedding cake. My mother insisted it was bad luck and that she herself would make the wedding fruitcake that had been in her family for generations."

Mrs. Cray asked how it was resolved.

"We had the fruitcake. No one on Izora's side ate it."

With some hesitation, Mrs. Cray asked about bringing up the children, where differences of opinion often caused major rifts with grandparents. "Not that Robert and I had to deal with it, but given how conservative his mother was, I was happy to avoid those battles."

Emm said his mother was a mix of modern and old-fashioned. The newest thing after the Great War was an emphasis on hygiene. Mrs. Benbow scrubbed the children until their skin was raw, which made Izora wince. On the other hand, she pooh-poohed the latest Freudian theory that children were physically fragile and emotionally vulnerable. "For example, our second born was sensitive and easily frightened. She was terrified of the bogey man in the basement. My mother thought the best way to get over her fear was to face it. So, whenever she needed something from the root cellar, she'd send Bruna down to get it. If Izora offered to go, my mother insisted, 'Let the child do it.' After a while, Bruna stopped saying she was afraid of the bogey man."

Mrs. Cray shuddered. "I'm not surprised. Your mother took his place. She was scarier."

"Nonsense. She was right. My mother had more experience raising children than Izora's mother. And looking at Izora's ne'er-do-well brother, it's obvious my mother did a better job." Emm snapped his fingers and smiled. "Mrs. Benbow, good as gold. Her children did as they were told."

Mrs. Cray was stone-faced. "So, no second thoughts or doubts about how you raised your children?"

Emm stared at his feet. "Just one. I wish I'd spent more time with them. My mother held that too much attention spoiled children. Of course, when you have a houseful, you can't worry about each of them. I'm sure she had to believe that what she did was best. Izora wanted to enjoy each child, but she ran out of time, and energy, too." Emm looked to his left. "It was different with Arvil, our first born. We both doted on him. Until all the others started to come along."

Mrs. Cray glanced toward Arvil's headstone too. "He didn't turn out to be spoiled."

"I wish he was alive, but it's Izora I miss every day. I can't believe she's been dead more than half again as long as we were married. After Arvil was born, she continued to sing Christmas carols year-round. The walls of the house still ring with them." Emm pushed his walker back to the bench. Mrs. Cray sat beside him. "Izora turned everything into a celebration, even the first day of school, or learning to ride a bike. She made each child feel special on his birthday."

"I have eighty-year-old clients who to this day complain a sibling's party was better."

"Izora let them choose the kind of cake they wanted—from the bakery. And in addition to getting their own presents, they could pick one to give to each of the other children. They were so proud to be the 'giver' and took great pains choosing just the right gift."

"What a lovely idea. It's clear your son extended the thoughtfulness he learned at home to his friends at school, and later to his comrades in the service."

Emm nodded. He'd always taken credit for raising his first-born to be a leader, in front of the pack. Maybe, in her behind-the-scenes way, his wife had done as much, or more, to turn Arvil into the fine young man he became. "Then the celebrations stopped."

"When Arvil was killed?"

"Before. Soon after one of the younger children was born. I can't remember which. Izora became ... listless." Emm's shoulders drooped, as if in sympathy. "I used to do crossword puzzles in the paper. They kept my mind sharp, and I learned odd facts that amused my customers. After Izora lost heart, I bought her a book of puzzles, thinking it would bring back her old spark. I checked now and then to see if she used it, but the squares were as blank as the look on her face."

"How terribly sad."

"After she was gone, I looked for the book, thinking it might help light a spark under me." Emm closed his eyes and did a mental walk through the house. "I never found it. Maybe one of the kids took it. Or threw it out."

"They wouldn't have understood its value."

"I suppose you're right. It wasn't worth much. But they were also careless about things that cost a lot. Spoiled, I dare say. Most of them were too young to remember the Depression."

"Children do take things for granted unless they're very poor. Fortunately, between your parents' help and your ability to find work, your children never went without food and shelter."

"I didn't stint either. I bought them nice clothes and expensive toys. Unfortunately, they lost or tore the clothes before they outgrew them and broke the toys hours after they took them out of the box. I'm as good at math as Arvil was, and if I calculated how much money I'd have if my children hadn't wasted my hard-earned dollars,

I could move into Woodmere tomorrow." Emm glanced sideways at Mrs. Cray. He didn't want to push his hard-luck story too hard.

She wasn't looking at him, though, but at a small nearby head-stone. "Like your children, Jorgie and I were lucky enough to survive the Depression with tightened belts but not empty stomachs. Losing their mother must have been a much bigger trauma for your children. You, too." She asked to hear more about the years after Izora died.

Deciding to hold off before making the next pitch, Emm told her about working at Inglis Munitions Factory during the war and going into sales when it ended. "It suited my personality. I began with small appliances. Returning soldiers were starting families, so there was a demand. I sold radios, irons with settings for the new synthetics. Our best seller was fancy kitchen clocks."

Mrs. Cray scrunched her face. "Robert and I received one as a wedding gift, with a big orange sunburst. It was too hideous to hang, but we left a nail in the wall so that whenever the aunt and uncle who'd given it to us visited, we could put it up for their benefit."

"A pox upon clocks whose bursts are the wursts." Emm waited for her smile, which came quickly. "A few years later I read about the surge in Canadian automobile production and decided cars were the future. My first sale was a blue and white Dodge Kingsway, with big headlights and huge fins. The salary wasn't much, but I made good money on commissions."

"It sounds like you found your calling." Mrs. Cray nodded encouragement.

"Reading *How to Win Friends and Influence People* was what really helped me succeed. I was depressed after Izora died and that book helps you break out of mental ruts. Not just in work, but in life. I tried to pass on Mr. Carnegie's lessons to my boys. Some of them have my head for business." Too late, Emm realized he'd sabotaged his case. Bragging about his own recovery and the sons who could help support him hardly qualified as "extenuating circumstances." He looked toward Mrs. Cray, who merely nodded. As much as Emm liked her, he barely knew her. Had she been unaware of his secondary motive in visiting the cemetery or cagey enough to deflect him?

"Aside from Mr. Carnegie, I'm sure your knack for rhyming helped you recover and stay lighthearted after Izora's death. Did you make up silly verses to cheer up the children too?"

Emm shook his head, as much in resignation about his future as in answer to her question about the past. His talent hadn't emerged until ten years later, when he entered a jingle contest: "Bad household smells making you sick? Clear the air with a spritz of Air-Wick." The stakes were lower than the Stork Derby, but the waiting period was only a month. "I got twenty-five dollars and a box of air freshener sticks. Since then, I win a few hundred bucks a year and more useless stuff, but it's fun to keep my hand in it." Emm had nothing to lose by bragging now. "Perhaps I'll write a few verses to read to Izora the next time I visit. If you're kind enough to bring me again."

"Did you ever try your hand at serious poetry?" Mrs. Cray suggested writing about aging and loneliness. "The funny bits are a good escape, but if you don't also face your fears, they hang around and fester." She adjusted her scarf. "There was some wisdom in your mother's advice."

"She was talking about children. Not grown-ups."

Mrs. Cray cocked her head but said nothing more about writing poetry. Instead, she asked about the rest of Emm's life, outside of work, after Izora's death. He talked about going out for drinks with the guys from the salesroom now and then, a habit that continued for a while after they retired, when most, like Emm, had switched to tea and coffee. He rarely saw them now.

"I meant, what about your life with the children once Izora was gone?"

"I felt left out, not being part of the baby boom. Not that I wanted more kids, but I was sad that the person I'd had them with wasn't around to make more. Does that make sense?"

Mrs. Cray nodded sympathetically. "Do you think Izora would have wanted more?"

"Hmm. Our youngest was nine when the war ended. Maybe after such a long break, and without the pressure of the Stork Derby, she'd have warmed to the idea. That is, once she got over grieving for Arvil." Emm recalled Izora's excitement before the first couple of children were born, but somewhere along the way that sense of anticipation had vanished. Perhaps Dr. Marsh had been right after all. It was motherhood itself, not the loss of Arvil, that had killed her.

Mrs. Cray looked at her watch.

"Do you think that in my haste to bring so many lives into the world, I was responsible for ending hers too soon?" Emm peered anxiously at Mrs. Cray's face.

"I can't answer that question."

"It's too late to ask forgiveness, but perhaps I can make it up to her. Do something for our children." Emm looked up at the steel gray sky. "What, though? I'm the one asking for their help, not the other way around. Any bright ideas?"

"I can't answer that either, Mr. Benbow. I have no idea what your children need, nor do I know you well enough to say what you can offer them."

"Other than sharing my meager pension check." He sighed, letting go of Woodmere.

"It's a place to start." Mrs. Cray opened her briefcase. "Have you decided who?"

Emm ran through the list in his mind. One child was as good, or bad, as another. With "A" for his son Arvil an impossibility, he might as well begin with "B" for his daughter Bruna. If she didn't work out, he'd move on, alphabetically, to each of the others in turn.

A hearse stopped two rows over. Emm heard the mourners' high-pitched keening as they circled the fresh grave. The sound reminded him of the anguished cries he'd heard yesterday at Kingsbridge. He swore to use every lesson from Dale Carnegie to win over his children, so they'd welcome him in their homes. The ever-present cloud between his resolve and failure would be the threat of "upstairs." And the silver lining, from a place higher still, would be Izora's forgiveness.

PART THREE:
BRUNA
MARCH 1976

Once home, Arvil was as easy to care for as he'd been to bring into the world. The rare times he fussed, Izora quickly soothed him by humming Christmas carols, even after winter turned into spring. When their son was barely five months old, Emm suggested to his wife that they start on baby number two.

Rocking in the chair that Mrs. Benbow had used to nurse Emm and his siblings, Izora planted her feet on the fraying braided rug. "I'm just getting to know Arvil. What's the rush?"

"A hundred thousand dollars. Maybe hundreds of thousands by the time the contest ends." Articles about the Stork Derby had stopped appearing a month after it was announced. Emm was confident that most families had forgotten it, increasing their odds of winning.

"We have to wait until Arvil is weaned before I can get pregnant again."

"Wean him now." Emm gently pulled the baby off his wife's breast. Arvil sucked air but didn't cry at the interruption. His dark blue eyes studied his father's face. Emm hefted the baby in his hands. "Look how big our son is already. He'll be fine."

"I don't know that I will." Izora said she'd miss the tug of Arvil's soft lips at her nipples. "Even if I gave up nursing now, it could still take a while before I get my monthlies again."

"All the more reason to get started as soon as possible." Emm felt the baby's wet bottom and handed him back to his mother. *"I kept my part of the bargain."*

Izora held Arvil close and entwined her fingers in his curls. *"What do you mean? We made a deal to enter the baby contest, and I've done my part by starting us off with this marvelous little boy."* She cooed at Arvil, who gurgled back and kicked his chubby legs.

"I put down a deposit on a house last week. A three-bedroom bungalow on the edge of town with a garden in back. The lot is big enough to build extra rooms when we're ready." Emm waited for his wife to beam with excitement. She'd always wanted a house of her own, but her parents couldn't afford one. Nor did they see the need for more space with only two children.

Izora's brief smile quickly gave way to nervous dismay. *"How far is it from the markets? Is the street safe for children to play outdoors?"* Arvil rooted at her breast and she began to feed him again. *"We ... I don't want to fill up the house too quickly. Or add on too many rooms."*

"Come on, Izora." Emm wrapped his arms around her and the baby. *"My folks agree that going for the prize is a good idea. They're willing to help out until the ten years are up."*

"What about after that?"

"Don't you trust their judgment? And mine?"

Izora conceded that the Benbows were sensible people, with lots of experience raising children. Also, that Emm worked hard at being a good provider. She buried her lips in the folds of Arvil's belly until he giggled and grabbed her hair. *"Okay,"* she said at last, *"it's a deal."*

Emm kissed her and left for his parents' house. While he helped his father install some shelves in the basement, his mother went to Emm and Izora's apartment armed with baby bottles and tins of sugared, diluted cow's milk. She announced that she would feed Arvil and sent Izora to bed *"to build up her strength for the next one."*

It was weeks before Izora could rest properly, her breasts swollen *and aching. The baby, on the other hand, seemed unperturbed. He snuggled against whoever fed him, including Emm, who gave him the bottle now and then so his wife could take a nap. "See," he told her, "Even Arvil agrees it's time for us to make him a brother or sister."*

As if to affirm what he said, two months after Izora's periods resumed, she was pregnant again. It was another easy labor when their daughter was born on April 10, 1928. They brought her home to their new house. Izora called the baby Bruna on account of her brown eyes, a name sufficiently odd to satisfy Emm. Unlike her big brother's outgoing personality, however, Bruna was a quiet, serious child, slow to warm up. Rather than smile and giggle when her mother sang, Bruna watched as if to inquire, "What am I to make of this?" When Arvil toddled past or poked at this new creature, she didn't cry out, merely observed to see what he would do next.

Only once did Bruna cry loudly. Izora, busy bandaging Arvil's knee after a tumble, was late nursing her. When Bruna whimpered, Emm picked her up until Izora was free, but the infant, soon frantic with hunger, sobbed and flailed. Nothing Emm did could soothe her. He thrust her into her mother's arms when Izora finally rushed over. After that, Emm didn't trust himself to take care of his daughter, and the child became as wary of him as he was of her.

CHAPTER 6

Emm waited in the hospital lobby for Bruna to get him. The morning after visiting the cemetery, he'd phoned, told her about his fall, and asked if he could live with her. There were several seconds of silence, before she finally said, "This is rather sudden."

"What do you mean? I've been in this place for weeks. The doctor says I'm ready to be discharged, but I can't stay on my own anymore. My blood pressure could drop too low or shoot too high. Either way, I've got to stay with someone who can keep a regular eye on me."

"I meant, I wasn't expecting you to want to move in. With me. Have you asked any of the others?"

"No. I haven't even told them what happened to me yet. I was hoping you would."

Bruna sighed. Emm knew she'd make the calls. It was in her obedient nature. "Besides," he continued, "you're the oldest. And it's not like you have anyone else to take care of."

After Izora died, Bruna had dropped out of high school to help raise her siblings. Not until the youngest left home did she go back for her diploma and then to college. She'd never married or had children of her own, instead devoting herself to her nieces and nephews. Bruna was also a responsible, if not enthusiastic, daughter. As if checking off an item on her "to do" list, she called her father on the first Monday of every month. Unfortunately, as it turned out, her most recent call had been the day before his fall. Emm couldn't remember the last time he'd seen her, though, and it had been years, if not decades, since they'd hugged.

"So, you're saying it's my duty?" It was more a statement than a question. Bruna sighed again. "Okay, Father. But give me a few days to get ready."

"What is there to get ready?" Emm was eager to escape the confines of the hospital and that nagging rehab therapist, even if it was only to his daughter's two-bedroom apartment. The place was already child proofed. Her nieces and nephews came over all the time when they were growing up, and now there were great nieces and nephews to entertain. Surely, the apartment was safe enough for an old man shuffling around with a walker. "It's not like you have to spoon feed me. Or bathe me. I'm not a baby. I can take care of myself. I just can't live by myself."

"There are still a few matters I ought to attend to. Things are set up to keep children from getting into them, but you'll need to be able to reach and take things out of the cabinets. That means I'll have to move some things lower down, where the little ones could get them. Child-proof locks should solve the problem, assuming you don't have arthritis yet?

Emm said his fingers were as nimble as ever. He waited for Bruna to ask why, in that case, he'd let the house go downhill. It's not like *he* had anyone or anything else to take care of either. Instead, she said, "I guess I also need time to get used to the idea." She asked if Emm could request that the hospital permit him to stay another week or if she should call someone in administration.

Emm said he'd take care of the matter himself. Delaying his discharge was the last thing he wanted to do, but it would give him another opportunity to talk to Mrs. Cray. She'd understand his impatience and wish him well. Emm needed her sympathetic sendoff. It had been a long time since he'd made a significant change in his life, and he didn't know what to expect.

A week later, when Bruna finally pulled up, she was ten minutes late. Given how punctual she was about her telephone calls, Emm wondered what had kept her. The paint on her old Chevy wagon was riddled with rust spots, but it was solid and roomy. Big enough to take a carful of kids to the zoo, and more than ample to drive Emm, his walker, and one suitcase to his new home.

While Bruna signed a form accepting responsibility for him and pocketed instructions for Emm to check in with his case worker once a month, he studied her. She was slightly overweight, and her mostly gray hair was pulled back into a bun that was coming loose. When had she aged so much? He shuddered to realize she was only six years older than his wife had been when she died. By then, Izora was thin and pale, however, a contrast to all those years of being swollen and flushed with pregnancy, whereas Bruna still looked robust and full of efficient energy. With another jolt, Emm realized that his daughter was only a few years younger than his case worker, whose advice he valued, even if he didn't always agree with or plan to act on it. Maybe Bruna would turn out to be someone he could lean on after all, and not just until he was more mobile.

Emm enjoyed the ride through the city. He didn't get out much, even before this latest fall. Occasionally he met one of the other retired salesmen for lunch, although one by one, they'd grown homebound too. He envied those whose wives were still alive and spry enough to take care of them. After the first couple of grandchildren, and the obligatory sharing of photos, none of the men talked about their families. Emm didn't know whether they'd lost interest or could no longer keep them straight. He himself had given up long before the great-grandchildren arrived.

When they got to her apartment, Bruna settled Emm on the couch and sat opposite him in an armchair. The living room furnishings were clean but worn, like the car and Bruna herself. Emm saw a bookshelf stocked with children's books, bins with toy cars and trains, and dolls in different states of undress. A square of linoleum had replaced the carpet in one corner, on top of it a small table strewn with paper, paints, and crayons. Along one wall, there were baskets of yarn filled with Bruna's knitting projects—a baby blanket, the sleeve of a child's sweater, a pair of tiny socks.

Bruna suggested they have tea, and Emm followed her to the kitchen, surprised that it was so large. He sat at a table, surrounded by eight chairs, but expandable to hold more, and gaped at a rack of hanging pots and pans, enough to cook for a small army. Early spring sunlight streamed through a south-facing window lined with containers of growing herbs. Bruna took a tin from her well stocked pantry, and milk and lemon from the stuffed refrigerator. Emm wondered whether she remembered that he liked his tea with lemon and extra sugar, but her routine movements suggested that she was simply in the habit of setting out everything her guests might want.

Emm was watchful, as though he were visiting a foreign country. His own kitchen, once a hub of activity, was now a gloomy room in which he did little more than heat canned soup or toast a grilled cheese sandwich. Would he ever feel at home in this hive of domesticity? Not until Bruna closed the refrigerator door, and Emm saw the drawings taped to it, did he feel a twinge of familiarity. He was taken back to a time when Izora was alive and the children were young. Only instead of shaky and backwards letters spelling MOMMY and DADDY, the ones he saw now were for AUNT BRUNA. There was no reason for Emm to expect pictures made for him, but a few empty spaces anticipating his arrival would have been a nice welcome.

He and Bruna made small talk while they sipped their tea. Emm asked if she had watched any of the Winter Olympic Games in Austria last month; she hadn't. Actually, neither had Emm; he just thought it might lead to a conversation. Bruna asked if he'd been following the Patty Hearst case in California. Emm said he had, until his stay at the hospital had cut him off from the daily paper. He missed it and asked Bruna whether she had the *Toronto Daily Star* delivered.

"I sometimes read a copy at work, but mostly I catch the news on the radio while I cook dinner."

"Would you mind transferring my *Star* account to your address?" Emm asked. When Bruna hesitated, he added, "Don't worry. I'll pay for it. I don't intend to be a freeloader."

She gave him an exasperated look. "I don't care about the money. I'm just opposed to clutter." Then she smiled. "Although you probably think my place is already cluttered with all of the kids' paraphernalia." Her serious face softened into an amused look that Emm thought she must easily give to a child. Not that he wanted to be treated like one, but he wouldn't mind more of those smiles himself. He promised to carry the newspaper to the incinerator after he finished reading it each day, and Bruna said she'd call the circulation department tomorrow.

Emm closed his eyes and, when Bruna asked if he was tired, admitted he wouldn't mind a nap before dinner. As she led him down the hall to his bedroom, he peeked into hers, small with a single bed and a dresser covered with family photos. Emm wondered if he was in any of them. His room, across from the bathroom, thank goodness, was a little bigger, but there was still barely space for a bunk bed, one night stand, and two dressers. Bruna set his suitcase on the lower bunk. "The kids like the top one," she explained, "now that they're old enough to climb the ladder." Did she think Emm would feel bad about displacing a great grandchild from the bottom bed?

Bruna opened the drawers of one dresser, and the closet. She'd already fetched all the clothes he'd left behind when he was rushed off in the ambulance as well as his toiletries and pills, which were now on his own shelf in the bathroom. His radio was on the night-stand. "Your house is in bad shape," she commented, "Much worse than I remember from my last visit."

"Well, that was a long time ago. Very long."

Bruna emptied Emm's suitcase, stowed it in the closet, and turned out the light. He pulled back the quilted spread, relieved to see plain blue sheets on the bed, but looked warily at the top bunk. He didn't relish trying to sleep with a child bouncing overhead or crawling into bed with him after awakening from a bad dream. How often did one of them spend the night up there?

***

Emm awoke to the smell of food, a good, familiar smell. He went to the bathroom, sighed when he saw the clean sink, and pushed his walker to the kitchen. Bruna had set two places, opposite each other, at one end of the big table. She pointed to the chair that would be his from now on. As she dished out the food, Emm smiled in recognition. Maple-cured bacon casserole, Izora's speciality.

"When did you learn how to make this?" he asked, breathing in the sweet-salty aroma.

Bruna looked puzzled. "I made it all the time after Mother died. You don't remember?"

Emm shook his head and closed his eyes before taking the first bite, the better to focus his senses on the taste. His daughter gave him seconds without having to ask if he wanted more. "Now that I think of it, you loved helping your mother in the kitchen. You were like her shadow."

"I was happier being with her than playing with my friends. What else do you remember about Mother and me, especially from when I was very little?"

Truthfully, Emm couldn't recall much of anything good, but he saw no harm in making up positive memories if it made Bruna happy. "You were the oldest girl, so your mother fussed over your hair and clothes. With your dark brown eyes, your best color was light blue. Everyone told your mother blue was for boys, but she stood her ground. She was right. You looked so pretty. And you were always well behaved. All you had to do was gaze at people with those peepers, and they were mesmerized. They stopped criticizing your clothes and praised your manners."

Bruna looked thoughtful. "Being well behaved mattered then. Nowadays, children are supposed to be independent. At least, that's what I aim to teach them." She smiled. "Only so far, none has shown an interest in learning to cook for themselves They're happy to leave it to me."

"I hope they say thank you." Emm did and congratulated himself on his decision to live here. He'd regain his strength in no time. His eyes opened wide when Bruna brought out dessert, a dense cake topped with shaved chocolate swirls. She told him it was a butterscotch torte.

"I'm sure I don't remember your mother making anything this fancy."

"She didn't have time to fuss. Nor did I back then. It was hard enough to feed everyone the basics." Bruna cut them both generous slices. "It's a luxury to bake treats for the family now."

Emm ate three mouthfuls before telling Bruna the cake was delicious. She blushed. "I'm glad you like it, Father. I enjoy baking. It will be nice to have another regular customer."

Bruna cleared the table and served them tea. She put lemon wedges and the sugar bowl next to Emm. "What do you think you'll do all day while I'm at work?"

Emm hadn't given it any thought. For the past several weeks, his days had been taken up by physical therapy and the hospital's other routines. Before that, at his house, he'd filled up the hours reading the newspaper, preparing plain meals, and napping. He couldn't remember what else occupied his time. Nor, he suddenly realized, could he remember what kind of work his daughter did. Rather than admitting this lapse, he simply said, "Tell me what your day is like."

He gathered that she was an elementary school teacher, left for work at 7:30 and was home by 5:30. That meant Emm would have ten glorious hours to himself. Bruna would feed him breakfast and dinner and prepare whatever he liked for lunch. She offered to bring books from the library, and once Emm felt up to it, he could catch the bus there on the corner. It was only two stops away. She asked if there was anything else he needed to keep him busy during the day.

Emm shrugged. "Not really. I sleep a lot."

"That's not a problem while I'm at work. But I'm giving you fair warning. One night a week, one of the kids sleeps over, to give their parents a break. And on weekends, the house is busier than a downtown bus station. All the Benbows, along with their children and grandchildren, hang out here." Bruna did a mental tally. "Fourteen—well fifteen—if everyone shows up."

Emm's vision of a restful existence, all meals provided, began to fray. Bruna would pay more attention to everyone else in the family than to him. That's what she'd done for the past thirty plus years. It was silly of Emm to expect that things would suddenly change. He stood; Bruna stood too. Emm wondered whether she was going to give him a good night hug or was waiting for one from him. The second hand on the kitchen clock ticked five times. "Thank you," he said at last and headed down the hall, eager to enjoy a night of solitude while he could.

"Don't forget to take your blood pressure medicine," Bruna called after him. "The label says you're supposed to take it at bedtime."

"I know," Emm called back. In fact, he'd forgotten, having grown used to a nurse's aide bringing the pill to his hospital room. Nevertheless, it irked him to be reminded, as though his daughter had become his mother. From now on, he'd show Bruna he was perfectly capable of taking care of himself. He wasn't a baby. Nor was he a patient any longer.

***

Two days later, Bruna brought Jonah home for a sleepover. Emm guessed the child was about five. He couldn't recall which of his children's children he belonged to and was too embarrassed to ask. Jonah, on the other hand, didn't hesitate to pepper Emm with questions. How old was he? Did he like baseball? Could Emm drive a motorcycle? Was he going to die? Soon? At Bruna's suggestion, Jonah called Emm, "Great Gramps." Emm had no idea whether the boy's other great grandparents were alive.

Right after dinner—macaroni and cheese, a gingerbread cake Jonah helped decorate with raisin eyes and white chocolate chip buttons—Emm pleaded fatigue and crawled into the bottom bunk. In fact, he wasn't the least bit tired, and lay awake, listening to Bruna and Jonah in the living room, setting up the train set and crashing cars. An hour later, his daughter helped her great nephew get ready for bed and climb the ladder. She tucked him in and kissed him good night.

The minute she left the room, Jonah prattled on about a child at school who had taken another child's lunch and had to miss recess. Emm pretended to be asleep, snoring as loudly as his roommate at the Kingsbridge Home. Soon, Jonah began to snore for real. Emm spent a sleepless night. He couldn't wait to get back to bed the next morning once Bruna took Jonah home and herself to work. Emm didn't even bother to read the newspaper first. He dreaded the weekend.

CHAPTER 7

Saturday left Emm dazed. A procession of his grandchildren dropped off their kids at Bruna's, while they ran around doing errands or, he suspected, going back to bed. The little ones tried to draw Emm into their play, but he couldn't crouch on the floor with their blocks and puzzles. Instead, he watched from his armchair and tried to amuse them by making up ditties about their toys. He told the girls that "Barbie doll was a gangster's moll. Her boyfriend Ken was good with a sten." With the boys he tried "A pox on Brix-blox." Coming up with a rhyme for GI Joe would have been easier, but Emm was silenced by the toy soldier, thinking of the real Arvil and the family he never had.

The children stared blankly when Emm recited his rhymes, then resumed playing without trying to engage him again. He sat quietly after that, marveling at their concentration, until they began fighting over whose turn it was to bang with the xylophone mallet or steer the locomotive. Only after one child got conked by falling blocks, and another was poked with a paintbrush, did Bruna separate the combatants and appease them with ice cream and sugar cookies.

"Wouldn't it make sense to step in a little sooner?" Emm ventured, as a boy ran his truck across Emm's foot and crashed it into the girls' tea party. "They're getting rather worked up."

Bruna shrugged. "Have you forgotten what young children at play are like?"

Emm stiffened. He remembered the mayhem all too well. The house was a battlefield of scattered toys and shrieking children until his own mother had countered Izora's permissiveness by imposing some much-needed manners and decorum. "I haven't forgotten. In fact, your style of discipline reminds me of your mother's."

"I take that as a compliment, although I doubt it was intended that way."

Emm glared. "It wouldn't hurt you to take a lesson from your grandmother instead."

Bruna glared back. "Grandma Bessie? She was a great role model. Like the stepmother queen in *Snow White and the Seven Dwarfs*, only instead of waging a beauty contest, she had to prove she had greater authority when it came to raising children. Grandma Bessie even criticized Mother for sprinkling a teaspoon of sugar on our Cheerios. She accused her of not feeding us properly." Bruna snorted. "As long as we're trading insults, you remind me of Grandpa Henry."

Emm cocked an eyebrow, waiting for the unflattering comparison to his father.

"You were both cold and distant, and deferred to Grandma Bessie. It was worse when you did it, though, because you were betraying your own wife when you took your mother's side."

Mrs. Cray's words echoed in Emm's head. She, too, had questioned his mother's behavior and his deference to her when she disagreed with his wife. Nevertheless, he defended his mother, and his father too. "Maybe you were too young to appreciate everything my parents did for us during the Depression. They made sure you children got fed and went to school nicely dressed, put presents under the Christmas tree, and even treated you to the movies. Their generosity didn't stop once I got back on my feet either. They helped hold our family together after your mother died. Unlike the Oxmoors, who were barely around while Izora was alive and pretty much disappeared after their daughter was gone."

While conceding that was true, Bruna insisted that a little less Grandma Bessie would have been better. She brought up the time Emm's mother had taken her grandchildren to see *The Wizard of Oz*. Bruna had been terrified of the Wicked Witch, and her grandmother had taunted her for being a "scaredy cat." Seeing how agitated the memory still made Bruna, Emm recalled what Eudora Cray had said about Mrs. Benbow turning into the bogeyman. An image of her looming over Bruna gave way to one of her towering over him as a little boy. He wished it away, and repeated that Bruna wasn't sufficiently thankful for everything his mother had done for them.

Bruna snapped that Emm was insufficiently appreciative of everything she had done after Izora died, dropping out of school to raise her brothers and sisters and keep house for him. She turned back to the children, but not before snarling, "Maybe you'll be more appreciative of the sacrifice I'm making now."

***

Sunday was worse than Saturday. Mid-morning, three generations of his descendants began to arrive at the apartment and settle in for the day. Bruna set snacks, drinks, casseroles, and dishes on the table. Grown-ups wandered between her living room and kitchen, eating, talking, laughing, and arguing. Children ran around, grabbing food and toys in one place, dropping them in another.

Emm watched warily from his armchair. He received a few obligatory kisses and questions about how he was feeling but was otherwise treated like the old piece of furniture he sat on. His attempts at conversation backfired. He asked one of the men how his son was doing and was told, "He's right there. Ask him yourself." Emm hadn't recognized his grown grandson, let alone his grandson's family. After that, it was safer to keep to himself, but Emm was irritated not to be acknowledged, and made a fuss over, as the patriarch of this outsized gathering.

Early afternoon he shuffled to his bedroom to take a nap. People stepped aside, or shooed children out of the way, but said nothing about him leaving. He closed the door and stuffed a towel under the crack, but the blare of *Sesame Street* permeated the walls. The kids sang along with jingles and kept the volume louder than at the old age home, even though they had perfectly good hearing. Emm couldn't tell which annoyed him more—Grover's cheerfulness or Oscar's grouchiness. Fed up with it all, he marched into the living room and turned the television down.

The outcry was immediate. "Dad," "Grandpa," "Great Gramps." Every possible name for him was paired with "Why'd you do that?" "Turn it back up," or "Look how you've upset them." Bruna scrunched her lips as if to say, "I warned you weekends would be like this." His hearing was acute enough to pick up some parent muttering, "Selfish old man." Only one person, perhaps a daughter-in-law, said in his defense, "He's been ill. Perhaps we can take the children outside to play for a bit." But no one stood or put on their coats.

Emm decided to go for a walk himself. For two hours, he pushed his walker around chilly streets, stopping now and then to rest on a bench. There was a sunny park nearby, but it was overrun with children whose parents let them run wild and sitting with them was no better than staying at Bruna's. Not until it was nearly dark, and he figured that all the Benbows and their offspring had left, did Emm go home. Or to the place he was now supposed to consider home.

"I was getting worried," Bruna said when he let himself in. "If you hadn't come back in the next ten minutes, I'd have gone out looking. Are you hungry?"

"No. Just tired." His voice sounded as petulant as a child's, even to Emm. Like a cajoling parent, Bruna nevertheless warmed a plate of food and made a pot of tea. Feigning nonchalance, Emm began to eat. Bruna sat opposite him, but he refused to speak to her.

"Enough." Bruna rose and began wrapping leftovers. There weren't many. "You're acting like the spoiled child you accuse the kids of being. I'm tempted to lay down the law with you like Grandma Bessie did with us." She shoved a covered casserole in the refrigerator. "If you can't stand being part of such a big family, you never should have had one in the first place. Especially to win that crazy baby-making contest. I don't care how big the prize was."

Emm winced. "It wasn't just for the money. I thought a houseful of kids would be fun. I enjoyed having lots of brothers and sisters."

Bruna pursed her lips. "I can't say that I did."

Nor, Emm admitted to himself, did his image of a rollicking brood of his own come true. He'd started out excited before each birth. What would this new child be like? Would he take after his mother or his father? When the child got older, what would Emm teach him? Emm tried to pinpoint when his balloon had burst. Being a father responsible for a big household wasn't the same as being a little boy who didn't have to worry. Emm sought sympathy from Bruna. "Maybe it would have been different if your mother hadn't died."

"Mother would have been happy with three or four kids, and she might have lived to enjoy the grandchildren and great-grandchildren you can't abide. Or even bother to learn the names of."

Emm put down his fork. "You never did like me, your own father."

"Because you didn't like me. Or spend any time with me. The only one you cared about and paid attention to was Arvil."

"He was the best of the whole lot of you."

"He wasn't the saint you claim. Big brother teased us, and he wasn't above giving us a good smack, a hell of a lot harder than one of Grandma Bessie's. He just knew not to do it when you and Mother were around." Bruna's chest heaved. "Arvil was even better at emotional torture. He knew that stories about monsters under the bed would scare us more than a raised hand."

"You never told us."

"Mother had enough on her hands. And you would have blamed *us* for provoking *him*."

Emm studied the drawings on the refrigerator. There were new ones from this afternoon. No child had offered to make one for him, but Bruna's name, crudely written, was on virtually every picture. "Did your name ever cause you trouble when you were a child?" he asked.

Bruna stopped bustling around the kitchen, surprised by the question. "No. I actually felt lucky that my first and last names started with same letter. It was easier to learn how to spell and write them. In college, my friends jokingly called me "Brünnhilde" because I was quiet and had a lousy singing voice. At one point, I even wore braids, but the look didn't fit me. Too childish."

"What do you think killed your mother?" The question popped out of Emm's mouth.

Bruna, startled, recited the words on Izora's death certificate. "Diabetes and severe anemia."

"Do you think one or both were caused by her having so many children?"

"I have no idea about the physical toll of bearing children. I never had any."

Emm looked at his well-nourished daughter, her comfortable kitchen. "I always wondered if your not marrying or having children was your way of repudiating your mother."

Bruna sucked in her breath but said nothing. Emm wasn't sure what her silence meant. Given her harsh words for his mother, he doubted she was too polite to speak ill of the dead. He wanted to break through her shell. "Earlier today you said that less interference by grown-ups was better for children. So how can you criticize me for standing back from all of you?"

"Don't twist my words. Laissez-faire doesn't apply to parents the same as grandparents." Bruna's eyes bore into him. "Admit the truth. You weren't a very good father. Or husband."

Emm's temples throbbed until he thought his head would explode. He tried to talk, but his throat was constricted, as if his daughter had shoved her fist down it. Bruna rushed over and leaned his body against hers as she helped him to the couch. She made him lie down with his feet elevated and fetched a cold compress for his forehead. For a second, he was afraid she'd sing him a lullaby and was grateful when she instead brought him a glass of water. They listened in silence to his breathing. After a few minutes, he could almost feel his blood pressure return to normal.

The concern in Bruna's voice sounded genuine when she asked Emm whether she should call his doctor, if there was anything else she should do. Emm shook his head. It was one thing to be taken care of by your mother or your wife, quite another to be dependent on your daughter. He let her walk beside him to the bathroom to take his pill, and she stood outside his bedroom until he turned off the light and closed the door. Emm slept until the next morning, not even waking during the night, as he usually did, to use the toilet. His urgency when the sun rose was painful.

CHAPTER 8

Bruna cancelled that week's sleepover so Emm could get another good night's rest. They spent evenings in front of the television, their eyes on the screen so they wouldn't have to talk. He watched the sitcoms she liked—*All in the Family*, *Maude*, *Mary Tyler Moore*—and felt a soft spot for the beleaguered Archie Bunker. Bruna listened to his news programs and gave him tea.

They both sat forward the day the CBC announced the verdict in the Patricia Hearst trial: "The famous heiress, who took the nom de guerre 'Tania' in honor of Che Guevara's martyred lover, was convicted of armed bank robbery and given the maximum sentence of thirty-five years. The jury decided that Hearst, kidnapped two years ago, was a willing accomplice of her captors, a left-wing guerilla group calling itself the Symbionese Liberation Army. Her flamboyant attorney, F. Lee Bailey, who spilled water on his pants during the closing arguments and was suspected of being drunk, has not said whether the legal team will appeal the decision."

"I've been following the case in the *Star*," said Emm. "The defense argued that she was brainwashed, but I say she was a rich girl getting back at her father. She got what she deserved and can rot in prison. I'm just glad it's not our country's tax dollars paying her room and board."

"How can you say she was a voluntary participant in the robbery? The poor young woman was held in a closet and raped. She was a victim. It's a classic case of the Stockholm Syndrome."

"What?" Emm recalled reading about it but couldn't remember what the term meant.

"It's when hostages identify with their captors and express sympathy for them. They even take on their beliefs and behaviors."

"To the point of becoming terrorists and toting machine guns?" Emm sneered. "I still say she was a spoiled rich girl, rejecting her parents' values. In the deadliest way possible."

"She was a neglected rich girl, and the SLA gave her the close family she never had as a child. Patty didn't want to reject her father. She was hungry for his love, and this was the sad and misguided way she showed it." Bruna looked down at her hands. "It's not so hard to understand."

Emm was incredulous. "You're taking her side because you identify with her? You think I neglected you?" He snorted. "Well, none of my children, including you, turned out that bad."

"We didn't turn out that great either."

Emm couldn't dispute that. All the same, he refused to be judged so harshly, as if he were somehow responsible for Patricia Hearst shooting up a bank and plotting to overthrow the United States government. He struggled to his feet. "I'm not going to live here if that's how you feel. I won't walk on eggshells around you. At my age, I deserve peace and quiet. And respect." Emm pushed the walker toward his room. "Sons appreciate their fathers more than daughters do. They know what it means to work hard to feed their families. I'll move in with Cleon."

"Be my guest. If he'll have you. Let me know by tomorrow if I should call your case worker or if you can declare your innocence and independence yourself." Bruna turned off the television and brushed past Emm, headed for her own room. "To answer a question you didn't ask, Father. I never had children; not because I don't like them. Just the opposite. But I prefer to take care of other people's kids so I don't have to face the coercion and abuse of their fathers. My decision not to marry or have children wasn't a rejection of Mother. It was a rejection of you."

CHAPTER 9

"Mr. Benbow. You weren't due to check in with me until next month. I hope nothing is wrong."

Emm had hoped Eudora Cray would be happy to hear from him. Not that she sounded unhappy, but her voice was uncertain. "More a case of 'not right' than 'wrong,'" he said.

"You've been at your daughter's for less than two weeks. Why not give it a little longer? Another move so soon may jeopardize your healing. Consult with Dr. Sawyer before you decide."

"Humph. That man is barely competent to look at my bruised ribs, and I've got a case of bruised feelings. You're the expert when it comes to human behavior."

"Well, that is my domain." The lilt in Mrs. Cray's voice told Emm his compliment had pleased her. "Tell me, how did Bruna hurt your feelings?"

"She's angry at me all the time. I've read enough articles to know that some older children never forgive their parents for having more kids. They feel cheated of affection."

"Using that logic, Arvil should have been the angriest of your children. According to you, though, he was the sweetest and kindest."

Emm hesitated. "Yes, Arvil was a wonderful boy and grew up to be a fine man. I can't say the same of his sister."

"Now, now. You mustn't be too hasty. Let's start with the basics, which I was going to review during your home visit. Is your daughter taking care of your essential daily needs?"

"The apartment is cramped, except for the kitchen. I have to share my bed with a child."

"I thought Bruna lived alone. Did she have to take in the child of another family member? A foster child?"

Emm heard Mrs. Cray rifling papers. "It's a great niece or nephew," he answered.

"Well, which is it?"

Emm realized that he sounded as if he were losing his marbles. "It rotates," he explained.

"Oh my. That can't be good for the children."

"Well, it's only one a day a week."

Mrs. Cray took a deep breath. "Ah, you mean a sleepover at their auntie's? How lovely." Emm pictured a slow smile spreading across her wide face. He coughed. "Of course, children can be restless sleepers," she added. "Do they kick you in bed? That's quite bad for your bruises."

"No. They sleep in the top bunk."

Another breath before Mrs. Cray asked, "So you actually have a bed to yourself? Every night of the week, even when a child is there?" Emm conceded that he did. "What about meals? Is your daughter feeding you adequately?"

"Quite well, in fact. Bruna enjoys cooking, and she's rather good at it, I admit."

Mrs. Cray finished going through her checklist. She asked if there was a problem with ventilation, heat, bathing? Anything that would qualify as a reportable offense? Emm answered no to each item. Bruna had even reminded him to turn up the heat if he felt chilled after she left for work in the morning. And she bought the soap and toothpaste he favored. "Okay, Mr. Benbow. It sounds as though your daughter is making an effort to take good care of you. Physically."

"But not mentally. She's doing her duty, but she begrudges my being here. Nearly fifty, yet she still complains I paid more attention to her big brother than to her. Remember, you were the one who said that in the families you counseled, grown siblings never got over their rivalries."

"So I did. But every family has its squabbles. That doesn't mean they're unfit to live together. I often find that if parents simply acknowledge how their adult children are feeling, and apologize for any hurt they inadvertently caused them, the children can get over a sense of having been treated unfairly. Sometimes it's too late—the parents are dead—but you're still alive."

Bile rose in Emm's throat. "I have nothing to apologize for. Bruna was loved and well taken care of as a child. Of course, I mostly left that job to Izora. I was too busy trying to earn a living. Besides, girls naturally cling to their mothers, not their fathers. Didn't you?"

"No, actually. I had more in common with my father. We spent hours hiking together or at the library. It left my poor mother to deal with my rambunctious sister, which wasn't fair to her, but it was bliss for me." Mrs. Cray sighed. "Don't forget. I was the older sibling."

Emm would not be convinced. "You're the exception that proves the rule. There's nothing I can do to make things work out with my daughter. She's too set in her anger."

"You're sure you won't reconsider?" Emm again heard Mrs. Cray consulting her notes. "I see that the next oldest child, Cleon, is your son. Daughters generally make better caregivers."

"I still maintain I'll have better luck with one of the boys. Men don't hold grudges." Emm thought back to the hullabaloo last weekend when he'd turned down the children's television show. It was the women, wasn't it, who'd raised such a ruckus? "All the same, would you call Cleon and ask for me? Kind of pave the way, put in a good word for him being nice to his old man?"

"I'm sorry, Mr. Benbow. I can arrange the transfer, but you'll have to call him yourself." Mrs. Cray hesitated. "If I may offer a piece of advice, however. Give some thought to what you might do differently so your stay with Cleon is not a repeat of the troubles you had at Bruna's."

Emm agreed. Not because he thought he'd done anything wrong, but to please Mrs. Cray. Unlike his daughter, her heart was soft and her kindness toward him was genuine. Eudora's anger toward him would be more upsetting than Bruna's. He also owed it to Izora to try harder. She'd been too timid to lash out at him in life, so Bruna had become her avenging angel in death. Emm was no saint, but he wouldn't follow the dictates of a child. He'd reform on his own terms.

PART FOUR:
CLEON
APRIL 1976

Bruna was even younger than Arvil had been, barely four months old, when Emm told Izora they should get started on the next baby. Her menstrual cycle soon resumed, but she begged him to wait. "Please, Emm. I'm only twenty-four and already I feel like The Old Woman Who Lived in a Shoe."

"You're not backing out, are you?" He heard his voice rise on the last two words.

"No. I mean, I don't think so ..."

"It's been a long time since we made love." Emm took Izora's hand and leaned in close, like a ten-year-old schoolboy revealing a secret. He said he'd read in the paper that abstinence increased a man's virility, although he didn't mention it was written for those desperate to have their first child, not seed a large family. "My little general and his soldiers are all rested up and ready to fight," he whispered. Desire for his wife, and the prize, aroused him in equal measure.

"But I'm not ready," Izora insisted and, for the first time, refused to have sex when they went to bed. In the middle of the night, she got up to give Bruna a bottle and tuck in Arvil's blankets. His legs, still running in his dreams, always kicked them off. Before she could drift back to sleep, as she usually did, Emm mounted her. "Please, no," she tried to push him off.

"I'll be gentle," he said. *"You don't have to do anything, just lie still and rest."* Izora stiffened, but this time she didn't resist, and Emm hastily finished.

The next morning, she was tightlipped. Emm, contrite, brought her breakfast in bed and played with Arvil before going to work, leaving an hour late. When he got home, she was still agitated and impatient with the children. She said her mother once told her a woman couldn't get pregnant if she didn't want to. Emm scoffed that it was an old wives' tale. Nevertheless, his guilt was assuaged when, the following week, she leaned against him as he nuzzled her neck.

Emm held back from saying *"I told you so,"* nine months later, on May 13, 1929, while Izora lay on the maternity ward enduring her first difficult labor. Dr. Marsh administered extra doses of morphine and scopolamine, and Izora awoke groggy and in pain, nothing like the peaceful state Emm recalled after her other deliveries.

"You might want to slow things down," the doctor said the following day, standing beside the bed as she tried to nurse their new son, Cleon. The baby was having trouble latching on and screamed and writhed in frustration. *"It's not good for you or for your children."*

Izora inserted her left nipple into Cleon's mouth, and he managed to start sucking. *"What could go wrong?"* she asked, her eyes wide.

"For you, low iron in your blood. A greater chance of miscarriage. And an even harder labor if the amniotic membrane ruptures." Cleon lost the nipple and began to wail. Dr. Marsh guided his mouth back into position and continued. *"I think this little guy will be fine, but your next baby could be born too early or have defects like poor eyesight, even retardation."*

Izora had looked at Emm as their son continued his struggle to nurse. He'd debated telling the doctor about the contest but was embarrassed to admit it to this man who was the opposite of competitive, and probably wouldn't understand Emm's driving ambition to win.

Cleon, either sated or having given up, had by now fallen asleep. Izora collapsed on the pillows and closed her eyes. Dr. Marsh patted her hand and said he'd check on her tomorrow, after she was back home. He turned to Emm. "Call me immediately if your wife starts to bleed."

It was clear from the moment they walked in the front door that Cleon was a colicky baby. It didn't help that Izora's milk was slow to come in and not plentiful when it did. Perhaps that was why, two months later, Izora was pregnant again. She didn't know until she started bleeding and Dr. Marsh, responding immediately when Emm went to fetch him, said she'd miscarried. He took Emm into the sitting room and told him to leave Izora alone for a while. Emm bristled but said nothing. He left with the doctor and returned shortly with his mother, who was more than happy to help with Arvil and Bruna. She promised to restore order to the house.

Oddly, after the miscarriage, Izora's milk began to flow copiously. Cleon almost choked at first but soon got the sucking rhythm that had eluded him since birth. He was still small, especially compared to his older siblings at that age, but he lost that sunken, hollow look.

"He'll be a bruiser yet," said Emm, as much to reassure himself as Izora. She remained unconvinced, however, until Dr. Marsh examined the baby and said there was nothing wrong with him. Whereupon Emm, his bluster justified, promised to personally guarantee their son grew up strong. Izora turned over worrying about the third child to him while she devoted herself to the other two. Arvil continued to thrive, and Bruna relaxed with her father in the background.

Three years into the Derby, life began to seem more manageable. With Cleon at her breast, Bruna at her knee, and Arvil racing about, Izora admitted to her husband that she'd overreacted. "You're right. It would be foolish to stop now."

Emm danced around the kitchen. Millar's dollars danced around in his head.

CHAPTER 10

"Cleon, it's Dad." Emm tried to make his voice sound weaker than he felt without seeming too needy. It was like closing on a car; you wanted the customer to think you were eager to make a sale and thus offering him a good deal, but not so desperate that he doubted your competence.

"Oh, hi. How are you feeling? Bruna taking good care of you?" Cleon turned down the television, but not before Emm heard a sportscaster shout "Another save for Wayne Thomas!"

"Actually, that's why I'm calling. I'm not healing as fast as I should here. Bruna's doing her best, but she's gone during the day and there's no one around to help me." Emm waited for a cluck of sympathy, but Cleon was silent. "We thought it would work better if I lived someplace where a person was home all the time. To keep an eye on me. The social worker agrees."

"Well, I'm at work too, Dad." Cleon was a high school coach. "Hockey season is finishing up, and the baseball team is already starting spring practice."

"Hold on a second while I sit down." Emm held the receiver near the wheels of his walker so Cleon would hear them as he pushed it across the floor. "There, that's better," he sighed. "I was thinking of Betty. She's home alone all day now that the boys are grown up with families of their own." Emm was proud that he remembered Cleon had two sons, Mark and Paul, even if he couldn't recall the names of their wives, let alone the number and names of Cleon's grandchildren.

Cleon was quiet a long time. Emm wondered if he was watching the game, or coming up with a reason to say no. At last, he spoke. "The thing is, Dad, Betty likes it just being the two of us. You know how she keeps the house spic and span. She doesn't even want the kids to come over. She'd rather visit at their houses or see them when the family gets together at Bruna's."

Emm hid his irritation behind a chuckle. "I'm a seventy-five-year-old man. I don't make a mess like a little kid."

"I know, Dad, but ..."

"Suppose I fall again, after Bruna leaves for work? I could lie there for hours before she found me. What if I hit my head? Or cut open a big gash?" Emm waited for Cleon to imagine him lying in blood and excrement, dying without dignity. "Remember all the times I was right there to pick you up whenever you fell. Which you did a lot as a boy. Before I helped you muscle up."

"You threw the ball to me a few times when you got home from work." Cleon clicked off the television set. "But to tell you the truth Dad, it wasn't until I sent away for the Charles Atlas Dynamic Tension Program, when I was fourteen, that I turned into a body builder."

"That's not how I remember it." Emm groaned and coughed, but not too loudly.

"I'm sure you did your best, Dad. I know what it's like to be a father, and you had a much bigger family to support than I did. You were tired at the end of the day."

"Even if I didn't spend much time with you, I didn't hold back on encouragement. That's more than you can say for a lot of fathers. They run down their kids, always criticizing them."

Emm counted to five before he finally heard his son answer. "Okay, Dad. We'll give it a try. I'll talk to Betty." Cleon took a deep breath. "When were you thinking of moving in?"

"Is tomorrow too soon?"

CHAPTER 11

Two days later, Emm stood in the foyer of Cleon's small but immaculate house, stunned by his son's appearance. Once a trim athlete with a full head of dark hair, he was now bald with sunken cheeks, and wearing a Toronto Maple Leafs sweatshirt stretched over a beer gut. Emm couldn't remember when he'd last seen his son—was Cleon at Bruna's last weekend?—but he'd clearly been through a long slide, not a sudden downfall. Cleon put Emm's suitcase at the bottom of the stairs and waited while his father made his way to the couch.

"Want something to drink, Dad? Hungry?" Emm shook his head no. Bruna had prepared a big lunch, whether as a final dutiful gesture or to celebrate his departure, he wasn't sure. When Cleon excused himself to go to the kitchen, Emm looked at the knickknacks carefully arranged on the end tables and studied the collection of trophies on the mantle. He recognized a few from the body-building competitions Cleon had won decades ago. There were later prizes given to the high school teams he coached, but even the most recent of these was from ten years ago. Nonetheless, every trophy was dusted and polished as brightly as if it had been awarded yesterday.

There was murmuring in the kitchen, then the sound of a can being popped open. Cleon returned to the living room alone and sat in an armchair opposite Emm, drinking beer and eating pretzels. "Maple Leafs had a so-so year. They finished the regular season with 34 wins, 31 losses, and 15 ties. It gave them 83 points, enough to make it to the preliminary round in the playoffs."

Emm used to keep up with sports. He memorized the standings to make small talk with his customers. It was the camaraderie that helped him close the deal. Since he'd retired, it was a relief not to have to feign interest. Now, however, if he wanted to sell himself to Cleon, Emm would have to change back. He leaned forward. "Remind me, who are they up against?"

"Pittsburgh Penguins. You got a hunch who's gonna win?"

"I always put my money on Toronto. Gotta stand behind the home team."

Betty came in from the kitchen carrying an empty plate, which she put in Cleon's lap to catch his pretzel crumbs. She crossed her arms and remained standing beside his chair, her blonde hair as stiff as her posture. "Hello, Emm." She didn't sound welcoming. "I've made up Paul's old room for you. It's right across the hall from the bathroom." Betty looked down at Cleon. "Honey, carry your father's suitcase upstairs and help him settle in. I'm sure he'd like a nap before dinner. Transitions can be quite tiring."

"Not upstairs," said Emm. The word made him shiver, even though the April afternoon was warm. Betty's hands moved to her slim hips. "I can't, with the walker," he explained. That wasn't actually true. Dr. Sawyer had said he was ready to switch to a cane, but Emm decided to wait and use the walker as an excuse to sleep downstairs. By the time he got a cane, he figured, he'd be settled in a room on the ground floor and the issue wouldn't come up again. Or, if it did, he'd say the doctor thought it was a bad idea to risk another fall on the stairs. "You've got a convertible couch in the den, right?" Emm vaguely recalled watching hockey games there with Cleon and his sons when the boys were little. "I can use the bathroom off the kitchen, with the stall shower. It's easier and safer than getting in and out of the tub anyway."

Betty stood in front of Cleon. "I am not going to open and fold up the couch every day."

She was going to be a tougher customer to convince than her husband. Like most wives.

"Don't worry, honey. I'll do it." Cleon carefully put his empty beer can on a coaster, then picked a few crumbs off the shelf that was his waist and placed them on the plate.

"I'm going outside to finish clearing the dead stalks from last year's garden. Don't forget to call Mark to see when he can come over to help you with the mulch." Betty went through the kitchen and out the back door. It closed quietly, was reopened, and then slammed shut.

Cleon excused himself and returned to the kitchen, where Emm heard him dial and talk to his son. "Really? All As? Good for Melissa! And Jonah?" So, the boy who'd slept at Bruna's was Cleon's grandson. "Yeah, that's why I'm calling." Cleon listened. "I know you're busy, but you promised ..." Long pause. "It's just that your mother wants the yard done before the garden party she's giving for my birthday next month." Emm cringed at Cleon's wheedling tone. "I see. Like you said, you're busy." Cleon's voice sank. "Well, mark your calendar now for my fiftieth, in three years." Emm heard Cleon's goodbye, followed by another can of beer popping open.

***

Dinner was Chinese take-out. Betty said she'd worked in the yard too late to cook and sent Cleon to pick up the food. Emm hadn't eaten a Chinese meal in a long time. It was high in salt, and he was under orders to avoid it, which Bruna had taken into account when she fed him. Emm would miss her food. Nevertheless, he ate heartily because he wanted to show Betty that he belonged at her table. She left for her weekly bowling night before they'd even opened their fortune cookies.

Cleon read his. "Winning streaks end. Invest wisely to make profits last." He popped the entire cookie in his mouth. "First, I need to have a winning streak, then I'll worry what to do with it. What does yours say, Dad?"

"Big changes are coming. Buckle up." Emm pocketed the fortune and pushed his cookie toward Cleon. "Hopefully, this is my last stop. Until I reach the end of the line, that is."

"Give Betty time." Cleon ate Emm's cookie. "Change is hard for her, but once things settle into a new routine, she'll be fine. I'll sweet-talk her if need be." Emm was doubtful. He knew from Dale Carnegie that "those convinced against their will are of the same opinion still."

Cleon washed the dishes. He put the leftovers in plastic containers, which he labeled, and sponged off the counter. Then he used a whisk broom to sweep up grains of rice. At last, after surveying the kitchen, he took a Molson's out of the refrigerator. "Can I get you a brew, Dad?"

"Not until I'm steadier on my feet," Emm answered. In truth, he'd have loved to have a beer, or something stiffer. He thought he could resume having an occasional drink now and then. The days when one would have led to too many others were far behind him now. But he had to keep up the appearance of mild frailty for a while, at least until he'd convinced Cleon that his father needed taking care of. Emm licked his lips. "I wouldn't mind a glass of water." He hoped Betty's own cooking was less salty than the Chinese food they'd just eaten. He knew he couldn't ask her to prepare food especially for him. She'd probably order Cleon to make it.

"How long before you can give up the walker for a cane?" Cleon sat down and leaned back. "When a kid on the team breaks something, it heals fast. Of course, they're a lot younger than you." He cocked his head. "But you didn't actually break anything. Or did you?"

"No." It was irksome that Cleon didn't remember the extent of Emm's injuries, but he'd make it work in his favor. "I got bruised up pretty bad, though. I'd like to switch to a cane soon, but the doctor said not to rush it." At least the first part of what he'd said was accurate.

"One change at a time, huh? You following the countdown to the Olympics?"

Montreal was hosting the summer games in July. Emm knew that from the headlines, but he had no idea which athletes the world was watching or who Canadians were pinning their hopes on. He listened to his son recite countries, names, and world records, forcing his eyes open when the lids drooped. After a few minutes, Cleon got another beer. This time it was Labatt's Blue.

"Can't make up your mind?" Emm was unable to keep the annoyance out of his voice. He switched to a kinder tone, falling back on the wisdom of Dale Carnegie. "Remember what I taught you, son. To be successful, act definitive about what you want and go after it, even something as small as choosing your brand of beer." He gulped his water. "Arvil knew what *he* wanted."

Cleon nodded. "He was something, wasn't he? God, how I worshiped him." He stood up. "I gotta show you something. Stay right there." Did he think Emm was going to take off? Cleon came back from the den with a 1938 comic book, encased in a plastic sleeve. "Arvil gave me this on my ninth birthday. It was the first *Superman* comic ever published." He handed it to Emm.

"Must be valuable." Emm unwrapped it. The magazine was in better condition than Cleon.

"I'd never sell it. It's worth more than money to me." Cleon got a third beer and wiped his hands on a dish towel before putting the comic away. "I followed Arvil around like a puppy."

"He let you," remembered Emm. "That's more than I can say for my big brothers."

Cleon picked at the Labatt's label. "But when I got older, I wanted a way to stand out. Be my own person. I got good at body building, but I couldn't beat Arvil at the sports people cared about. Hockey. Baseball. So, I decided to bone up on the stats for our favorite teams."

"You have a good head for numbers." Emm regretted he hadn't encouraged Cleon to be an accountant, once Arvil was gone.

"Arvil thought it was cute, at first, but starting my freshman year, he'd ask trick questions whenever there were girls around, then laugh when I flubbed the answers. He embarrassed me to make himself look better." Cleon blushed.

"Boys are naturally competitive," said Emm. "I'm sure Arvil meant no harm."

"It was mean," Cleon's tone was matter of fact. "I tried to fill his shoes after he died, but it was hopeless. Not just because you saw him as perfect, but because you ignored me. All the rest of us, really. You didn't care about who we were, only that there should be more of us. The opposite of that expression nowadays, 'quality over quantity.' You bragged that the Benbows were going to win. At the time, I didn't know exactly what we were supposed to win, but later Bruna clued me in about the derby. What a lousy reason to become a dad."

Emm was on the verge of retorting that Cleon had no reason to resent Arvil, but then he remembered Mrs. Cray saying that grown-up siblings never got over their feeling of being slighted as children. Instead, he asked if Cleon was still angry.

"Not at my brother. How could I be when Arvil was killed, only a month after I turned fifteen?" Cleon stroked his gut and ran a hand over his bald head. "These days I look like I was the one in the trenches."

Emm sat up straight, silently urging his son to do the same. He wondered whether Cleon was always so self-pitying or if all the beer made him worse. "Remember the Dale Carnegie lesson about the four ways we have contact with the world?"

"What we do, how we look, what we say, and how we say it." Cleon burped, loudly.

Emm ignored it. "Think of the second one. Take more pride in your appearance. Like Betty takes in hers." He hated praising her, but his wife's example might inspire Cleon. Emm himself had long since lost any influence.

"She looks great, doesn't she?" Cleon wiped his mouth, with a napkin, and sucked in his stomach. "I should do it for her."

"You should do it for yourself too." Emm warmed up to his subject. "You probably don't remember, because you were only seven, but I read *How to Win Friends and Influence People* the year it came out. The book changed my life. I vowed to use it to help change yours. You felt bad about being small, so I tried to bolster your self-confidence. One of my favorite sayings was 'If only the people who worry about their liabilities would think about the riches they do possess ...'"

Cleon completed the quote. "'They would stop worrying.'"

Emm clapped him on the back. "See, you did learn those early lessons. All you have to do is apply them." Emm hoped his smile looked more sincere than he felt. He'd never approved of Cleon's choices, thought body building a waste of time, and coaching a thankless job. "Use your talent for remembering statistics to sell sports equipment. It's a growing field. A manufacturer or store would jump at the chance to hire an experienced, responsible adult to talk up its products."

"Well, I can't do any worse than I'm doing now." Cleon began to blubber. "My kids and grandchildren used to idolize me. Now, I'm like that Rodney Dangerfield line. I don't get no respect." He leaned forward until Emm could smell his breath. "The only one who still stands by me is Betty. If it weren't for her, I don't know ..." Cleon shook his head, unable to continue.

Emm reared back and spouted another quote. "'Feeling sorry for yourself and your present condition is not only a waste of energy, but the worst habit you could possibly have.'" He waited for his son to say it was good advice and admit it was time he stopped pitying himself.

Instead, Cleon gave him an exasperated look. "You must be tired, Dad. I'll get the sofa bed ready." He tossed out his last beer can, wiped the counter again, threw back his shoulders, and stalked off to the den. Emm left his dirty water glass on the table and followed.

CHAPTER 12

The next two weeks passed by pleasantly enough. Emm lay on the unmade sofa bed, surrounded by Maple Leafs memorabilia, reading the newspaper, then the books and magazines neatly stacked on the shelves and end tables. Betty cleaned around him, making a big show of moving his walker to vacuum under the couch. She seemed irritated that he rose earlier and got to the paper first, pointedly re-folding it before taking it to the kitchen to read with her morning coffee. After the second time Emm saw her do it, he scattered the open sections, willy-nilly, around the den. He knew he was risking his new home by aggravating its mistress but couldn't stop himself. He'd vowed to reform on his own terms and resented this woman dictating standards for his behavior.

In the evenings, Emm watched the hockey playoffs with Cleon. His son was ecstatic when Toronto beat Pittsburgh in the preliminary round and took the first two games out of seven in the quarterfinals against Philadelphia. Emm hoped these victories would strengthen his son's resolve to turn himself back into a winner and tried to mirror Cleon's excitement to bolster him. "'If you want to be enthusiastic, act enthusiastic,'" were the words of advice Emm gave himself. Alas, they didn't work. The games bored him, and for the first time, he doubted Mr. Carnegie's wisdom.

He had no trouble, however, drumming up enthusiasm for annoying Betty. Remembering the filthy bathroom at Kingsbridge, he marveled that here, even the grout between the shower tiles looked bleached and scrubbed. In response, when Emm washed his razor, he didn't rinse the hair down the drain. Same with the toothpaste he spit from his mouth. He half expected Betty to let him live with his own mess, but she used that bathroom during the day too. It was either clean it herself or walk upstairs every time she had to go. Daytime meals were another opportunity for Emm to get under her skin. The morning after Emm arrived, as soon as Cleon left for work, Betty told him he was on his own to cook breakfast and lunch. Whatever he couldn't find in the cupboards, Cleon would pick up for him. Emm made himself soup or a sandwich, same as he'd done at home, leaving his dirty pots on the stove and dishes on the coffee table in the den.

One night at dinner—the only meal that Betty did cook, competently if unimaginatively—she announced, "Before we eat dessert, it's time we set some ground rules around here."

Cleon smiled nervously. "Sure, honey. What seems to be the problem?"

"I'm not the hired help, and I didn't sign on to clean up after your father." Ignoring Emm, she addressed her complaints to Cleon. "I don't see why your father can't wash up after himself. It wouldn't take long, and it's the least he can do in exchange for having a roof over his head."

"What do you say, Dad?" Cleon eyed the chocolate cake on the sideboard.

"That takes two hands, and I need one to hold onto my walker when I stand at the sink."

This time Betty spoke directly to Emm. Her nostrils flared. "You manage to cook and shave using two hands. There's nothing to prevent you from leaning against the counter."

"Dad's still regaining his strength and mobility. I'm sure he'll be able to help more before much longer. Meantime, I'll wash his dishes first thing when I get home, before we sit down to eat." Cleon cleared away the dinner plates and walked toward the sideboard.

Betty held out her arm to stop him. "What about the bathroom?"

"Okay. Dad's up early and shaves before I leave for work. I'll swab the sink before I go."

Betty persisted. "And do his laundry?" Cleon agreed to wash Emm's clothes on the nights she went bowling. Betty stood and embraced him. "Thank you, honey. That will help a lot." They waltzed around the table, deftly circling Emm's walker, like two lovers alone on the dance floor. Then Betty kissed Cleon and released him to finally bring dessert to the table.

Cleon took a large slice and a large bite. "Wonderful cake, honey." Betty ate a small slice and went to work in the garden. Emm helped himself to seconds, then wheeled to the den where Cleon would join him after he finished cleaning the kitchen. As far as Emm could recall, there was nothing in *How to Win Friends and Influence People* about emboldening henpecked husbands.

***

Despite Emm's misgivings, the added cleaning responsibility seemed to make Cleon downright chipper. A few days later, at dinner, he announced that the baseball team he coached had won their first two games. "Honey, that's wonderful." Betty had squeezed his hand. "I just know those boys are going to have a great season." Emm thought back to the early days of his own marriage, when Izora had offered similar encouragement. When had her support for him waned?

Then, as suddenly as his mood had lightened, Cleon plunged into despair. Toronto lost the next two games. Betty offered to skip her bowling night and go to the movies to cheer Cleon up, but he told her, "Nah. You go on ahead. The girls need you to make the league finals this year." Betty promised to come straight home instead of going out for her usual drink and suggested that Cleon watch something funny on television. Cleon said that was a great idea, but after she left, he was too despondent to decide on a show. Emm chose *Happy Days*.

The sitcom's canned laughs only depressed Cleon further. "See how the Cunningham kids respect their parents? Mark and Paul used to be like that with me. They asked my advice all the time. Now they can't spare a minute to say hello." He drank and slumped on the couch.

Emm couldn't summon any wise words about how to be a father. He tried a different tack. "Buck up. The games are tied, two-two. Toronto can still pull off a victory." Cleon stared morosely at the row of beer cans and broken potato chips. Emm exploded. "For God's sake, it's just a game. You don't know what real disappointment is. You never lost your job because of the Depression. You never lost ..." He stopped. Cleon was nearly prone.

Emm felt disgust and wondered if Betty's support actually caused his son's decline. Did her being so in control, and competent, emasculate him? Was there a chance he'd sink so low, he'd go bonkers and finally blow his top? Rally against his wife and become certifiably slovenly?

Cleon rose abruptly. Emm waited for the eruption. Instead, his son gathered the empties and chip bowl, washed up in the kitchen, and called out, "Goodnight, Dad. I'm headed upstairs."

Angered on his son's behalf, Emm escalated his campaign to undermine Betty. He left his walker where it would get tangled in the vacuum cleaner cord or wheeled it across the freshly mopped linoleum. Betty said nothing, seeming as determined to keep her manners as much in check as her home. However, she jotted down notes, likely a compilation of grievances to present to Cleon.

One day, when she was preparing to wax the floor, Betty suggested that Emm go outside. "Why not take your walker around the block? The weather is nice now and the air will do you good." She opened the door and handed Emm his sweater. "I'm sure the doctor would approve."

Although the urge to defy her was strong, the lure of being outdoors was stronger. Emm made two circles around their street, then crossed over to the next one, where he strolled past the small but well-kept houses and tidy front yards. It was clear that he was capable of giving up the walker and getting about with a cane. He felt almost jaunty heading back to Cleon's. As he turned into the front walk, however, Emm spied Betty watching him from the window. He swayed, as though dizzy, and then slowly wobbled forward. Staring back at Betty, Emm swerved his walker into a flower bed where daffodils and crocuses were blooming. He coated the bottom of his shoes with dark soil. Then he stumbled through the door and tracked dirt from the foyer to the kitchen, where he gulped a glass of water, then into the bathroom, and finally the den. As soon as Betty appeared in the doorway, mouth agape, Emm closed his eyes and faked an exhausted sleep.

Betty was waiting in the driveway when Cleon came home. From behind the curtains in the den, Emm saw her pounce on him like a big cat stalking its prey and lead him around to the backyard. Cleon followed, holding his suit jacket close to his side and gripping his briefcase. Emm crept to the back door to listen. Betty's voice was loud, Cleon's barely audible. Emm couldn't make out most of the words, but "honey" wasn't one of them. When it began to turn dark, he fixed himself a bowl of cereal, careful to scatter crumbs, and went to sleep. After what he judged to be a couple of hours, Cleon came into the den and asked if he could share the sofa bed. Emm scooted sideways, and the two of them lay there, silent, staring at the ceiling all night.

Betty was gone most of the next day, returning with her hair freshly dyed and styled and carrying several department store packages. Cleon came home early, carrying Chinese take-out. Their argument resumed over dinner. Betty spoke through tight lips. "I am not a nanny. I am not a maid." She shoved a notepad covered with tiny, neat handwriting, across the table. Cleon put down his fork and read it, flipping through all five pages.

Emm kept quiet and ate. He felt like a child whose father has come home, been told by his mother of his offenses, and is awaiting punishment. Emm knew he deserved it but felt helpless to tamp down the urge to be naughty. He thought of Kingsbridge and blamed it on his fear.

"I'll start tonight," Cleon told Betty. "Vacuuming and mopping." She nodded. "Saturdays I'll scour the shower and wash the sheets." He enumerated the other chores he'd thenceforth do on weeknights and weekends. Apparently, Cleon, not Emm, was the person who would bear the punishment. Betty posted the list on the refrigerator door and left to go bowling.

Cleon waited until the sound of the car had faded before clearing the table, on the verge of tears. Emm was angry at him for not being the man in his own house but felt partly responsible for this latest humiliation. He was also embarrassed to see his son cry—again—so he tried to joke. "Men are supposed to marry their mothers, but I guess you chose the opposite of yours."

"You didn't marry your mother, either Dad. Mom was nothing like Grandma Bessie. Mom was kind and patient. She never pushed me to do something I wasn't capable of. Whatever I was, was good enough for her." Cleon wrung out the dishrag. "Grandma Bessie purposely bought me sports equipment I was too small to use. I dreaded opening her Christmas presents."

"My mother was just trying to toughen you up. She meant well."

"Grandma Bessie mocked me. She called me clumsy and stupid. She said I would never amount to anything and that you and Mom were ashamed of me. She said if I didn't learn how to run faster, jump higher, and throw a baseball, you were going to put me in a cripples' institution."

Emm was dumbfounded. His mother was strict, often pushy, but cruel? And to a child, her own grandson, no less? "Perhaps my mother worried that your mother was being overprotective."

"Do you think Mom was?"

At the time, Emm had thought so. He saw Izora as sabotaging his own attempts to fortify his son. Now, in hindsight, he wasn't so sure. "It was your mother's way of loving you. You were so frail when you were born, she never got over her fear of losing you."

Cleon snorted. "Why? There were plenty more of us."

"To her, you were each precious." The right thing would be for Emm to claim that it was the same for him, but the words wouldn't come. Maybe someday, for the sake of his children and for Izora, he'd be able to say them, and mean it.

Cleon took a deep breath. "Betty has high standards and she's an exacting taskmaster, but she's never told me I'm not a good person. You married a woman who didn't dare contradict you, but as a grown man, you let your mother boss you around. What's worse, you let her boss your wife around. At least I've got the guts to put myself in the middle between you and Betty." With that, Cleon stalked out. A few minutes later, Emm heard the whirr of the vacuum cleaner.

CHAPTER 13

Emm couldn't bring himself to wash dishes or make the bed, but he began to carry his dirty plates to the sink and rinse his stubble and toothpaste down the drain. He told himself he was doing it to make life easier for Cleon, but Betty noticed too. To Emm's surprise, he was pleased with himself for pleasing her. Perhaps because it had been his choice to do so. He hoped Izora was taking note.

With the new routine, Betty seemed calmer, just as Cleon had predicted. Emm applied the same thoroughness toward cleaning that he'd brought to every challenge he'd set himself, whether selling cars or adding to his household. Betty slowly warmed to him, at one point admiring his fastidiousness. Emm felt like a hungry child who was fed praise after a steady diet of criticism.

Not that there was a complete thaw in their relationship; Betty still expected him to make his own lunch. But she invited him to sit with her at the table. Since they were both newspaper readers, they found plenty to talk about. "So, are you excited about the Olympics?" she asked.

Emm confessed he wasn't, then waited for her disapproval. Would she banish him again?

Instead, Betty laughed. "To tell you the truth, except for gymnastics, neither am I. But Cleon follows all the events, so I'll watch them with him. In the den." She raised an eyebrow.

"I'll make sure it's straightened up," said Emm. "Perfect den, score of ten."

Betty smiled. "I hope you'll join us. It'll boost Cleon's morale if we're both there."

Emm agreed. It might even be fun. Cleon knew enough about the athletes' stats to act as an in-house commentator. He and Betty chatted next about Queen Elizabeth's trip to Canada this summer, part of her silver jubilee tour. Betty was sympathetic when Emm said he was anxious about adapting to metric units when the road signs were converted in the fall. "Maybe it's a good thing I'm getting older," he said. "I don't have to worry about driving under the new system."

Betty admitted she was nervous about the switch too. "I don't like change either, although I am looking forward to the opening of Eaton Centre next year." Emm confessed that except for buying houses and cars, he thought shopping was best left to women. Betty chuckled. "Like every other man. I will say this for Cleon, though. When I ask, he comes with me and is unbelievably patient, whether I'm choosing new curtains or trying on clothes."

Emm wasn't sure if he saw this as a virtue, or flaw, but he liked hearing Betty laud his son. He accepted a glass of lemonade. "I hope I'm improved enough to visit the new CN Tower when it opens in June. I read it will be the tallest free-standing structure in the world." Emm thought a minute, afraid his memory was going. "Darn. I can't remember how tall it is."

"I can't either, but Cleon will. We can ask him at dinner." Betty poured them both more lemonade. "I'd love to take the grand-children to see the Tower. Although I don't know if I'm any more capable of keeping up with them than you are." She laughed, then frowned. "I wish the boys treated Cleon better. It breaks his heart that they brush him off these days."

"Don't all grown children do that with their parents?" Emm asked. Not that he had, at least with his mother, but his children had certainly turned their backs on him. He wondered, if Izora had lived, whether they would have been kinder to her, and maybe, by extension, to him.

"I suppose every family is different." Betty brightened. "Wait until Mark and Paul's own children reach adolescence and start to disrespect them. I bet they'll develop more sympathy for their old dad and come running back to Cleon for advice." Emm was doubtful, judging by how his adult children treated him. But, as Betty had said, every family was different.

The lightened mood between Emm and Betty prevailed and changed the tenor in the household as a whole. Even after Toronto lost their final two games to Philadelphia, Cleon's spirits didn't plunge. He was only mildly disappointed. Betty was sympathetic and Emm told his son not to lose hope, there was always next year. Cleon smiled at the sports cliché and said it was enough that they'd had a good run. It was he, not Emm, who quoted Dale Carnegie. "'Success is getting what you want. Happiness is wanting what you get.' I'm happy with what I have."

***

Betty drove Emm to his next doctor's appointment. When he came out of the exam room with a cane instead of his walker, she actually hugged him. "Stick close to your father-in-law," Dr. Sawyer told her as he saw them out, "until he gets his sea legs back. Er, land legs. Make sure he practices an hour or two a day to start. Once he's steady, all restrictions are off. Even climbing."

As soon as Emm could move easily between the den, kitchen, and bathroom, he ventured outside every day. Betty accompanied him around the block, and then through the neighborhood, timing their walks and increasing them a half hour every other day. She encouraged him, the same way she did Cleon, saying she had faith in his full recovery. At dinner, she told Cleon about his father's daily progress. Emm thought that Cleon himself moved better, with a lift in his step.

"You're like your son," Betty told Emm one day at lunch, after their longest walk yet. "Strong on the inside. Of course, that shouldn't come as a surprise. The apple doesn't fall far from the tree."

Emm glowed at the compliment. "Is his strength what attracted you to Cleon?" he asked.

Betty laughed. "I didn't know about the body building until later. It was his name. I thought he was French and would be more romantic than the other boys I dated."

Emm was surprised. He'd expected odd names would help his daughters get husbands, not help his sons attract wives. "Do you know if he got teased for his name when he was younger?"

Betty shook her head. "Not that he ever said." She grinned. "Just the opposite, in a way, when he began coaching. The students thought 'Cleon' sounded kind of sci-fi, and they liked it. Of course, they never called him anything other than 'Mr. Benbow,' but their playing took on the warlike aggressiveness of Klingons. It helped them win some of those early trophies."

"I guess I haven't kept up with the television shows kids watch these days."

"I don't care for them either, but you have to keep up to connect with your grandchildren. It was the same with dance crazes when our boys were young. Personally, I prefer the old ones." Betty smiled as shyly as a young girl. "Cleon was, still is, a good dancer."

"A woman accepts the advances of a man who dances." Emm thought back to early in his own marriage. "Izora and I used to waltz around the kitchen table. Until the pregnancies began."

Betty touched his arm. "Before you know it, you'll be able to waltz me around the kitchen table. Soon, you can even help me vacuum. I appreciate a man who's spic and span." She stood and wrinkled her nose. "Ouch. I'll leave the rhyming to you and stick to the work I'm good at. It's early in the season, but I want to get the flower beds cleared to plant annuals next month."

Emm headed for the den. He turned around to thank Betty for practicing with him. "This might sound silly, but you've been like a parent helping a toddler learn to walk for the first time."

Betty blushed. "Seriously, Emm, at the rate you're improving, you'll be able to move into the upstairs bedroom in no time."

Emm's legs began to shake. His throat felt dry. "I don't want to ... shouldn't overdo it," he stammered. But Betty was already outside.

***

That evening, on his way to dinner, Emm made himself trip and grab onto the tablecloth to regain his balance, upending a glass of water. Both Cleon and Betty helped him into his seat. Cleon knelt to make sure there wasn't a bulge in the linoleum; Betty pulled up a fourth chair for Emm to rest his leg on. At lunch the next day, Emm dropped his soup spoon carrying it to the sink, and later in the week, he stumbled into the coffee table, knocking a stack of magazines to the floor.

"I'm worried about you, Dad. I think Betty should take you back to Dr. Sawyer. Maybe you've got a blood clot in your leg. Is it swollen?"

"No, I just need to take it slower," Emm answered. "It's not a race."

Cleon looked toward Betty for her opinion. She narrowed her eyes but said nothing.

For the next two days, Emm told Betty he wasn't up to walking. She tapped her foot and said no doubt it was a temporary setback. On the third day, she waited at the door. When Emm shuffled past her to the kitchen, she bypassed him and moved his soup cans to a higher shelf. He eyed the step stool before slinking off to the couch. Then, on Saturday, when they were all in the den and Cleon said he hoped Emm was getting better, he banged into an end table, toppling Betty's two favorite porcelain figurines. They broke into small pieces and sprayed fine white dust.

Cleon rushed toward Emm, arm outstretched, but Betty grabbed her husband and dragged him into the kitchen. Emm, trembling for real now, sat on the folded sofa bed. Once again, he was that child who could not control himself, but nevertheless felt like the victim, not the perpetrator.

"Can't you see he's doing it on purpose?" Betty spoke loud enough for Emm to hear. "He wants to go back to when we waited on him hand and foot. Or when your mother, or his mother, did. I'm not Emm's wife or his mother. He's your father, and you have a choice. Either he leaves, or I do, and you can spend your forty-seventh birthday, and every one after that, without me."

Emm heard Betty stomp up the stairs. Minutes later, she came down and told Cleon she was going to stay at Mark's house while he made up his mind. "Sleeping with the grandkids and tolerating their mess can't be any worse than living here." Then she was gone.

Cleon didn't come into the den immediately, so after ten minutes, Emm ventured into the kitchen. His son was at the table, drinking a Molson's. He motioned for Emm to sit opposite him, in Betty's chair. Emm eased himself into the seat. He eyed the beer thirstily and waited for Cleon to get him a glass of water. Cleon didn't move.

"You heard what Betty said, Dad?"

"She threatened to leave you, but she'll back off. Women do, even those as ... tough as Betty." Emm nodded. "Things will settle down again. I just have to be careful not to overdo it."

Cleon shook his head. "Going back to how it was a couple of weeks ago would be another change. Betty won't stand for it." He got a second beer, another Molson's. "Neither will I."

Emm looked around the neat kitchen and conjured a memory of his kitchen, during and after the Stork Derby: baby bottles boiling on the stove, wet diapers hanging on drying racks, streaks of mud tracked in by the children making crazy patterns on the floor. "I'll leave if that's what it takes to save your marriage." He gazed up at the ceiling, as if to appease Izora, but self-sacrifice was only a small part of his motivation. Emm could no longer watch Cleon kowtow to Betty. If that's the kind of man his son had turned out to be, then Emm had failed him as a father.

Cleon said nothing, just wrapped his hands around the bottle.

The blood pounded in Emm's temples. He told himself not to say more but was unable to keep quiet. "You should have married a woman as agreeable as your mother, after all. If you don't put your foot down, you'll lose what little self-respect you have left."

"I made the right choice when I married Betty, and I'm making the right one now. If you hadn't offered to leave, I'd have told you to." Cleon took a third Molson's from the refrigerator. "Sometimes, making up your mind is easy."

***

Early Monday morning, Emm called Mrs. Cray. She didn't hide her disappointment. "I was just reading Dr. Sawyer's latest report. You were doing so well, Mr. Benbow. What went wrong?"

"I don't blame my son," Emm said, "It's his wife. I'm an old man with health problems, and her demands are unreasonable."

"Did your son speak up for you?" Mrs. Cray asked.

"Hah! Those two would defend each other against provable charges of treason." The moment the words were out, Emm envied them. He tried to think of a time when he'd taken Izora's side, and all he could come up with was defending her flapper dress against his mother.

"I'll record your move," sighed Mrs. Cray, "but you're going to run out of options."

"I'm only down two, three counting Arvil, with a long roster to go. When I started my family, I was planning ten years ahead. Who knew that having a lot of children would come in handy fifty years later?" From Mrs. Cray's sharp intake of breath, Emm sensed she heard the bluster in his feeble laugh. Time was running out and not because he was in a race with other derby contestants. This time, the only one threatening Emm was himself.

PART FIVE:
DAROLD
MAY-JUNE 1976

Their fourth child, and third son, Darold, was born after a perilous ride to the hospital on October 31, 1930. An early frost had turned Toronto's roads icy, and they were in a rush since each of Izora's previous labors had progressed more quickly than the one before. Despite the scare, Emm took it as a good omen that the baby was born on the fourth anniversary of Millar's death. With their head start, few other families, if any, would be in such an enviable position.

Izora's reaction was in stark contrast to her husband's. "What good does it do to be so far ahead when I feel so far behind?" She dragged herself from room to room, as if trying to slow down time itself. Her lethargy made Emm more impatient.

"This is no time to hold back. We need to pick up the pace." Determined to maintain the lead he'd convinced himself they had, Emm forbid his wife to nurse Darold at all. "The sooner we start the next one, the faster we'll secure our place at the front of the pack." Mrs. Benbow brought ice blocks wrapped in dish towels to reduce the swelling in Izora's breasts and Emm occasionally helped bottle feed the baby in the wee hours. But Darold often cried through the night and was sick and fussy during the day, with bouts of diarrhea, runny noses, and coughs.

Izora had no proof, but she swore that her other babies had been healthier because she'd breastfed them. "Mother's milk is made for babies," she said. "Cow's milk is for calves."

"Nonsense," said Emm when she told him her theory. "That's another old wives' tale."

He grew concerned, however, when the bills from Dr. Marsh arrived. The kind doctor told them to take their time paying, but they were still hard pressed to come up with the money. The Depression was forcing people to make do with their old appliances, and business at the toaster factory had fallen off. There was no Christmas bonus that year. When Darold was four months old, Emm lost his job altogether. Two months later, when the bank repossessed their house, the family moved in with Emm's parents. Mr. and Mrs. Benbow had plenty of room.

Emm saw himself as a failure. Being in the company of so many other laid-off men was no comfort. Not until he was back in the home where he'd grown up did he begin to feel better, like a child who was going through a bad patch but still had his whole future ahead of him. He also welcomed the extra space. His plans for adding onto the house he'd bought as he and Izora added on children had been put on hold when the economy turned sour. In his parents' house, Emm no longer faced that daily reminder. He began to see the move as a temporary setback, a blessing that would let them move forward once his luck turned. Which he was sure it would.

Izora didn't see things that way. Instead of expanding to fill the spare rooms, she shrank before the constant criticism from Mrs. Benbow, who declared her daughter-in-law too lenient with the children. Emm, believing his mother had done a fine job with him and his siblings, deferred to her judgment. It made sense that Arvil, age three, learn table manners; that Bruna, age two, be toilet trained; and that Cleon, still catching up at eleven months, be forced to walk. Mrs. Benbow tantalized the little boy by holding toys out of reach and around barriers. Another child might have screamed in frustration, but Cleon kept trying, no matter how many times he tumbled or got bruised. Emm held Izora back from rushing to pick him up, convinced the tactic would help make his son stronger. Izora shed the tears that Cleon wouldn't, or couldn't.

She was most upset, however, when Emm's mother insisted that Darold begin eating solid foods. She was terrified he'd choke during a coughing fit and asked, for the first time, if Emm would speak to his mother about letting them decide what was best for their children. Instead, he'd deployed the look and told Izora to be more appreciative of the advice and help they were getting. It was obvious that she couldn't manage on her own and he couldn't be of assistance. Either he was off looking for work or doing the occasional carpentry job that let him contribute something, however small, to the household. Besides, it wasn't a father's place to take care of little children. His role was to be the breadwinner. Other men had been driven over the brink after letting their families down. Acting like a nanny would have driven him there too.

After she failed to change Emm's mind about his mother, Izora next ventured that, given their dire straits, they pull out of the contest. She tried to enlist her in-laws' support. One night at dinner she looked across the table at Mr. Benbow, pushed the limp hair off her forehead, and said, "According to the papers, one man in five is out of a job, with no end in sight. You've been very kind, but the only way we'll get back on our feet is by not having more mouths to feed."

Emm had thrown down his fork and scowled. "Since when are you the expert? You leave the papers, and financial decisions, to me." He'd drummed his fingers on the table. "Things will turn around before you know it, and that pot of gold will be worth a lot more than what Millar left behind. In fact, if other families think like you and give up, we'll be sitting prettier to win."

Mrs. Benbow had instantly agreed with her son. Emm's father said that things couldn't stay this bad much longer, and he was inclined to side with Emm too. Given the likelihood that other families would drop out of the Derby, they should redouble their efforts to win.

Izora had looked down at her uneaten food, then excused herself to check on Darold. She kept her thoughts to herself after that. Emm interpreted his wife's silence as agreement.

CHAPTER 14

The thought of calling his son made Emm's bowels contract and his breathing grow as labored as Darold's had continued to be all his life. Living with him might merely capitulate the problems he'd run into with Bruna and Cleon. For one thing, Darold was as devoted to the family as Bruna. After Izora died, he'd helped his sister take care of the younger ones and now had grandchildren of his own. Five, as Emm recalled. The house would be overrun with them on weekends. Second, Darold's wife Virginia resented her husband's attention to his siblings and all their offspring. On the rare occasions when Emm had been invited to their home, Virginia's temper had made the hair on his arms stand on end. It seemed to just roll off Darold's back, but Virginia's anger over Emm moving in, which could prove worse than Betty's, might be harder for his son to shrug off.

Then again, Emm expected Darold would be more sympathetic than Bruna or Cleon. Darold's own chronic health problems had made him stoic; his son accepted illness as a way of life and wouldn't push Emm to hurry up and get better. Moreover, unlike Bruna, he'd never acted bitter toward his father. Emm debated these pros and cons, but ultimately, they didn't matter. Quite simply, it was Darold's turn. "As sure as the number four follows three, the letter D comes after C." Emm went to the bathroom, took a deep breath, and dialed Darold's number.

"Hi, Dad. How are you? You looked shaky at Bruna's, but I'm sure she's taking good care of you. Sorry I haven't gotten over there to see you in a few weeks. Virginia insisted I use those Sundays to clean out the gutters and oil the garage doors."

Emm had to explain that he'd moved out of Bruna's and was now living with Cleon, but that things weren't working out there either. "You know what a meticulous housekeeper Betty is. I don't have it in me to meet her standards."

Darold cleared his throat. "Standards around here are significantly lower, but I'm afraid Virginia won't be any more welcoming toward you than Betty." After a pause, he chuckled. "Oh well, my wife's already pissed at me so I don't see that your moving in will make much difference. With the kids grown, we've got plenty of empty bedrooms. I expect you'd prefer James's, but I can repaint Barbara's or Brenda's old room. Unless you favor pink. It's your choice."

"The thing is, Darold, if all the bedrooms are on the second floor, then ..."

"Of course. Sorry. You can't climb stairs. There's a maid's room off the kitchen with its own bathroom. Virginia uses it for junk. I'll clean it out this weekend. Do you need a ride here?" Emm thought Cleon would be happy to take him, and Betty would be glad to watch his departure. She'd want to make sure it went according to plan. Which is what happened. Cleon packed Emm into the car, while his wife stood in the doorway, chest puffed out, a triumphant grin on her face.

They drove to a neighborhood with boulevards and houses twice the size of the one they'd left. Darold, a manager at Eaton's Paper, had done well for himself. Emm was struck by the carefully tended homes and lawns, until they arrived at Darold's. The house was as grand as the others, but paint peeled off the south side and the shingles on the covered porch had a child's gap-toothed grin. In place of spring blooms were wilted shrubs. His son didn't look much better.

Despite his pallor and sunken chest, however, Darold welcomed

Emm with a big smile. Cleon hugged his brother, waved goodbye to Emm, and strode to the car with a young athlete's confidence. Darold stumbled as he helped Emm over the threshold, laughed at himself and said to be careful of the loose nail. Then they were inside the sprawling, none-too-clean house. It reminded Emm of the disarray their home had fallen into after his parents moved out and left it to him and his family. After Izora died, Bruna had tried to restore order, but even her iron will wasn't enough to prevail.

Emm peered around the first floor. Virginia was nowhere in sight, but Foy sat on the living room couch, mesmerized by a *Brady Bunch* rerun. He waited until a commercial break to acknowledge his father's arrival, at which point he jumped up like an excited puppy. "It's Popsy!" he exclaimed. His six-year-old speech was at odds with the pudgy stomach and thinning hair of the middle-aged man he was.

Looking at Foy, you wouldn't know he was slow. It was the same when he was a boy. Emm had been relieved that Foy didn't have the slanty eyes and puffy jaw that other children like him did. But once he opened his mouth, you could tell there was something wrong with his head. Emm had avoided being around him in public and stayed clear of him at home too. He told himself he wasn't repulsed, just that he didn't know what to do with a child who smiled at everyone without understanding a word they said. Foy caught the tone of others' remarks, though. The few times Emm had spoken to him sharply, the boy's face had crumbled. Izora hadn't scolded Emm for scolding their son. Instead, she'd hustled Foy out of the way and humored him until his good spirits were restored. Emm's one attempt to apologize, to her, was met with a stony look. He never tried again.

"Watch television with me, Popsy." Foy tapped the head of Emm's cane. "Jan is sick. She coughs a lot, like Darold. Oh no, what if they have to get rid of Tiger?"

Darold explained to Emm that Jan was one of the Brady children and Tiger was their dog. "Don't worry," Darold reassured his brother. "The ending is always happy." Foy breathed a sigh of relief and turned his attention back to the show.

"Does Foy visit often?" Emm asked. He vaguely recalled that a decade ago, the city had licensed a nearby group home for Foy and five other men. After an ugly neighborhood protest, the approval was rescinded and Darold found another place for his brother a couple of miles away.

"Most weekdays I bring him here for an hour after work. Every weekend too, unless we go over to Bruna's."

Foy clapped his hands and asked if Bruna was coming to play too. "Not this evening," Darold answered. "We have to take you home before Virginia gets back."

Foy's hand flew to his mouth. "Can I have a Blow Pop?"

"You already had a box of Gobstoppers. That's enough candy for today." Darold relented when Foy pouted and gave him a cherry gumball. "Careful you don't swallow it." When Foy was again too absorbed in the show to listen, Darold told Emm that Foy's obsession with sweets was becoming a health problem. He tapped his heart. He had to monitor Foy to make sure his brother didn't sneak candy from here or from Bruna's to take back to his room at the group home.

"I assumed Virginia made herself scarce today to avoid me," said Emm. Foy looked up at the mention of her name. Emm lowered his voice. "I gather she's not thrilled having Foy around either." Nor was Emm. Living in this house could be worse than Bruna's. Here there would be no child-free days and Foy was less easily dissuaded from getting what he wanted than the little ones.

"Virginia uses the time that Foy is here to go grocery shopping." Darold grinned. "We eat lots of fresh food."

It would likely be the only fresh thing in the house. Emm had just arrived, and already he wasn't sure that this third move would work out any better than the other two. Unlike Darold's wife,

Emm couldn't escape Foy's high-pitched prattling by running errands. The best he could do was plead an old man's fatigue and go off for a nap. It was almost a shame that the bedroom he'd chosen was just down the hall, instead of upstairs, out of earshot.

***

Emm accompanied Darold when he drove Foy home; he didn't want to be alone in the house if Virginia returned first. She was unloading groceries when they got back, and after saying a casual hello to Emm, served dinner and chatted about a neighbor she'd met at the market. After they ate, Virginia gathered the plates and left them in the sink. She didn't wipe the table or counter. They all watched television. Darold coughed frequently, but neither he nor Virginia made a fuss about it, other than turning up the volume during one prolonged fit. When the nightly news ended, Darold helped Emm throw some sheets on his bed, found him a clean towel, and everyone turned in.

The next day, Emm and Virginia nodded when they crossed paths, but otherwise stayed clear of each other. Emm made do with the leftovers he found in the refrigerator and spent the rest of the day in his room, leafing through old magazines and listening to the news on his radio. Despite lazing about, he had a mild headache after lunch. In all the confusion of moving in, he'd forgotten to take his blood pressure medication the night before. Dr. Sawyer had told him that if he missed a dose, but it was less than half a day until the next one, he should wait. "Don't double up," he'd said. "It's like kids. Two at once is more than twice as hard on the body." Emm turned his wristwatch upside down as a reminder to take his pills before bed. He tried to remember when he'd learned that trick. His mother didn't wear a watch so it must have been his father.

Late afternoon, soon after Virginia left to go shopping, Darold came home with Foy. Instead of turning on the television, Foy asked to see the photo album. Darold told Emm that other than watching family sitcoms and eating candy, looking at family pictures was Foy's favorite activity. They settled on the couch, with Foy taking the middle spot. Emm felt odd about three grown men sitting so close together but reassured himself that Foy was more like a child.

Foy told Emm to turn the pages. The photos, like the rest of the house, were in no particular order. Many were of Darold's children, with Foy often playing beside them. Others were taken at Bruna's, the older siblings and cousins mixed up with more recent shots of their grandchildren. Emm wasn't in any of them, but he couldn't remember if he hadn't been asked or if he'd turned Bruna down so often that she'd stopped inviting him. He calmed himself, thinking it no longer mattered, but then his heart lurched whenever he came upon long-ago photos of Izora and their children, his parents, or himself looking young and proud.

Foy pointed and named the people in each photo. Emm raised his eyebrows at Darold, who said, "He knows everyone, don't you Foy?" As weak as his mental capacities were, Foy had a good head for people and social events. He even remembered the stories behind the pictures.

"Halloween. Darold's a cowboy. Cleon is Popeye. And that's me under the sheet. Boo!" Foy doubled up with laughter and Emm couldn't help smiling. "I got lots of candy." Foy's face clouded over. "Grandma Bessie made me throw it away. I could only eat the toffee apple. Right?" He looked at Darold. Emm remembered his mother making those when he was little. Her attitude was that if you had to eat sweets, they should be nutritious. Emm hadn't cared for them either.

Darold put his arm around his brother. "Grandma Bessie loved us and didn't want us to get sick." Foy smiled again and asked if Halloween was coming again soon. Darold said not for another six months. Foy accepted this and nudged Emm to turn the page.

As Foy rambled on, Emm looked over his head at Darold. He wanted to know what Darold really thought of his mother but was afraid to ask after what Bruna and Cleon had said. He tried to phrase the question neutrally. "What do you remember about your Grandma Bessie?"

"We stayed with her and Grandpa Henry until I was ten, then they moved out and we kept the house. While we all still lived together, Grandma packed my favorite sandwich for lunch—peanut butter with stripes of raisins—and helped me with my spelling."

"I can spell," said Foy, and rattled off his siblings in alphabetical order. He asked how to spell "Popsy" and practiced it over and over until Emm distracted him by turning to the next photo. Emm gasped. It was of Arvil in his Army uniform, the picture enlarged to fill the whole page.

"Arvil," said Foy. "He got shot dead. Right?" Emm wondered if Foy had any concept of death. Its finality had been hard for Emm to grasp. He kept waiting for his son to come home.

Darold quickly flipped past Arvil's photo to scenes from a recent picnic. Foy began to enumerate the guests. Then Darold continued to answer the question that Emm, stunned by the sight of his eldest child, had momentarily forgotten he'd asked. "Grandma Bessie bought me a dictionary when I won the school spelling bee, but she took it back after I lost the first round of the regional contest. She said I didn't deserve it after she'd worked so hard to prepare me."

"Maybe she thought it was too much pressure and was worried about your health."

Darold, uncharacteristically, looked as upset as Foy had a minute ago. "Just the opposite. I loved looking up words. I couldn't run around like other kids, so print was my best friend. Sometimes I think that's why I went to work for a paper company."

"Uncle Cam and Aunt Leona." Foy, impatient with their talk,

had turned the page himself. Emm was surprised to hear the names of his own siblings, whom he hadn't seen in years. The photo showed them here, in Darold's living room, along with the rest of his family. While Bruna kept up with her siblings and their families, it turned out that Darold had also stayed in touch with Emm's. Foy named his great uncles and aunts, and, unlike Emm, knew all of his second cousins,

Tucked inside the album's next page was a family tree Darold had drawn of his parents and siblings, and their children and grandchildren. Foy, unable to read, skipped over it but Darold took it out and handed it to Emm. He offered to make him a copy. Unlike the house, the tree was orderly. From that Emm concluded that Virginia was to blame for the messiness of their home. As further proof that Darold was organized, Emm considered how successful his son was at work.

"I see you took the Dale Carnegie lessons I taught you to heart. For example, the one about putting your own house in order before managing the affairs of others."

"His advice does make sense," said Darold. "Except that I learned it from reading the book in school. I don't remember your telling me about it." Emm's prodding continued to elicit blanks from his son. Was it possible he'd only quoted Carnegie to Cleon, thinking Darold would never have the strength to be a leader?

Emm looked back at the scores of names on the family tree. There were too many great nieces and great nephews to count. He handed the chart back to Darold. "It's nice that you stayed in touch with my family too." Why hadn't he? Emm had fond memories of his childhood. Giggling tickling matches and giddy Christmas mornings. Chasing each other up to the second-floor playroom, down to the basement root cellar, and outside where they hid among the sheets drying in the sun. He'd wanted to create that same happy pandemonium with his and Izora's family. Instead, there was chaos and sadness, his wife's gradual decline, and then her premature death.

Mr. Carnegie believed that "People rarely succeed unless they have fun in what they are doing." Emm wondered at what point the fun had gone out of making a family, when the pleasure of having children had turned into an obsession with winning the derby. He remembered laughing with Arvil, but were there happy times with the others? All Emm knew was that the more children he'd had, the more he wanted. He was never satisfied. Like Foy's never-ending desire for candy.

"Turn, Popsy." Foy's command cut short Emm's thoughts. On the next page, were photos of Izora's parents. Darold had kept in contact with the Oxmoors too. "With Mom dead, I wanted to make sure my kids knew her side of the family." Emm listened for any reproach that he hadn't done more to maintain those ties but heard none. Darold merely went on to say that he was the only one of his siblings who'd gone to Lewis and Clara's funerals.

On the facing page were people Emm didn't recognize. "Uncle Reggie," said Foy, naming Izora's brother, sporting a full beard, and a woman Emm assumed was Reggie's wife. Emm asked what had become of that shiftless man. "Marginal jobs," answered Darold. "I hired him as a truck driver for a while, but he quit. We lost touch after his second marriage and third child."

"Where's Uncle Reggie and Aunt Fiona?" Darold told Foy he didn't know. Foy turned to Emm. "Can you take me to see Paul, Edna, and June?" Emm guessed they were Reggie's children. He said he had even less knowledge of their whereabouts than Darold.

Foy slammed the photo album shut. "I want a Jawbuster." Darold reminded him he could no longer eat those after he'd broken his tooth. Foy settled for a Jolly Rancher and calmed down as quickly as he'd gotten upset. He reopened the album and peppered his father and brother with questions about a new set of people Emm didn't recognize. They were friends of Darold and Virginia, so at least Emm wasn't embarrassed not knowing them, but he was bored and annoyed by Foy's chatter. What if he himself turned into a blithering idiot as he got older? To obliterate such a thought, Emm made up couplets about the people in the pictures. "Poor Georgie wears a frown. Puts his pants on upside down." Foy looked confused but smiled tentatively. "Jane was plain but rather vain. Fluffed out her hair like a lion's mane." Foy turned to Darold, who laughed. Foy took that as a signal that it was okay for him to laugh too. When that made the Jolly Rancher fly out of his mouth and stick to the carpet, Foy looked scared—until Darold laughed harder. Then so did Foy. Darold wrapped the gooey sucker in a tissue and gave him another.

Emm continued to make up rhymes and Foy responded, even though they seemed to go over his head. It wasn't clear to Emm whether his son understood that laughing was something you did in a social situation, or he was simply happy to be with his father and brother, doing what he loved. Darold was patient, treating Foy's endless questions with respect. After finishing his candy, Foy leaned against his brother like a child would lean against a parent who was reading him a book. After an hour, Emm looked at his watch and excused himself for a nap before dinner.

"Rats," said Darold. "I lost track of time. We better leave right now."

It was too late. Before they'd gotten up from the couch, Virginia walked in. She threw her keys on the coffee table where they bounced off the album onto the floor. "Why is he still here?"

"Hold your horses. We were just heading out." Darold ushered Foy toward the door, but when Foy whimpered, he stopped and faced his wife. "My brother has a name and when it comes to knowing how to act around other people, Foy is a hell of a lot smarter than you." Darold put his arm around Foy and looked at Emm. "You coming with us, Dad?"

Emm nodded and sat in the back seat, where he wouldn't have to see Foy's dejected face. "Why doesn't Virginia like me?" Foy asked his brother. "I'm not mean to her."

"It's not you she's angry at," said Darold. "It's me. She's jealous of the time I spend with my family. Do you know what jealous means?"

Foy perked up. "It's when you want something that someone else has. Right?" Darold said that was exactly right and patted his hand. Foy clapped and turned on the radio. He bounced in his seat the rest of the way and was still bouncing when he got out of the car. Halfway to the door of his group home, Foy ran back to say, "Bye, Popsy. I'll see you tomorrow."

Darold wheezed on the ride home. Emm couldn't tell if this was an ordinary episode of troubled breathing or whether he was agitated about the argument with his wife. He wondered whether Darold would defend him against Virginia as forcefully as he'd spoken up for Foy. "You know, son, another Dale Carnegie quote is apropos here. 'Unjust criticism is often a disguised compliment.' Maybe Virginia secretly admires your devotion to Foy and the rest of the family."

Darold managed a deep breath and smiled. "Nice try, Dad." He turned the radio back on.

Emm admired Darold's gentleness toward his brother. He was even more patient than Emm recalled Izora being. Perhaps she'd been so exhausted by the time Foy was born that she'd left his care to Bruna and Darold. In truth, Emm's feelings were closer to Virginia's. He too found Foy irritating, a reminder of the slowness and confusion that lay ahead. He wondered, if Izora had lived, whether she would have been kind and patient with him as he aged.

No matter how much Emm tried to follow his idol's advice about putting others before yourself, he always came back to his own needs. Mr. Carnegie would be very disappointed in him. It was Emm's turn to feel dejected.

CHAPTER 15

Despite the daily annoyance, Emm thrived in his new surroundings. Darold's physical weaknesses, and Foy's mental ones, made him feel stronger and sharper by comparison. Within two weeks, he was almost nimble with his cane. Even better, no one said anything about him moving upstairs.

Emm began to take pride in keeping his bedroom and bathroom clean, more than he had in his own house for many years and the opposite of his behavior at Cleon and Betty's. As he grew more confident getting around, he started straightening the living room and kitchen too. He wasn't sure why. To irk Virginia with the implied criticism of her housekeeping; to thank Darold by getting rid of the dust and mold that aggravated his lungs; or to prove himself to Dale Carnegie by putting his life in order after all. On his best days, Emm dared to hope he'd get well enough to return home, alone, with Eudora Cray checking in on him once a month and staying for tea.

The last room Emm began to clean, once he could maneuver around the narrow space, was a den Darold called the study. It held little more than a desk littered with yellowed news clippings, cancelled checks, and dried-out ballpoint pens. One day, sorting through the clutter, he found Izora's obituary from *The Toronto Star*. The survivors listed were him and their children, and her parents and brother. It also said she'd been predeceased by her son Arvil, a war hero. The photo of her Emm had chosen for the announcement was a youthful one from their courting days.

He put the clipping in a folder he labeled "Keep," along with articles about Darold's various promotions and the awards his children and grandchildren had won over the years. As he slipped the folder into a drawer, Emm pulled out a soft-covered book he found at the back. It was the volume of crossword puzzles he'd bought to amuse Izora when she seemed ground down by the children. The puzzles had been filled in, but not in her handwriting. It looked like that of an older child who was still experimenting with the style of certain letters.

That evening, when Emm asked, Darold said he'd found the unused book in Izora's vanity table after she died. He was fifteen. "Doing the puzzles kept me company. Words were still my best friends."

Emm had an image of Izora snuggling with Darold in his father's brown tweed armchair. "Do you remember your mother reading to you every night? She never skipped that half hour with you, even if it meant the other children had to wait before she gave them her attention."

"She told me to ask you to read to me too because you were smarter than her and knew more big words."

"Did you? Did I?"

"Not that I recall."

Emm leaned on his cane. "I suppose I thought reading to a child was something only mothers did. From what I see in the papers, times have changed. Fathers do more nowadays."

"Parents do what their own parents did until the pendulum swings and something changes. Hopefully for the better."

"Why did you save the book after you finished the puzzles?"

Darold thought before answering. "First, as a remembrance of Mom. Later, thinking how much pleasure it gave me to work on it, as a reminder that effort can overcome adversity."

Emm stroked the book's wrinkled cover. "Your mother wasn't able to. She succumbed."

"Which made me that much more determined not to." Darold looked at Foy, who was lost in a soap opera, *As the World Turns.* "I've lived my life trying to rehabilitate her legacy."

***

A month into Emm's stay, Darold's son James visited with his wife Cynthia and their children—Thomas, seven, and Sharon, three. While their parents drank beer and Darold grilled hot dogs, Sharon drew with Virginia at the picnic table and Thomas asked Emm to play catch with him.

Emm's instinct was to turn down his great grandson. He was too unsteady on his feet to chase after a ball. On the other hand, he was so pleased to be asked, after being ignored at Bruna's, that he proposed standing in place and throwing the ball for the boy to catch. As they played, Emm was reminded of Arvil. Thomas had his thick brown curls and long lashes. The same behavior too. He cheered himself after every catch. If he missed, he'd say "I know I'll get it next time." With his brash confidence, the boy could have been a miniature disciple of Dale Carnegie.

Ten minutes into their game, Virginia went inside to make a salad. Sharon came over and asked Emm to throw the ball to her too. Her big brother told her that girls couldn't play. Emm waited for Sharon to give up and follow her grandmother into the kitchen. Instead, she fought her brother for the ball. They elbowed and kicked each other, crying "Give it to me."

James, their father, sauntered over, took the ball, and calmly handed it to Emm. "Hold this for a minute," he said, then knelt between his children and put an arm around each one. "What's the problem?" He listened as first Thomas and then Sharon told him why they were mad. Keeping his voice neutral, James summed up the situation. "So, Sharon wants to play catch and Thomas says girls don't know how?" The children nodded. He asked if they had an idea on how to solve the problem. When they shrugged, he offered a suggestion. "What if Great Grandpa Emm throws the ball to each of you, and we'll see if Sharon can catch it?" The children agreed to give it a try.

Thomas took his place behind the line and caught the ball. He gave his sister an "I told you so look," and returned the ball to Emm. Then Sharon stepped up to the line. Emm lobbed a gentle throw, and she caught the ball too. Thomas looked surprised, but thereafter brother and sister took turns until they were told it was time to eat, whereupon they raced to the house together to wash up.

Emm slowly followed, shaking his head in wonder. He'd never done anything like that with his children. Not that he'd needed to. Regardless of what Bruna and Cleon told him, Emm couldn't remember their big brother Arvil teasing them. By comparison, he had just seen Thomas taunt Sharon. Just as he'd seen their father James solve the problem with them. Although he'd been a bystander, Emm nevertheless felt that he'd helped too, simply by being a witness and not taking sides. He wished Mrs. Eudora Cray had been there to see how well he was fitting in.

Eudora rhymed with Izora. Why hadn't Emm noticed that before? It was a pity his social worker wasn't there, but Emm hoped his late wife was looking down in amazement at him playing with their great-grandchildren. He let go of his cane and turned both palms up toward heaven.

CHAPTER 16

At Virginia's insistence, Foy hadn't been at the backyard picnic, but on Monday, after work, Darold brought him home as usual. Foy stationed himself in front of the television to watch another rerun of *The Brady Bunch*, whose members Emm was still no better at keeping straight than those in his own family. Foy pouted at being given a snack of grapes instead of candy but was soon distracted singing the show's theme song. When the tic-tac-toe board introducing the cast came on, he touched the screen and named each character. His finger, wet with grape juice and pulp, left a big streak. Darold didn't care. Virginia wasn't likely to mind either, but the smear bothered Emm. He'd cleaned the house that morning after the weekend gathering.

The episode was about friends of the Bradys who bought a bigger house after adopting a little boy. Foy grew upset because he didn't recognize the unfamiliar characters. When he asked what their names were, Darold told him to watch a while longer and see if he could figure it out. After another minute, Foy proudly announced, "The daddy is Ken, the mommy is Kathy, and the little boy is Matt. Right?" He repeated their names the next few times they appeared on screen and settled back with his bowl of grapes. It wasn't long however, before he had trouble following the plot and his agitation returned. He demanded of Emm, "Why is Matt so sad, Popsy?"

Emm, imitating Darold, suggested he wait and watch. Foy turned back to the set, only to give up after hearing more names he didn't recognize. "Who are Dwayne and Steve?" he whined. Darold said they were Matt's friends at the adoption home and that the little boy missed them. He said it would be like Foy leaving the group home and missing the friends he left behind.

"Like if I moved here?" Foy asked, his voice a mixture of hope and fear.

"Yes," said Darold, "but that isn't going to happen. I take you back every day."

Foy's sigh of relief was tinged with sadness. Emm wondered whether, if he were forced to move to Kingsbridge, his old work friends would visit him there. Would he make new friends? He couldn't recall meeting anyone at the home who interested him and even if he had, there was no point getting to know people who would soon die. And yet, while he hadn't minded keeping to himself when he lived at the house, being alone surrounded by others would feel ... lonely. Strange as it was to admit to himself, ever since he'd begun living with his children, Emm had gotten used to having other people around and talking with them every day.

Once more, Foy tried to follow the show's plot but was soon perplexed by a reference to three musketeers. Darold explained it was the nickname of three men in an old storybook, as well as the name of the candy bar that Foy liked to eat. At that point, Foy's brain became overloaded. He yelled at the television set to play a story with the Brady Bunch people he knew. Then he overturned his bowl of grapes, smashed them into the carpet, and demanded to be given candy.

Before Darold could calm Foy down, Emm blew up too. Foy's incessant whining and addled brains brought back frightening scenes from the old age home. Only now, instead of being on the side of the residents, Emm had sympathy for the staff. If he became like Foy, he deserved to be locked away upstairs like Mr. McCreedy. He almost wished he had died when he'd fallen.

"Damn it, Darold. No wonder Virginia gets the hell out of here when Foy is around. He's going to be the death of me this afternoon. Take him home now." Emm stomped off to bed. He fell into a deep sleep and didn't wake up to eat dinner. Or to take his blood pressure medication.

The last thing Emm remembered, as gray morning light seeped underneath the window shade, was stumbling when he put his good leg on the floor. He tried to call for help but all that came out was a low gurgle. His head pounded until, mercifully, he lost consciousness.

***

"A second stroke of good luck, Mr. Benbow." Dr. Sawyer stood at Emm's hospital bedside, again, and chuckled. "Sorry, bad choice of words." He explained that just as Emm had avoided breaking anything when he'd fallen three months ago, this time the stroke he'd suffered appeared to be mild. Furthermore, his son had brought him to the emergency room right away, which boded well for his recovery. "Either partially or fully. Eventually, that is. Depending."

Emm saw a shadow out of the corner of his left eye and assumed it was Darold.

"We won't know the residual effects for a few weeks or months, but here are some things you might notice." The doctor rattled off a list of problems, some bearable, others horrible, in no particular order: muscle weakness on one side; impaired vision; trouble swallowing; loss of bowel and bladder control; trouble speaking or understanding speech and print; depression; anxiety; loss of inhibition; irritability; impaired sense of taste. He motioned Darold closer. "Call immediately if your father complains of numbness or shows the same symptoms as last night or this morning."

Darold looked at the floor. "The thing is, doctor. I'm not sure my father will continue to live with me when he leaves here. I don't have the strength to look after him. You see, I ..."

Dr. Sawyer coughed impatiently and handed Darold a pamphlet. "Whether it's you or one of your siblings, you should all know the warning signs and act fast. Mr. Benbow will be in rehab for several weeks, so your family has time to work it out." The doctor left. Emm couldn't hear his soles squeaking down the hall and wondered if the floors were less polished than on his former ward or if he'd lost some hearing. He couldn't remember if growing deaf was on the list.

Darold took Emm's hand. "I'm sorry, Dad. It's not that I don't want to take care of you, it's that I can't. I can manage Foy. His head doesn't work right, but I don't have to help him with his body. The people at the group home take care of that." Darold suppressed a sob, muttered something about feeling like a failure, and said he'd be back later.

Emm told his son that he wasn't a failure. Or maybe he just thought to say it. He couldn't be sure. All he knew was that he was very tired, and the room was empty. He closed his eyes and entered a dark, quiet cave. It was peaceful inside. He didn't feel anxious at all.

***

This time when Emm woke up, Bruna and Cleon were standing on either side of him. He had no trouble rotating his head as they took turns speaking or understanding what they were saying.

Bruna spoke first. "We've been talking Father. Darold feels helpless and even if he could take care of you, Virginia has ruled out your moving back there."

"I guess you know how Betty feels," Cleon shouted close to his ear. Emm told his son that his hearing was fine, there was no need to yell at him.

"We think it makes sense for you to rotate among our houses." Bruna looked above Emm toward Cleon and said pointedly, "Yours included." She looked down at Emm again. "One month with each of us, so no one has to bear the entire burden."

Emm tried to sit up, then to raise his head. He wanted to speak forcefully but settled for talking clearly. "I can't do that. I need the stability of living in one place."

"The nursing home is one place. With, I assume, predictable routines." Cleon jiggled the ice cubes in the water cup on Emm's tray table.

"Stop," said Emm.

"The family is getting together at my house tonight to discuss how to pass you around. Meanwhile, get some rest. One or more of us will be back tomorrow. We'll take turns visiting while you're still here." Bruna's lips grazed the top of Emm's head. She walked to the door.

Cleon followed. He turned with his hand on the knob and spoke in a normal voice. "Need anything, Dad? Want me to stop at the nurses' station on the way out?"

Emm, mute, watched them leave. He sipped his water; it tasted like metal. Reflexively, he spat it out, soaking his hospital gown. Where was the damn call button? Were Cleon's words about Kingsbridge meant to encourage or threaten him? The stroke seemed to have taken away his ability to tell if there was a hidden meaning behind them. Suppose it was simply a statement of fact? Whatever the case, Emm should reconsider living at the nursing home. Only not right now.

***

Late afternoon, Darold returned with Foy. "He asked to come see you," he explained before excusing himself to confer with the rehab office. Emm saw it as a pretext to avoid facing him and feeling guilty. As his son had said, it wasn't that he didn't care about his father; he felt bad that he couldn't care for him. What puzzled Emm, however, was why Darold left Foy behind while he escaped. It was the first time he could recall being alone with him.

Izora had never asked Emm to help with Foy, and why would she? If she couldn't handle their son, she wouldn't expect Emm to.

Damn it. Hadn't aggravation with this man-child brought on Emm's stroke in the first place? And hadn't Dr. Sawyer said that irritability was an outcome of a stroke? What the hell was Emm supposed to do now? Getting old meant you were stuck wherever life landed you.

As soon as Darold was gone, Foy sidled up to the bed and put a finger to his lips. "Look what I snuck in for you, Popsy." From his pocket, he withdrew a handful of cellophane-wrapped candy. He lined up the pieces on top of Emm's blanket. Each was a different shiny color.

Emm frowned. "I thought you weren't allowed to eat candy."

"Not for me. All for you." Foy beamed.

Recalling the taste of the water, Emm shook his head. "I'm not supposed to eat it either."

Foy's face fell. "Not even one? I brought it special. To make you get better."

Emm popped the red piece in his mouth. Thank goodness it was small. If it tasted horrible, he could swallow it without choking and not risk hurting Foy's feelings. Or getting Foy worked up. Too late, Emm remembered that trouble swallowing was another symptom after a stroke.

Foy peered at him anxiously. "You like it. Right?"

Emm scrunched his face and rolled the candy on his tongue. It tasted sweet. His jaws relaxed. "Mmm. Cherry, my favorite flavor."

His son hopped around the room. "I knew you'd like it. Look what else I brought. Darold said I could." He took the photo album out of a shopping bag and sat on the edge of the bed. Emm tensed again, waiting for the nattering and barrage of questions. But Foy, with a sensitivity Emm hadn't expected, snuggled next to him and silently flipped the pages. When, an hour later, Darold came back, Emm quickly hid the remaining candy under his pillow and winked at Foy.

"Bye, Popsy. Feel better." Foy's hug was the first welcome phys-ical contact Emm could remember since losing Izora. He didn't ask what Darold had learned at the rehab office, or if that's where he had really gone. Instead, he asked if Foy could visit him again.

Darold raised his eyebrows. "Of course. To be honest, though, I wasn't sure about leaving him with you today."

Emm struggled to explain. "Foy is easy to be with. I'm tired, and it doesn't take much to make him happy. Remember what you said about his having good sense when it comes to people? It's true. You did the right thing, bringing him here to see me." This time Emm knew for sure that he'd spoken the words aloud. They brought a look of relief, and gratitude, to Darold's face.

"Dad, I can't take you back permanently, and I'm guessing you don't want to be shipped around like an orphan or go to the nursing home. So, tonight at Bruna's, I'll try to persuade one of the others to let you move in long term. It's the best I can do." Darold held out his hands.

Emm took hold, surprising them both with the strength of his grip.

That night, while his children debated his fate, Emm imagined what Darold would say to his brothers and sisters. He couldn't conjure the exact words, but he understood why his son felt compelled to say them. Quite simply, Darold, having suffered himself, had learned that he felt better by being kind to others. Foy was harder to understand. What made him kind? Did the holes in his mind, which he couldn't help, allow him to forget that Emm had been short tempered with him? Or, given his deter-mined streak, had Foy made himself forget that Emm had been unkind?

If only Emm were more like Foy, he too could disregard the mess he'd gotten himself into. Unfortunately, the stroke hadn't left holes in his brain, and he couldn't let go of what had happened in his life before. Even more, Emm wanted to take control over what would happen next.

CHAPTER 17

Following a restless night and uneaten breakfast tray, Emm called Eudora Cray. Just hearing the sympathy in her voice when he told her he'd had a stroke made him feel optimistic. He said he was disappointed that he couldn't live at Darold's anymore, and that he'd enjoyed playing catch with his great-grandchildren. He would miss being a regular part of their family.

Mrs. Cray sighed. "What a shame. You were recovering so nicely, and the medicine was keeping your blood pressure in check. Did the doctor say why he thought you had the stroke?"

Emm was tempted to blame it solely on forgetting his pills. What stopped him was worrying that Mrs. Cray might think he was becoming senile and that it was time to lock him away after all. He decided it was safer to confess the whole story. "I got irritated with Foy. He's the slow one. I was so fed up with him that I stomped off to bed and slept until the next morning without taking my medicine." He braced himself for a scolding, hoping it would be gentle.

"I see," was all Mrs. Cray said.

"The thing is," Emm hurried on, "my children now have the idea that I should move from house to house so that none of them is stuck with me all the time. But I don't want to be shuffled from place to place and I don't want to be stuck forever at Kingsbridge."

"You realize you're running out of options?" Mrs. Cray sounded stern. "Not only among your children, but the openings at Kingsbridge get filled quickly. They expect to have a waiting list by the end of the year. And the places that will still have room for you are not as nice."

Emm's vision blurred. He told himself it was tears, not the stroke. "I know you said you wouldn't call my children for me, but perhaps you'd make an exception this once. Seeing as how I'm ... disabled at the moment. Talk one of them into taking me in."

Emm heard the sound of pages being turned before Mrs. Cray spoke again. "You know, Mr. Benbow, you've inspired me to read Dale Carnegie's book. I've found several quotes that are proving useful with my other clients. So, here's one for you. 'The successful man will profit from his mistakes and try again in a different way.' If I were to speak to your children, what could I tell them you would do differently?"

There was no anger or pity in her voice. It was more like cajoling. That Emm could hear that tone, and knew the word to describe it, reassured him that his faculties were intact. "Say that from now on I'll do my best to fit into their routines. And I'll use the time in rehab to learn how to take care of myself, so they won't have to do as much."

"That's a good start." The word s-t-a-r-t was drawn out; she was waiting to hear more.

"Tell them I'll be kinder." Mrs. Cray agreed to make the call.

Emm thanked her for breaking the rules on his behalf. And for not giving up on him when he was ready to give up on himself. "Why?" he asked, genuinely puzzled.

"Because you've survived hardship and loss. And bounced back every time. I don't think you'll give up on yourself. As long as your mind is working—and you couldn't write poems if it didn't— you're still capable of learning and changing."

"If I can take words and rearrange them, I can take actions and change them." Emm hung up, reassured by Eudora's chuckle. A faint light shone on the wall opposite his bed as a cloud moved just enough to uncover a sliver of the morning sun. A few hours later, just before lunch, Mrs. Cray phoned back to say her intervention wasn't necessary after all. Darold had persuaded his siblings to give Emm another chance, and Erissa had volunteered to let Emm move in with her.

Emm asked what Darold had said to them. Mrs. Cray admitted she didn't know. "Do you think Erissa stepped up because she's next in the alphabet?" he asked her.

Mrs. Cray hesitated, as if she were now the one deciding whether to tell the truth. At last, she spoke. "Your daughter said your government pension would help her with rent and food."

"Oh well," said Emm. "It's a start."

***

Emm went back to using a walker. After soiling himself for a month following the stroke, he regained control, but the right side of his body, the one he'd fallen on, had momentary power outages. He examined himself for other symptoms, especially questioning how well his mind was working. It seemed sharp enough, but he occasionally had trouble following conversations. He didn't know if the problem was him or the jumbled speech of the people he met in rehab, all stroke victims like himself. The thought of not making sense to others, or the world not making sense to him, haunted the lonely minutes before Emm drifted off to sleep.

Another annoyance, by comparison a small one, was the awful hospital food. Emm blamed it on the fare itself rather than his impaired sense of taste. He regretted ending his stay with Bruna, not only because she was a good cook, but because her food brought back fond memories of the tasty meals Izora prepared. Emm hoped that if he reformed enough, he'd be invited to the weekly gatherings at Bruna's house. As near as he could remember, though, Erissa hadn't been at the one he had attended. If she were seen as an outcast, would he, by association, be treated like one too?

A week before he was released from rehab, Emm was allowed to go on one field trip away from the hospital grounds. He wanted to visit Erissa, to get a sense of where he'd be living next, but she told Darold to tell their father that she needed more time to get clean.

"You mean, get her house clean?" Emm asked.

Darold shrugged. "That's all she said. I didn't push her."

Emm asked to instead spend the day at Darold's, provided Foy would be there. Darold said of course, but on the drive to his house, said that he was curious about what prompted the request. Emm, struggling to explain what he himself didn't understand, resorted to another rhyme: "Fear comes from not knowing where you are going. But there is no fear if you've always been there."

"But Dad, you know where you're going. To live with Erissa."

"I don't mean it literally, but the older we get, the more we worry about our bodies or brains failing. If they've never worked, we don't have to adjust to the idea of them falling apart. Like you and your body. Losing your mind is scarier, but Foy is already comfortable in his. He's at peace." Emm looked out the car window. While he'd been hospitalized, the slow-to-bloom trees had finished leafing out. "It may sound backwards, but I think Foy has something to teach me."

From the corner of his eye, Emm saw his son nod. They drove in silence for a while. "Now I'm curious." He turned toward Darold. "Did your name cause you problems growing up?"

"Not really. It was so close to Harold." He chuckled. "In fact, on the first day of school each year, my teachers thought the office had made a mistake and assumed my name *was* Harold. It wasn't until the fourth grade that they decided I was old enough to know what I was talking about when I insisted it really was Darold."

"You learned to stand up for yourself. So, it wasn't bad, having an odd name."

Darold coughed. "Poor Foy was the one who got teased about his. Of course, he got teased for everything, but most of the taunts he didn't understand, so they didn't upset him. He got it, though, when they made fun of his name. It was one of the few things that made him cry. To him, if other kids didn't like his name, it meant they didn't like him. His sobs broke my heart."

Emm's heart ached too. For Foy, for Darold. Mostly for himself. His children didn't like him. Unlike Foy, he couldn't blame their rejection on his slowness. On the contrary, Emm had been too quick with them. With having them. He hoped it wasn't too late to pull out of the race.

PART SIX:
ERISSA
JULY-AUGUST 1976

Erissa was born on April 10, 1932, four years to the day after her sister Bruna, but the two girls were otherwise polar opposites. Whereas Bruna was stone-faced and withdrawn, Erissa was bright and outgoing, bringing much-needed joy to a household steeped in the bleakness of hard times. The child's happy gurgles and smiling eyes even managed to get the staid Mr. Benbow wrapped around her chubby little fingers. Emm's parents lavished her with gifts—a musical mobile with hand-carved animals, a menagerie of stuffed animals, and embroidered outfits she would outgrow in less than a month. Izora was muted in her thanks. Emm knew she felt bad that her parents couldn't match the Benbows' generosity, nor their continued help with the older children, all of whom, with the exception of Cleon, rapidly outgrew their clothes too.

One evening, when the rest of the family was passing Erissa from lap to lap at the dinner table, Emm came home late, waving the Daily Star. "The Ontario government is trying to nullify Millar's will," he cried, "so it can give the money to the University of Toronto." He handed the paper to his father and waved away the baby when his mother tried to hand her over.

Mr. Benbow skimmed the article, frowned, and turned to the editorial page, whereupon his lips turned up. "The newspaper accuses the government of resorting to 'communism in the raw' and predicts there'll be a huge public outcry," he read aloud. Which is just what happened. A week later, the government's suit was withdrawn, and the contest went on according to Mr. Millar's wishes.

Nevertheless, Emm fretted that the renewed publicity would bring more families into the race. The fewer contestants, the better his chances of winning. When he'd entered the race, it was with excitement and determination. Now he was driven by anxiety and desperation.

Izora wiped up the older children's drips and spills before her mother-in-law could scold them or give her a stern look of disapproval "What does it matter if more people know about the Derby?" she asked Emm. "It's too late for new families to start accumulating babies."

He told her she was being naive and oblivious to the danger. "Parents who missed the announcement six years ago but have lots of children will realize they could be in contention. See here." He pointed to another article that named half a dozen families who now planned to compete.

Coverage of the race soon became a regular feature in both the Toronto Daily Star *and the* Evening Telegram. *Emm, who'd started having a drink before dinner and sometimes one or two afterwards, gave his family updates every night. "Do you think we should go public?" he asked his parents, "to discourage anyone with less than five kids from entering the contest?"*

Mr. Benbow scowled. "Folks are so hard up for money, nothing will stop them."

Emm turned away from Izora's accusing look after his father's pronouncement.

Mrs. Benbow slapped Arvil's wrist as he reached across the table for the potatoes. "It's shameful how the other parents in this race allow the press to scrutinize them and their children. Yours are spoiled enough already. They don't need the added attention."

That wasn't how Emm saw it. He thought publicizing their advantage would persuade other families to give up. Nevertheless, he deferred to his parents' position that it was unwise to play their hand with four *years remaining. As he continued to give his daily reports, Emm sensed that Izora was hoping that another family, a child or two ahead of them, would in fact appear. That didn't happen. However, when it emerged that several families were tied for the lead, the Benbows cared for the children after dinner each night so he and Izora could retire to bed early.*

CHAPTER 18

As Darold drove to Erissa's, Emm wondered what awaited him. He knew his daughter would be nothing like the delightful child who'd been his second favorite, after Arvil. Erissa had already become wild by the time she was thirteen, when Izora died. Things went downhill from there. By fourteen, Erissa was drinking heavily and at seventeen she had a baby out of wedlock and left home. Bruna and Darold had helped to raise the little girl, Cheryl, who would now be twenty-seven. Emm had no idea what had become of her and often forgot to count her among his grandchildren. He realized now that when Bruna had been uncertain about how many would be at the weekly family gathering, the question mark must have been Cheryl. He asked Darold if Erissa ever saw her daughter.

"There's a kind of radar between them. On the rare occasions when Erissa shows up at Bruna's, Cheryl doesn't. And vice versa. Except once, when they both came." Darold steered across an invisible border separating the middle class and poor sections of town. "Erissa tried to talk to Cheryl, but Cheryl turned her back on her mother and left." Emm caught his breath and asked Darold how Erissa had reacted. "She blew her nose, and five minutes later, she left too."

Ouch, thought Emm, but Cheryl had good reason to be angry. When Darold told him that Cheryl was a home health aide, Emm perked up. "In that case, do you suppose ...?"

"If you're thinking about hiring her to take care of you, don't. She was fired from her last position, and it wasn't the first time."

Emm snorted. "Cheryl sounds about as dependable as her mother."

"They both keep trying, Dad. Give them credit for that."

Emm searched for a suitable Dale Carnegie quote, but all he could come up with was the old bromide, "If at first you don't succeed, try, try again." He wondered how many chances a person was entitled to. After dropping out of high school, Erissa had enrolled in a secretarial course but left a month shy of getting her certificate. She'd signed on to various sales schemes, never making it past the first level. Mixed in were stints in rehab and attempts at wedlock. He asked about Erissa's most recent marriage, her third if he was correct.

"That ended a while ago." Darold drove past a laundromat, convenience store, and pawn shop, then several boarded-up buildings. Even after Emm felt strong enough to walk again, he wouldn't feel safe wandering around this neighborhood. "As far as I know, there's no new fiancé in the picture," Darold continued, and when Emm asked how his daughter managed financially, he answered, "She finds jobs that come and go, like husbands. Bruna and I help out when we can."

"And now I'm coming to the rescue with my pension check."

"I won't dispute that, but I think Erissa is sincere about wanting to help you out too."

Just like Darold, thought Emm, always seeing a person's positive side. He wondered where his son got that habit from. Emm had always been an optimistic sort, but counting on the luck of fate wasn't the same thing as trusting in the goodness of people. Could it be that Darold took after Izora? She rarely said a bad word about anyone, even his mother. Then again, his wife never said much of anything. Perhaps Emm just hadn't been listening.

***

The car entered a large complex with a sign reading "Cityhome Apartments, Operated by the City of Toronto Nonprofit Housing Corporation." After a few more turns, Darold parked in front of a three-story building that looked identical to the others. Carrying Emm's suitcase, he helped his father up the front stoop and pushed the elevator button. "Glad it's working today," he said.

On the top floor, Erissa opened the door before Emm finished wheeling his walker down the hall. Darold moved slowly alongside him but raced ahead the last several feet to embrace his sister. Emm held back to take her in. Her once pretty face was deeply lined, its peachy cream skin ashen and blotchy. Her bouncy dark curls were now dyed a lifeless straw blonde. Hardest for Emm to look at were the multiple piercings. Three in one ear, four in the other, a stud in her nose and another stabbing her bottom lip. She wore a thrift-store ensemble—pink tank top, floral pants with a multicolored scarf tied around the waist—which in its mismatched way, nevertheless gave her a certain stylish flair. It reminded Emm of Izora's jaunty flapper clothes. It was a shame that the nasty metal bits in Erissa's face took your attention away from the one decent thing about her.

"Come in, Papa. It's been a while, hasn't it? I can't remember exactly. Darold, take Papa's bag into the bedroom. I'm turning it over to him until we move to a bigger place. Meanwhile, I'll sleep on the pull-out." Erissa looked at the tiny mound of belly that protruded from her otherwise skinny frame. "I'm not in great shape, but I figure I can handle the sofa better than someone your age. Remind me again how old you are. I'm good with numbers, but people's ages don't stick with me. They come in the front of my brain, then pop right out the back." She moved a pillow from the couch to the floor. "Oh, silly me, rattling on. Sit down, Papa. Do you hurt a lot? Bruna said you were lucky the stroke wasn't worse, but you gotta be careful from now on."

Emm thought how unlucky he was to be moving in with a

nonstop talker. Unlike Darold, Erissa didn't act anything like Izora. Even his own mother, who no one could ever accuse of holding her tongue, wasn't as bad as this motor-mouth daughter.

Darold returned from the bedroom. "I'll stop by to get you two on Sunday." Erissa said thanks, but she wasn't going to Bruna's. She had to work. Emm declined the offer as well. He'd use the time to take a long uninterrupted nap. Darold slipped a few bills into a jar on the kitchen counter, which was at the other end of the room from the couch. Emm wouldn't have to walk far to get from place to place in this apartment. "Call if you need anything," Darold said on his way out.

Panic crept from Emm's buzzing head to his quaking stomach and settled in his trembling legs. Suppose the elevator stopped working and he was stranded on the third floor alone? It was scarier than being upstairs at Kingsbridge. There, presumably, they had an evacuation plan.

He shifted his buttocks to avoid the broken spring in the couch and looked around. This room, the bedroom, and a bathroom, which, from what he could see through the door, was none too clean. Nor was the rest of the apartment. There were roach traps in the corners and grease stains on the bare wall. Pine-scented air freshener couldn't blot out the smell of mold and another odor that Emm couldn't identify. On a beat-up end table were a few photos of Erissa and her friends partying, but there were no pictures of her daughter, exes, or other family members.

Erissa followed his gaze and started to jabber again. "It was bad like this when I moved in, and I didn't see the point in trying to clean it up. You know what public housing is like. Silly me, of course you don't. Well, folks don't take care of these units; they figure they're going to move on to something better. Unless they get kicked out first." She sat next to Emm and grabbed his hands. "But with your pension, we can afford a two-bedroom unit. People usually take better care of those, I think because they rent them to women with children." Erissa bit her lip. "There are a few openings in this building, beginning next week. Do you want a ground-floor unit with a little patio and garden out back or an upper floor with a balcony?"

Emm, relieved by the thought of living at street level, said that he'd prefer a downstairs apartment. His daughter squeezed his fingers harder than he anticipated, given how frail she appeared.

Erissa crowed. "I knew it. That's what I picked. You're going to like it here. Promise."

Dinner was stale ham and cheese sandwiches from the convenience store. Erissa removed the stud from her lip before she unwrapped hers and set it on a paper napkin. Emm nibbled half his meal and said he'd save the rest for lunch. Erissa ate even less, either because she wasn't hungry or the constant movement of her mouth was incompatible with chewing and swallowing.

"I'm sorry I can't offer you something better, Papa, but just wait until we move into our new apartment. I'm not a bad cook, and once I get some pots and pans, we can eat in style. What do you like? Bruna makes a lot of Mama's old recipes, especially anything with bacon, but I'm more of a grilled meat and vegetable person. That's probably heathier for you anyway, right? I heard strokes come from having high blood pressure, and people who have high blood pressure aren't supposed to eat cured meats and salty canned soups." Erissa looked out the grimy window. "It's hard to find fresh food in this neighborhood, but with your pension, I can walk to one of the markets a couple of neighborhoods over and then take a cab back home. We'll eat like royalty."

Erissa swept the leftovers into the bag they came in and threw it in the trash. She'd already forgotten that Emm had planned to save his for tomorrow. She rolled up her sleeves to wash the breakfast dishes still in the sink. That's when Emm noticed the needle marks on her arm.

Erissa reddened. "Honest, Papa. I haven't used in months," she stammered, which made Emm wonder why she'd told Darold she needed more time "to get clean." She could relapse at any moment. Or had Erissa said "to clean?" If so, there was no evidence she'd used those extra days to do that either. Emm longed to ask if she'd stopped drinking too, but he didn't want them to get off on the wrong foot his first night here. He reminded himself to think more like Darold, and to find a Dale Carnegie quote about giving people the benefit of the doubt. All that came to mind, however, was his advice about getting others to do what you wanted them to.

He thought about what Mrs. Cray wanted him to do. Be kinder, more patient, give his remaining children a chance. Erissa had burned—drank, shot up, pierced—her way through many chances. Maybe Emm would offer her the one that worked. Of all his children, she was the worst off. The others didn't need Emm, but Erissa did. Lifting their fallen daughter might be Emm's best chance at winning Izora's forgiveness. He'd also validate Eudora's faith in him.

When the dishes were done—Emm sensed that his daughter took pains to scrub them more than she usually did—Erissa started to put the stud back in her lower lip. Emm must have winced because she immediately stopped. "Sorry, Papa. I won't wear it around the house if it makes you uncomfortable. I know a lot of folks get the willies when they see jewelry stuck in people's lips. Eyelids are the worst. Even I don't like to look at those." Erissa pocketed the small silver ball. "Is it okay if I wear it to work, though, since you won't be there to see it?"

Darold had said Erissa took odd jobs, but Emm had no idea what they were, so he asked. She said she was currently a clerk at a party store. Not the best position for someone with a drinking problem, he thought, but again chose to keep his mouth shut. Even if Erissa couldn't.

"I used to work the night shift, but it was scary. Being there alone with cash in the till and who knows what kind of crazies desperate for a drink or who knows what else." Erissa smiled, and for a moment, maybe it was the dimple despite her thin cheeks, Emm glimpsed the charming little girl she'd been. "So, I got friendly with the manager, Terrence, and now I work days. Mid-afternoons are slow, so Terry comes by to check on me. He likes to take out my stud before we kiss. And put it back in before he leaves. Like putting a period on the end of a sentence."

Emm thought of Erissa's three failed marriages and countless other relationships gone sour. He wondered if Terry was married and what his intentions were, but again saw no point in bringing it up. This was the third time he'd chosen to remain silent, and it was only the first day.

Erissa giggled. "He calls me Missa Erissa."

Emm couldn't help smiling. The manager was a poet like himself. "Missa Erissa is a good kissa. So says Terry, her Papa, and big brotha and sissa." He was rewarded with a grin. It gave him an inkling of the pleasure Darold must feel when he was kind toward others. "It's an odd name to rhyme. Do you like it or hate it?" He might as well get the question out of the way.

"I've always loved my name. It belongs to me alone. Plus, it's pretty and it got the boys' attention. Still does, I guess. I wear a name tag at the store, and guys are always coming on to me because of it. Well, not just because of my name. You know what I mean. Oh, silly me, of course you don't. Say, suppose I go buy us some ice cream to celebrate your moving in?"

Before Emm could object that ice cream was no healthier for him than bacon, Erissa was out the door. While she was gone, he checked under the sink and the bottom shelf of the cabinets for liquor. There wasn't any. He wished he could look under the couch or on the upper shelves, but of course bending and climbing were out. Perhaps he'd never be able to perform those simple acts again. "Emm Benbow can't bend his bow, nor neither flex his knee. He can't look low, he can't look high. All that's left him is to ..." He left the rhyme unfinished. It would complete itself.

CHAPTER 19

Erissa used every spare minute that week to get the new apartment ready. Maybe she really had told Darold she needed more time to clean. She bought plants for the garden, and Emm gave her money for paint and kitchen supplies. Tired as Erissa was, she looked years younger. She refused to let Emm see the place until everything was ready. Finally, Darold and James helped them move.

As Erissa had promised, the two-bedroom apartment was much nicer than her old upstairs unit, both bigger and in better repair. There was a small eating nook, less rust on the fixtures, and the former resident had left behind a comfortable couch. For Emm's safety, Erissa had asked the handyman to install handrails in the bath and shower and to make sure the carpet was tacked down at the thresholds. Best of all was the small walk-out garden. Erissa bought a patio chair with sturdy arms so Emm could lower and raise himself between the walker and the seat. Not only could Emm forget the fear of being trapped inside a burning building, he could step outside for fresh air whenever he wished. "Thank you, Missa Erissa. Living here will be a blissa."

Again, his daughter blushed with pleasure at the rhyme he'd made using her name and because she'd pleased him. "I'm happy you like it, Papa." Emm wanted to sit in the patio chair; just watching the move had tired him out. But Erissa insisted on showing him what she'd planted. "Shasta daisies because they stand for the sun.

That's anthurium, for hospitality. Not just because I'm welcoming you but because I feel like the apartment is opening its doors and windows and closets and drawers to welcome us. This is freesia. I'm not sure what it means, but it smells nice, like oranges and lemons. It's too late for tulips, but I'll plant bulbs in the fall so they'll come up next spring." She went on to name some ornamental grasses and pointed out the colorful octagonal paving stones she'd placed around the perimeter of the beds.

Emm peeked over the low brick wall at the gardens on either side, one bare dirt, the other with a few wilted blooms. Compared to those, their place looked like it belonged in a landscaping magazine with a feature on how to live big in a small outdoor space. He leaned on his walker with one hand and swept his free arm in a circle. "You have a real knack for this."

Erissa touched her hair, which she'd done up in a multi-colored scarf. "Oh, there's nothing to it. You think about what colors look nice together, and make sure to get a variety of heights and textures in the stalks and leaves. Also, what needs sun and what can take a little shade. And you check the time of year they bloom so there's something growing all the way from spring right through fall." Erissa ducked her head, suddenly shy. "Here, did I show you the chrysanthemums?"

"I mean it, Erissa. You're good at designing gardens. You should get a job at a nursery or a flower shop. Heck, get a degree at one of those two-year colleges the government is opening. They're practically free, and I'll pay your fees. Meanwhile, we can manage on my pension."

Erissa was uncharacteristically silent. At last, she hemmed and hawed, "That's awfully kind and it might suit me, but the thing is, I don't want to leave Terry in the lurch. He says I'm the best counter girl he ever had, and he wouldn't trust anyone but me to run the store for him all day." Erissa looked at the ground again, unable to meet Emm's eyes. "Why don't you sit out here and enjoy the garden while I go inside and start dinner."

At last, Emm eased himself into the chair and shoved the walker aside. For months it had provided a handy device that let him avoid people and places. Now he hated being dependent on it and couldn't wait to leave it behind in Dr. Sawyer's office. It was past time for Erissa to become independent too. Times had changed since he and Izora were married. These days, women could be on their own. As angry as Bruna made him, Emm admired her self-sufficiency. Erissa couldn't keep counting on being taken care of by a man. Not a husband, not a boyfriend, not a boss. Emm wouldn't be around forever either. And when he was gone, unlike Mr. Millar, he wasn't going to leave behind a fortune.

***

Erissa had overstated her skills as a cook, at least compared with her older sister, but her flair for decoration was still evident. The food was artfully arranged on the flowered plates she'd bought, and there was bubbly gold liquid in the new faceted glasses. Before proposing a toast, she held out the bottle so Emm could read the label: Non-alcoholic sparkling wine, product of California.

After dinner, they watched the Olympics. Emm still didn't care about sports, but the summer games were being held in Montreal and it was hard to avoid. Viewed on Erissa's black-and-white television, last night's opening ceremonies had been disappointing, but tonight was gymnastics, and his daughter was eager to see the events, especially the floor exercises.

"It's like dancing, only they fly through the air and instead of taxiing to a stop, bam, they hit their spot when they come down." Erissa jumped up from the couch, landed her feet squarely on the rug, and raised her arms over her head.

Emm held up ten fingers. "When you were a little girl, you danced all the time. You loved wearing your mother's old flapper dresses, so she taught you to do the Black Bottom."

Erissa slapped her buttocks. "I remember. I danced it for show and tell. My kindergarten teacher was *not* happy, especially when all the other kids ran around at recess spanking their butts too. Maybe the teacher was afraid parents would see the bruises and think she was paddling us."

"Your Grandma Bessie didn't approve of the Black Bottom either."

"Uh oh. Did Mama stop doing it?"

"No. She thought it was funny and I admit, the rest of us did too. It was one of the few times we went against your grandmother."

"Ooh, I wish I could remember that part. And more about Mama. There are a few things I haven't forgotten. She was really gentle when she brushed the snarls out of my curls. And she let me pick my own clothes to wear to school, no matter how outlandish the outfit I chose. It's too bad I don't have Mama's old dresses in my closet now. They'd be fashionable again today."

This was the moment Emm could have asked if Erissa ever felt bad about not being a real mother to Cheryl, but she seemed so buoyant lately that he didn't want to burst her bubble. Even if she'd been a more stable person to begin with, a question like that could be upsetting. Would he be rattled if someone asked whether he regretted not being a better father? It's true he wasn't the best parent in the world, but on a scale of one to ten, he would rate himself closer to his grandson James than to his daughter Erissa. All the same, that wasn't saying much.

Throughout the broadcast, Erissa and the CBC announcer kept up running commentaries until Emm's head pounded. He eyed the door to his new bedroom, but Erissa begged him to stay and watch the uneven bars with her. Suddenly, the broadcaster and the audience grew silent as a tiny Romanian girl named Nadia Comaneci, looking calm and determined, performed her routine. The arena erupted when she scored the first-ever ten. Shortly thereafter, she repeated the feat on the balance beam. The crowd went wild.

Erissa bounced and cheered too, then suddenly slumped back on the couch. "I'll never be perfect at anything."

"You just have to work harder. You'll get where you want to go. That's what your big brother Arvil did during the Depression. We didn't have money for the movies, so he got a job as a ticket seller and saw them for free."

"Oh, he saw them for free alright, but not because he worked as a ticket seller."

Emm had no idea what Erissa meant. He was surprised to see her grow animated again.

"After I started hanging out with the older boys, they told me that Arvil used to sneak into the theater manager's office and help himself to rolls of tickets. He'd keep a couple for himself and his pals, then trade the rest to the upperclassmen for cigarettes and booze."

Satisfied, Erissa turned back to the television, but Emm couldn't concentrate. He kept trying to make her bombshell fit with his idealized image of his son. He stared at the awards ceremony in silent thought until the Romanian national anthem ended. At last, having figured it out, he smiled and told his daughter. "Like I said, Arvil was very enterprising. That just proves it."

Erissa snickered. "You always made excuses for him. Not that your playing favorites bothered me all that much. Despite being second best, I still got a good share of your attention. But pardon my French, your treating Arvil like the greatest thing since sliced bread pissed the hell out of the others." She turned off the television. "Now, if you'll excuse me, I'm looking forward to sleeping in a real bed again." The telephone rang; Erissa walked past it to her room.

Emm fantasized that it was Cheryl on the other end, calling to make up with her mother in a sudden change of heart. Or it might be one of his own children, calling to wish him well as he settled into his new home. He took his pills and slowly guided his walker to his freshly painted bedroom. At this late hour, it was probably a wrong number.

CHAPTER 20

The first week in August, Erissa came home in the middle of her shift. Emm looked up from the newspaper and asked if anything was wrong. "Erissa dismissa," she snapped. "Terry's wife surprised us, and now I'm out of a romance and out of a job." She went to her room and didn't come out until dinnertime, when she dumped an unheated can of Dinty Moore beef stew onto two paper plates.

Emm thought, "I could have told you so," but said, "Mr. Carnegie says to accept the worst and improve on it. Maybe now's the time to go back to school. My offer to help still stands." Erissa pushed chunks of congealed meat and potatoes around with her fork and said she'd think about it. Then, the food uneaten, she returned to her room.

Over the next few days she stopped washing or changing her clothes. She wore the same torn jeans and, despite the summer heat, long-sleeve shirts. Her nonstop jabbering grew worse, yet at unpredictable moments she'd fall silent and stare at the wall or her hands. Never out the window. The flowers nearly died of thirst until Emm found he could carry a small watering can in one hand and push his walker with the other. It took several trips, but he felt he was doing something.

The following week, Erissa started sleeping all day and staying awake all night. Emm, waking to the suffocating stench of air freshener, suspected she was smoking marijuana. After he'd sniffed and made a face, Erissa began to use mouthwash. Emm searched the places he could reach but found no alcohol. He considered calling Darold. Or Mrs. Cray. Being a social worker, she might know how to deal with people who had problems like his daughter's, especially how to help their families help them. He decided to give it more time. He was determined to solve this situation on his own.

One afternoon mid-month, Emm awoke from a nap on the patio and went inside for a cold drink. The door to Erissa's room was open, but she wasn't inside. The house was eerily quiet, as if the absence of her patter had drained the life out of everything. Finally, when Emm wondered how he'd manage to cook dinner without her help, Erissa came home with a pizza. She was wearing clean clothes, and her hair was done up in a colorful scarf.

"Sorry, Papa, I was going to call out that I was leaving but I didn't want to interrupt your snooze, and I couldn't think of a place to leave a note where you'd see it. I should have left it on the fridge, assuming you'd get thirsty, but I didn't think of that until I'd left. Later, I couldn't find a phone and even if I had, I didn't want to call in case you were still sleeping and the ringing woke you up. You've been kind of restless in your sleep lately, and I figured you needed the nap."

Emm's pulse quickened when he heard Erissa babbling. She sounded like the person she'd been last month. When she took a third slice of pizza, he marveled that her appetite had come back too. Listening to her chatter about the heat and whether she should buy a wok and take up Chinese cooking, Emm dared to ask if she'd given more thought to going back to school.

Erissa took a big bite, chewed quickly, and swallowed. "It just so happens that today I registered at Centennial College. Classes start in September."

"I'm glad to hear that." Emm's face flushed. He wondered if his blood pressure could rise with happiness. "Do they have courses in horticulture and landscaping?"

"Um, I haven't looked at the catalog yet."

"Be sure you choose courses that will lead to a job." Buoyed by hope, Emm dared to say more. "You know, Darold told me that Cheryl wasn't doing too well. When you get your degree, you'll be in a position to help her. The same way I'm helping you." He put his hand over Erissa's. "I can't tell you how good it makes me feel to worry about someone besides myself. It actually makes me steadier on my feet. I bet looking out for your daughter will help you stay steady too."

Erissa pulled back her hand and threw the rest of the pizza slice back in the box. Her lips trembled, but no words came out. She grabbed a napkin and blew her nose.

"I'm sorry," said Emm. "I'm so excited for you that I jumped the gun. Let's back up and begin by celebrating your matriculation. Is it too late to buy daffodils?" Emm didn't know much about flowers, but to him they'd always signaled the end of a bleak winter and the start of brighter days. "I'll get you some money. I'm sure you can find a florist that's open until eight."

"Papa, I don't think ..." But Emm, propelling his walker, was already skipping across the floor like a gymnast. He got his wallet from his room and hummed the Olympic theme song while he rolled back to the kitchen. Erissa was twisting her scarf in her hands. Emm made a ceremony of reaching into his billfold but found only singles and fives. Two hundred dollars was missing.

Emm wobbled. He gripped the handlebars and sputtered. "You stole my money. You went out to buy drugs. And alcohol. You didn't come home happy, you came home high."

"That's not true, Papa. I took the money for school. I didn't tell you because I wanted it to be a surprise."

"That's a lie. Public colleges don't cost that much. I've given you every opportunity to move forward, yet all you've done is backslide. As your father, I'm entitled to some gratitude."

"Gratitude? For everything you've given me?" Erissa knotted

the scarf and pulled the ends tight. "All you ever cared about was winning that stupid prize money. You liked me because I was your lucky number five, but when the contest ended and you lost, I was as useless as the others. Except Prince Arvil. Later, when you could have turned me around, you were too busy moping over Mama's death. She was nothing to you but a baby-making machine."

"That's a lie. I loved your mother. I had a right to grieve."

"As for your so-called help now, it's just pressure to win another contest, like that Romanian girl. I can never live up to Arvil's standards, so why the hell should I bother trying?" Erissa got two beers from under the sink, one of the hiding places where Emm hadn't been able to look. She opened them and drank alternately from both bottles.

Labatt's, Emm noted, one of Cleon's favorites. At least she stuck with a single brand.

Erissa emitted a loud, three-part burp. "What do you have to say for yourself now, Papa?"

Emm shivered in the hot apartment. Whether it was drugs or alcohol that made Erissa talk like that, her words filled his body with a cold rage. "How dare you speak to me like that? Your addictions, all your wasted chances, are not my fault. You never lacked for a roof over your head or food in your stomach. You had me and my parents, plus your big brother and sister, to help raise you after your mother died. That's more than lots of kids have. More than you gave Cheryl."

"You put food on the table alright, but emotionally you starved us. Except for Arvil. Like a mother bird who gives the fattest worm to her favorite fledgling and leaves the others to fight over what's left. Or to simply fall from the nest."

"Don't blame your falling off the wagon on me. Since I moved in and started paying for your food, you've eaten better than you had in a long time."

"It's too late. I needed to be fed, with heaps of love, when I was growing up."

"Well grow up now and take responsibility for your own life. And, for once, your child's. I'm an old man, and I won't let you kill me with blame."

With halting steps, Emm headed to the bathroom. He would not let aggravation make him forget his medicine again. Still shaking, he hobbled to the bedroom he'd just settled into. Erissa's uncertain future cast doubt over his, but she had no right to trash his past. True, he could have taken better care of her at fourteen, but now she was forty-four. There was a time in the natural order of things for children to take care of their parents. And if his daughter couldn't do it, then one of his other children would have to. Erissa had given up, but Emm refused to.

CHAPTER 21

Darold paid for another round of rehab, after which Erissa would stay with Bruna until she was ready to live again on her own. Meanwhile, Emm moved back in with Darold while his children figured out what to do with him next. With time on his hands, Emm wasn't able to shake thoughts of Erissa. He tried to make sense of her behavior, comparing her addiction to drugs with Foy's insatiable craving for candy, but the analogy didn't hold. Foy deserved sympathy; he'd been dealt a rotten hand. Erissa had been given a better set of cards and had no such excuse.

Her accusation that Emm had treated Izora like a mere baby-making machine continued to sting as well. Emm asked himself whether the Stork Derby had been his personal addiction. He'd been drawn by the huge reward, but what was wrong with that? Everyone loves to win. He wondered what he would have done with the money. Paid for his children's futures? Lavished his wife with gifts? Taken care of his parents, maybe even helped hers? Emm told himself he would have been generous, but in his darker moods, he admitted it was nothing more than guess work. No one could say with certainty what he'd do if he met with good fortune. And now he'd been hit by bad.

"Mr. Benbow. How nice to hear from you. I was just about to call to see if things were all set in your daughter's new apartment." Mrs. Cray's voice was upbeat.

Her cheeriness only made Emm feel worse. He told her that instead everything had fallen apart and hurriedly explained what had happened. At the end of his story, he announced, "This time, no one can say it was my fault. Erissa did this to herself. And to me."

"I wasn't going to accuse you, Mr. Benbow. I'm sorry, for both of you."

Emm wasn't after even-handedness. He wanted all the sympathy for himself. Erissa, troubled as she was, still had decades to turn her life around. Emm was running out of time and children, while Kingsbridge was running out of beds.

"Let me know when you decide on your next stop, or should I say step. And Mr. Benbow, while no one would hold you accountable for your daughter's behavior, consider *if* you might have helped her more. There's nothing like early intervention to prevent later problems."

Emm agreed to give it some thought, but the implicit criticism riled him. Mrs. Cray was his social worker; she belonged in his corner exclusively. Erissa's older siblings had been there to catch her when she stumbled. No one had been there to catch him when he fell. And now, thanks—or no thanks—to his children, Emm was right back where he started.

***

The following week, Darold announced that Emm would move in with Garnish. It made sense; skipping over Foy, Garnish was next in the alphabet. Nonetheless, Emm asked how Darold had talked his younger brother into it.

"It was Bruna," he answered. "Unlike me, big sister is willing to make people feel guilty. She told Garnish that she and I were taking care of Erissa, and now it was his turn to take care of you." Asked how Garnish had responded, Darold chuckled. "Bruna didn't tell me that part. You'll have to find out for yourself."

"Will Foy be coming to your house on Saturday?"

"I don't see why not," said Darold.

Emm looked at the large, manicured gardens in Darold's neighborhood. He missed the small charming one that Erissa had created in their backyard, before she let it turn to weeds. The last thing she'd planted had been a holly bush, which she said stood for happiness in the home. "Would it instead be possible for me to spend the day visiting Foy at his group home?"

"I don't see why not," Darold said again. "But why?"

"To do you a favor. Let you spend a peaceful day alone with Virginia."

Darold playfully elbowed Emm's arm. "I'll be. Are you getting kind in your old age?"

Emm suspected there was more to it, but he was tired of trying to figure things out.

PART SEVEN:
FOY
AUGUST 1976

Despite frequent coupling, with days added before and after Izora's fertile period to increase the odds, it took longer than any previous attempt for her to become pregnant. Late getting started, Foy was perversely born one month early, on October 15, 1933. The house was shrouded in gloom until Dr. Marsh said the baby was out of immediate danger but cautioned that he'd likely be slow to walk and talk. Emm reread the terms announcing the Derby to make sure there wasn't a clause invalidating children with physical or mental defects. Thankfully, he couldn't find one.

Little Foy was a placid, amiable child who rarely protested when Erissa, an exuberant toddler, stumbled over him or grabbed his rattle. He watched his older brothers, especially Arvil, with adoration, but it was Darold, now age three, who was the most patient with him. Perhaps because Darold himself got winded whenever he tried to run, he was happy to sit quietly and play with his infant brother while the others raced around the house. Eventually, Mrs. Benbow would admonish them to slow down their steps and hold down the racket before she punished them with a spanking or no dessert. Only Erissa escaped her grandmother's tight reins, while Bruna, deeply attached to Izora, did her best to keep her other siblings out of her mother's hair.

Meanwhile, the contest in Toronto was garnering fresh attention, not only in Canada but in the United States too. On April 20, 1934, a gleeful headline in a Colorado paper announced that a mother of eight and the current leader declared she wasn't even trying:

> *Mrs. Grace Bagnato, who is in her early forties, has given birth to 22 children, 11 of them living, and expects to have 2 or 3 more by the deadline. She says the prize, which has already tripled in value, isn't an inducement, although it would come in handy. "But we aren't thinking of that," insists the Italian matron. "We're just raising the family we consider our duty." Mrs. Bagnato says if she wins, the first thing she will do is adopt a child. Then she and her husband hope to buy a small farm, about 15 acres, on which to raise their family.*

A Milwaukee paper, not long after, identified what it called "a dark horse" in the Derby:

> *Mrs. Arthur Hollis Timleck, a 36-year-old Irish-Canadian mother of 16, who has kept discreet silence for three years while other ambitious mothers have been advancing claims to the prize, says she now believes in birth control. Mrs. Timleck is dismayed that a dead millionaire has convinced Toronto women to have as many babies as possible, but nevertheless plans to stay in the race.*

The public was amused, but Emm, to whom this was serious business, became that much more determined to win. With less than two years to go, he decided the time had come to tell the newspapers that he and his wife were in the running. They'd just discovered Izora was pregnant again. News reports said that the judge assigned to the case, Justice William Middleton, might rule that some women's babies were ineligible. Emm hoped that other families, hearing about the impeccable credentials of the Benbow babies, would be intimidated and withdraw from the competition. He called the Star *and the* Telegram, *and invited reporters to the Benbow house.*

"My mother and I will handle the questions," Emm told Izora. "You just stick out your stomach, so you'll look farther along than you are."

Actually, this deception proved unnecessary. She was already larger than she'd been at this stage in her earlier pregnancies. Nevertheless, she seemed relieved that she would not be expected to talk during the interview. Mr. Benbow, perhaps feeling the same way, left for the hardware store before the press arrived.

Emm, wearing the clean but casual clothes of a busy father, stood before the reporters. "Some immigrants may have already been pregnant when they came here, or even lied to Vital Statistics about where their babies were born." Mrs. Benbow tsked and said she hoped the judge would be fair and rule against such pretenders. Emm continued, "I assure you both our families have been in Toronto for generations and each of our six children was born in this city, at the hospital, under a doctor's care." He smiled at Izora and motioned for her to show off her belly.

A reporter called out, "Ma'am, how many more children can you have before the contest ends?" Emm answered for his wife. "Don't embarrass the little lady, or should I say big lady, by inquiring as to her fertility or my virility." He winked. "The Benbow racetrack is good for a lot more miles." After a few more questions, his mother lined up Izora and the children for a photo. Emm collected business cards and promised to hand out cigars when the latest baby was born.

The next day, the Daily Star *headlined "Lucky Number Seven on Way for Baby Jockey and His Wife," while the* Evening Telegram *blared "Another Family in Contention Brings Derby Total to Twenty." Emm strutted, satisfied he'd timed the announcement perfectly. Mrs. Benbow began a scrapbook of news clippings. Mr. Benbow quipped that his son would not only be able to buy a house for his own young family, but a new one for his old parents as well.*

Izora, distressed at how old and tired she looked in the newspaper picture, took to bed, fussed over by Bruna and Darold who plumped her pillows and brought her tea. Hours later, Mrs. Benbow roused her daughter-in-law, claiming, "Exercise is precisely what you need if you don't want a repeat of what happened with Foy."

CHAPTER 22

Darold dropped Emm at the group home late Saturday morning. Foy was in the kitchen, carefully slicing frankfurter rounds and dropping them into a simmering pot of baked beans. Martha, who along with her husband Joe were the house parents, told Emm that of the six men who lived there, Foy was without a doubt the best cook.

"I know how to make pisghetti and meatballs too, Popsy. But franks and beans are more fun because I'm allowed to cut with a real knife. See how sharp it is? I'm also allowed to use real chemicals to clean the bathroom. Right?" He looked to Martha for confirmation.

She nodded. "Foy is a super-duper cleaner-upper. He likes to help with chores. That makes him a good member of our community." She smiled at Foy. He grinned, stood straighter, and gave the pot a vigorous stir.

The dining room had a table large enough for everyone to fit around. Foy brought an extra chair for Emm and set it alongside his. Lunch began with grace. Joe suggested that since Foy had company, he be the one to say it. Foy bowed his head and folded his hands. "The Lord is kind, the Lord is good. We thank Him for our yummy food." He raised his head and added, "Let's dig in." The others laughed. Apparently, he was allowed to add his own twist to prayers too.

As they ate, Foy introduced Emm to everyone, saying not only their names but something about them. "This is Johnny. He likes baseball," or "Malcolm wears red socks, even when it isn't Christmas." Halfway through the meal, one man dropped his fork and put his arms over his head as though he expected to be beaten. The others froze too.

"It's okay, Benjamin," said Foy. "I'll get you another." He raced to the kitchen and back, gently pried Benjamin's hands from his face, and did a silly dance before giving him the clean fork. Benjamin took it and smiled. Everyone resumed eating. If someone with Foy's knack for calming people down lived at Kingsbridge, Emm thought, fewer would be sent upstairs for bad behavior.

Dessert was ice cream. Two men dished out the servings. Foy asked for seconds. "Now Foy, you know you're not allowed to eat that many sweets," Martha told him. Emm braced for the kind of fit Foy had thrown at Darold's when told he couldn't have more candy. Instead, Foy said, "I thought maybe because I had company today ..." Then he grinned sheepishly and helped clear the table. When the cleaner-uppers sat back down, everyone joined hands and said what they were grateful for today. One man said, "Ice cream for dessert." Johnny said, "My new baseball glove." Foy said he was happy about his name because it rhymed with "joy" and "toy."

Emm smiled. He'd been afraid to ask after Darold told him that Foy cried when he was teased about his name as a child. Not only was Emm relieved that his son now liked his name, but he also marveled that Foy, of all his children, had inherited his affinity for rhyming.

"Can I have a second turn to say why I'm happy today?" asked Foy. Martha answered that in this case, since it didn't involve sweets, he was allowed. Foy squeezed Emm's hand. "Because Popsy came to play with me."

Everyone looked expectantly at Emm. He had no idea what he was going to say until the words popped out of his mouth. "I'm grateful that my son has such a wonderful home."

One by one, the men went down the hall to the bathroom to wash up. Foy headed in the opposite direction. "Foy," said Joe, "no TV or games until you do you-know-what." Foy looked at him blankly. Joe persisted. "Do you want to go back to Dr. Carlisle for another cavity? You hated going when you broke your tooth."

Foy hung his head and followed the other men to the john, dragging his feet.

"He hates to brush his teeth," Joe explained to Emm. "So, he pretends he doesn't know what Martha or I are talking about. It's the only frustrating thing about your son. Whenever he doesn't want to do something, or disagrees with what one of us is saying, he acts as if he doesn't understand the words."

A minute later, Foy's good mood restored, he helped lift Emm's walker over the threshold to the common room where they joined the other men. After watching one television show, he led Emm to a quiet corner to play Candy Land. "Do you remember your mother playing with you?" Emm asked. Foy looked up eagerly, his hand poised over the stack of game cards. "You liked to build tall towers with blocks, but you got upset when they crashed and made a loud noise. So, your mother bought you a set of rubber blocks."

"I miss Momsy," said Foy. He drew the card with the picture of gumdrops and moved his piece to that square, advancing six places.

"I do too," said Emm. He drew a card with a plain blue square and moved ahead one space.

***

Mid-afternoon, Joe announced there would be no more television until after dinner. Some men shambled off for a nap, others to a small room called the library that was filled with magazines and picture books. Foy said he wanted to go outside. Emm gestured at his walker and said it might be too much for him. He wasn't sure if Foy understood until he said, "It's not far, Popsy, and you can lean on me if you get tired. Right?"

The place where Foy led them, walking slowly and asking often if Emm was okay, was an old-fashioned corner candy store. Shyly, he asked Emm to buy him a roll of Smarties. "They're my most favorite candy." He touched the display. "Darold doesn't have them in his house."

Emm was torn. He wanted to return the favor Foy had shown him by sneaking candy into the hospital. On the other hand, he knew Darold struggled to keep Foy's weight in check. Seeing the longing in Foy's eyes, Emm made up his mind. He hadn't indulged him as a child and since, in a sense, he was still one, he could make up for it now. Emm bought five rolls. "Don't tell Darold." Foy put a finger to his lips. For a moment, father and son became two little boys, up to mischief.

"Why are Smarties your favorite?" The irony of the name made Emm's heart ache. Foy said he liked that each pack had so many colors. "Do you have a favorite color?" Emm asked.

Foy frowned. "It's not nice to play favorites. Right?"

Emm was flummoxed by this odd turn of logic. He wished his grandson James were there to help him out. Finally, Emm said, "It's only bad to play favorites with people. Candies don't have feelings. You told me you like Smarties best and the Tootsie Pops didn't start to cry."

Foy thought hard. Then, as suddenly as the cloud had descended on him, it lifted. "Yellow is my favorite. It tastes like sunshine. Will you also buy me a Ring Pop, so I can make a wish?"

"I'll buy you five."

"Oh no, Popsy. Only one at a time. Otherwise, your wish won't come true."

***

Emm was surprised that Foy didn't open even one roll of Smarties on the walk back to the group home. He assumed he'd eat all five right away. Instead, Foy saved them to share with his house mates, including the yellow ones. At first, Emm wanted to protest that he'd bought the candy for Foy and here he was giving it away, but when he saw how happy and proud it made Foy to treat his friends, Emm felt like he was the greedy and selfish child. His son put him to shame.

The men sat in a circle in the commons room, passing the candy until it was gone. Foy saw that Malcolm had brought in a book from the library and asked what it was. *One Fish, Two Fish, Red Fish, Blue Fish*. Malcolm looked around for approval. Emm wondered if he'd actually read the words or just knew the title by heart. Malcolm struck him as being slower than Foy, which gave Emm an unexpected sense of fatherly pride.

"Can I see?" Foy reached for the book. "Red, just like your socks." Malcolm looked at his feet and smiled. Foy pointed to another picture. "Who are they?" Malcolm explained they were Jay and Kay. Foy continued to ask questions about Dr. Seuss's characters until Emm grew bored, but all the other men seemed spellbound. After finishing the book, Foy raised his hand and Johnny tossed him his baseball mitt. "Did you play catch this afternoon?" Foy asked. Johnny answered that he'd caught every ball Joe threw him. One by one, Foy asked all the men what they'd done while he and Emm were at the candy store. Each sat up straighter when his turn came to answer.

Emm followed Foy to the kitchen when it was time to prepare dinner. Foy chattered the whole time he worked. He asked Martha how she knew the exact number of tomatoes to slice for the salad, and whether the tools Joe used to repair the back porch railing were like the ones Foy used at the sheltered workshop where he went three days a week. Although the conversation was lopsided, dominated by Foy, their camaraderie was fifty-fifty. Emm thought of the Dale Carnegie saying, "You can make more friends in two months by becoming interested in other people than you can in two years by trying to get other people interested in you." Seeing his son in action, he finally knew what those words meant.

After they ate, Martha played the piano, and each man chose a song for everyone to sing together. Foy picked "Away in a Manger," despite its being August, and led them in a clear alto that would have blended well with an adult choir. Emm remembered how Izora sang Christmas carols year-round too. It seemed as natural to sing them in the group home this summer evening as it had in the Benbow house, so many years ago. Emm closed his eyes and harmonized.

***

Darold picked Emm up when the day's last light was fading. "How did it go, Dad?"

"I'm beginning to understand what you like about your brother."

"Being with Foy gives your brain a rest, but it gives your heart a workout."

Emm was tired, yet he also felt more awake than he had in months. "Parents often say they never want their children to grow up. If wishes like that came true, then Foy is the kind of grown-up child a parent would be happy to hold onto forever."

Darold considered. "The luckiest parents are those whose children grow up to be the kinds of adults their mothers and fathers want."

"Like your son James?"

Darold nodded. "I think that growing up around Foy made my children more sensitive to their own kids." He chuckled. "It's a shame it didn't also rub off on Virginia, but I guess she was too old by then. The window of opportunity had closed."

"Do you think I'd be allowed to spend Monday with Foy at his sheltered workshop?"

"I'll check, but I'm sure it's okay. I'll drop you off at the group home so you can ride in the van with Foy—there's a lift for wheelchairs and walkers—then bring you both home after work." Darold pulled into the garage. "Are you thinking that you want Foy to rub off on you?"

Emm wasn't thinking. His brain was at rest. But his heart was working overtime. Right?

CHAPTER 23

Foy was one of ten handicapped men and women who did mechanical repairs on small electric appliances, working alongside a crew of non-handicapped people responsible for fixing the wiring. With pride, he showed his father the metal toolbox with his name on it, reading the letters aloud, and the swivel stool where he sat at a long counter that functioned like a reverse assembly line. Foy dragged over an ordinary chair so Emm could sit beside him and watch him work.

"See, Popsy, I use this flat screwdriver if the screw has a straight line and the pointy kind if it has a cross on top." As he disassembled a clock, Foy described which tool he used for each part of the operation. He was like an eager little boy explaining a matching game to a curious adult.

Emm watched Foy press his lips together in concentration and said that he was proud of his son for being such a good worker. "You know, before you were born, I worked in a toaster factory."

Foy's mouth dropped open. "Did you fix the broken ones?"

"No, the company only made new toasters. My job was to take orders and make sure the toasters got shipped to the stores where people bought them."

"Were you a good worker too?"

Emm replied that he was. It had been years since anyone had asked about his job, and it was gratifying to remember a time when he was a productive man and the family's wage earner.

Foy passed the dismantled clock down the line and selected needle-nosed pliers and a thin metal file to take apart a radio. "If your old toaster ever breaks, bring it to me. Sometimes I forget stuff, but I always remember how to fix things."

"Everybody forgets now and then, but you have a good memory for people in our family. You can name everyone in the photo album and even tell me when the pictures were taken."

"I can tell you things that aren't in the pictures too." Foy glanced around like a child afraid of being caught telling secrets. He hunched over and whispered, "Bruna has favorite people. She likes me and Darold best. That's bad, isn't it?" Emm told him it was okay as long as you acted nice to everyone. Foy relaxed, then the worried look returned. "Does Bruna like you, Popsy?"

"Bruna was very nice to me. She cooked my favorite foods just like she does for you."

Foy mulled this over while he pried apart a blender motor. "She doesn't like Cleon." Emm asked how Foy could tell. "She wrinkles her nose when he opens another beer, like he smells bad. Or the beer does." Foy scrunched his face too. "I once snuck a sip of his beer. It tasted yucky."

Emm wondered what brand, or brands, Cleon had been drinking that day.

Foy, sounding emboldened that he hadn't gotten in trouble for talking, put down his tools and continued. "Bruna acts nice to Erissa, but I don't think she likes her either."

"Because Erissa drinks too?"

Foy shook his head. It was something else.

"Then how do you know?" Emm asked.

Foy pointed to his heart. "Sometimes you just know. In here." He picked up his tools and went back to work. He'd said enough, and Emm didn't want to hear more anyway.

***

162

A buzzer signaled the start of lunch. There was a stampede to the break room, but Foy walked slowly beside Emm, protecting him from whoever rushed past. Emm saw several empty seats near the front, under a window and close to the vending machines, and started wheeling his walker toward them.

"Not there, Popsy." Foy led him to the back where all the men and women like him crowded around one table. Not until they reached it did Emm realize that the only people sitting up front were the non-handicapped workers.

They squeezed over to make room for Emm, and Foy introduced him to everyone, the same as he'd done at the group home. Wedged that close together, Emm could smell their body odor and see creases of dirt in their necks. Wherever they lived, they weren't cared for as well as Foy. The table looked like it hadn't been cleaned in a long time either. It was littered with crumbs embedded in dried ketchup and mustard, and the entire surface was sticky from spilled drinks.

Emm looked toward the front of the room and saw a man wearing a badge walk in. He beckoned him to the table. Foy stood and introduced him. "Mr. Johnson. He's the boss man." He told the manager, "This is my Popsy," and smiled as Mr. Johnson extended his hand to Emm.

Emm's hand gripped the front of his walker as he struggled to get up. He kept it there once he was on his feet. "My son Foy and his friends work as hard as everyone else here. They deserve to sit wherever they want, and to eat at a clean table. It's disgraceful to treat them like they ... don't count as much as other people."

Mr. Johnson lowered his hand and narrowed his eyes. "I'm doing them a favor by hiring them in the first place, and I pay their caregivers a decent wage so they're not a complete drain on society. You don't know what you're talking about, mister, and besides, it's none of your damn business." He snorted, turned on his heel, and stomped back to a front-row table, where the loud word "asshole" elicited a round of laughter, followed by other labels like "idiots" and "retards."

Emm trembled when he sat down, but it was from anger, not weakness. He wished that Darold and Eudora Cray had been there to hear him defend Foy and his co-workers. He glanced around the table, anticipating their gratitude. Most simply continued eating, a few looked puzzled. Foy rocked in his chair, crumbling the cookies Martha had packed in his lunch. Then he said in an anguished voice, "Why did you yell at Mr. Johnson? Why did you yell at him?"

"I was standing up for you," Emm said. "What he's doing isn't right."

Foy pursed his lips in concentration, trying to understand. His mouth went slack. It made no sense to him. He threw away what was left of his lunch, including his daily piece of candy.

Emm scooped the crumbs into a pile and wrapped them in a napkin, wiping a clean space before Foy sat back down. "I'm sorry, son. You're right. A smart man named Dale Carnegie once said that you can only get people to do something by making them want to do it. Yelling doesn't make people want to change. It only makes them keep on doing what they did before."

He wished he could take it all back. Upsetting Foy was the last thing that Emm intended to happen today. Words of blame ricocheted in his head, but yelling at himself wasn't going to make Emm change either. The time to stand up for Foy was over forty years ago. He had to—wanted to—find a different way to help him now.

***

The opportunity came a few hours later, while Emm and Foy waited outside the group home for Darold to pick them up. Foy pointed to his chest and said, "You like me, Popsy. I know. In here."

"You're right, Foy. I like you so much that I love you."

Foy grinned. "You're my best pal." He looked up the street for Darold's car. "So is Darold, but if I don't tell him you are too, then his feelings won't be hurt. Right?"

Emm said yes, and that even if Foy did tell Darold, it would be okay. Foy's face took on the sunshine that the day was giving up. Emm brightened too. He was freeing Foy to be himself and to stop worrying about having favorites. Meanwhile, Emm had been feeling guilty the last few months about favoring Arvil. Now he knew that wasn't the problem. What he should feel guilty about was not being just as nice to the others.

Darold arrived and helped Emm into the front seat. Foy bounded into the back and said, "Guess what Darold? Popsy is my best friend. He said it was okay. Right?"

Darold laughed. "It sure is." He reminded Foy to buckle his seat belt and headed home.

Emm leaned back against the head rest. Foy didn't need another father. Between Darold and Joe, he had enough. Foy was happiest among his friends, and that's what Emm had agreed to be. As Emm got older, and Foy remained a child, they would become more like peers anyway. He told Foy that he would come to his house to play with him again soon.

CHAPTER 24

When the time came to move in with Garnish, Emm couldn't wait to get away from Darold's. He was uneasy about what lay ahead, but eager to leave behind Virginia, who was less welcoming than during his first stay. She flicked her crumbs toward Emm's place at the table, and he could swear that after he made his bed each morning, she rumpled it while he was in the bathroom.

He was also worried by a change in Darold. A month or two ago, Virginia's barbs had rolled off him. But lately, as Emm's return had increased their frequency and intensity, Darold coughed more after each of her outbursts. His chest sagged under the weight of her incessant disapproval. Emm hoped that his going would ease the tension between them. Ditto his spending more Saturdays with Foy and leaving the pair to themselves. He'd never appreciated the importance of a husband and wife having time alone together. Now he regretted that he and Izora hadn't had more time with each other before the babies began coming and was even sorrier that they'd never had a chance to be alone again after the children left home. Izora had died too soon.

It was time to call Mrs. Cray. Today, when she asked what he'd learned, he would have an answer. For the third time, with a third child, Emm called to mind the Carnegie quote, "If only the people who worry about their liabilities would think about the riches they do possess, they would stop worrying." He told the social worker that he'd become more accepting of his limitations and less angry at life for having disappointed him. He explained what he'd learned from Foy.

"You've taken a big step forward, Mr. Benbow. But don't just apply the lesson to your waning physical and mental abilities. Your dwindling list of children is also a liability."

Emm was confused. "Are you saying that the riches I possess are shrinking?"

Mrs. Cray laughed. "Well, the central office limits the number of times you can register a change of address to mail your pension checks to, and you are running out of those."

It took Emm a second to realize that she was joking.

"I'm saying that you can afford a decent old age home, like Kingsbridge, provided they still have an opening by the end of the year. Consider changing your attitude and behavior to make living in that kind of setting an acceptable alternative. In case none of your children work out."

Emm did consider it as he set about tidying Darold and Virginia's house. Could he accept Mrs. Cray's premise that living in an institution would not be so bad? His days would be orderly. He could shed his unnecessary possessions and no longer witness the house falling apart around him. The newspaper could be delivered to his room and taken away by the janitor when he was done with it. The food, while bland, would not endanger his health. He could dine with the ladies. There would be people around if he fell or got sick, and he might even make friends, as Foy had, and get them to join him in the common room for activities livelier than watching television.

But for all that he'd changed, Emm was not Foy, and Kingsbridge was not a cozy group home. The fear of living in an institution persisted and grew into a new obsession. Only in this case, Emm's need was not to get something, but to avoid it. The threat of "upstairs" loomed larger than ever, a reverse descent into hell.

PART EIGHT: GARNISH AND HELMA AUGUST-SEPTEMBER 1976

Given the speed with which Izora's belly grew, it shouldn't have come as a surprise when Dr. Marsh informed her and Emm that she was expecting twins. Nonetheless, Izora said she wasn't prepared to have babies seven and eight arrive at the same time. Even with Mrs. Benbow to help, she couldn't imagine how she would juggle two babies at once. Or get a moment's rest.

While his wife was busy wringing her hands, Emm pumped his fists. Despite bragging they were a shoo-in to win the Derby, the newspaper coverage of all the contestants had made him fearful that they were falling behind. Now he had a reason to crow to the reporters. "Twins give us a leg up. Make that four legs!" He splurged on four boxes of cigars, two wrapped in blue cellophane and two in pink, to cover all the possible combinations.

The bigger surprise was that Izora carried the babies to term. On July 13, 1935, as she was wheeled into the delivery room, Dr. Marsh said he was proud of her and that compared to the scare they'd had with Foy, this birth would be twice the work but half the worry. First to come out was a boy with a head full of dark hair, delicate features, and a powerful set of lungs. When the second baby emerged, and Dr. Marsh proclaimed it a girl, they waited to hear another lusty cry. Instead, there was silence, followed by frantic activity, followed by more silence. Izora, catapulted awake from the twilight reverie of the anesthetic, was the one whose cry pierced the hushed room when the doctor said he was sorry, but their daughter was stillborn.

Emm named the boy Garnish. He was ready to bury, or preferably cremate, the girl without calling her anything. He hid his grief behind a mask of anger and regret. "A baby born dead doesn't count in the Vital Statistics," he railed. "She didn't even take one damn breath." Izora rose from her bed to insist that their daughter be given a name, Helma, and a proper burial as well. Emm acquiesced to the name, but still resisted having a formal funeral.

In a rare show of unity, his mother took Izora's side. "There's scarce consolation with such a loss," Mrs. Benbow said. "At least rituals provide some comfort." She admitted that she'd lost two children, one before and one after Emm, both under a year old. "I wasn't myself for weeks afterward. I could hardly get out of bed and I cried at the least little thing." She helped Izora choose a tiny casket lined in pink velvet and told Mr. Benbow to spare no expense on the service or cemetery plot, which was located on the edge of a ravine overlooking the Don River. She told her son, "I don't give a hoot whether the government or the Derby judge recognizes this baby, our family does."

Not Emm. He didn't attend the funeral or visit the grave, nor did he utter the dead twin's name. When people asked how many children he had, he didn't count Helma among them. Izora glared at him, but Emm ignored her. He ignored Garnish too. Seeing the lone boy only brought fresh waves of disappointment. As near as Emm could tell, however, Garnish was unaffected by the loss of his companion from the womb. Out in the world, he seemed a perfectly normal and self-contained child.

CHAPTER 25

As he had last time, Darold drove Emm to his next home. Darold hadn't volunteered much about Garnish, and Emm had been too anxious to press him. He regretted not having paid more attention to his son as a boy, so he'd have an inkling of what to expect in the man. The mental turmoil had taken a toll on Emm's body too. He'd had a power outage in his right arm and was too weak to pull the car door shut. As Darold closed it, Emm finally got up the nerve to ask about Garnish.

Darold went around to the driver's side and checked the map twice. Emm didn't know if he was genuinely unfamiliar with the route or was stalling while he decided how to answer his father's question. "I've only been to his place once, but I remember it being a lot neater than ours." He grinned. "Don't worry, Dad. My brother isn't a crazy cleaning fanatic, like Betty."

Emm was too tense to laugh over the jibe at Cleon's wife.

"Seriously, Garnish is a talented graphic designer. In fact, he did some projects for Eaton. Not in my department, but my colleagues were impressed with his work. Outside of that, he directs community theater. Musicals, I think. We've never gone to see one. When our kids were young, he took them to the Art Gallery, but I don't think he kept that up with the grandchildren."

Darold turned the wheel so sharply that Emm grabbed the dashboard with his left hand to keep from falling over. Once steadied, he asked his son what he really wanted to know. "Do you think he'll be easy for me to get along with?" If Mrs. Cray had been in the back seat, she'd have said it wasn't up to Garnish, but to Emm, to smooth the way. He was glad she wasn't along for the ride.

"Garnish is a … sweet man." Darold shrugged. "That's about all I can tell you."

Emm was uneasy. For a man who kept tabs on the family, Darold was surprisingly silent about his brother. Was he hiding something? Emm tried to reassure himself. Darold had his hands full with Foy. And Erissa. It was understandable that his contact with Garnish was limited.

When they reached Garnish's apartment, Darold carried in Emm's things. He refused the mint iced tea and hand-dipped chocolate strawberries, shook his brother's hand, and hugged Emm goodbye. He told his father to call him after he got settled and was ready for his next visit with Foy.

Emm avoided looking at Garnish, afraid he'd see something that would knock him off balance. He let Garnish lead him to a chair with a straight back and wide metal tubes for arms. "I think you'll find this comfortable, Father." The other seats were low slung or soft and shaped liked giant bean bags, and the cushions on the curved sectional sofa were only inches above the polished wooden floor. Emm would never be able to sit down on those, let alone get back up.

After Garnish left to fix them a snack, Emm looked around the rest of the large living room. He saw floor-to-ceiling bookshelves with leather-bound volumes and a stereo turntable with enormous speakers. In front of the couch was a low glass-topped table holding enameled ash trays and glossy magazines. There were hanging plants in the wide street-facing window and two shaggy rugs, one on the floor and the other hung on the wall opposite him. An abstract painting of geometric figures in bright primary colors took up the entire wall to Emm's left. He saw Garnish's signature and a date, March 1971, in the bottom right corner.

Through an open archway, Emm saw his son filling tall glasses with tea and sprigs of mint. The kitchen was almost as big as the living room. Black and white ceramic tiles, in alternating diamonds, covered the floor. Pots and pans of all shapes and sizes hung on hooks over a counter that held racks of knives and other, less familiar, utensils. Between the oversized living room and kitchen, Emm couldn't imagine what a single man would do with so much space. Compared to the old-fashioned, shabby furnishings of the house where he'd lived, Emm felt tiny and shopworn. On the other hand, the smooth floors would make it easy to slide his walker along, provided he didn't trip on the scattered rugs. Thankfully, there was no "upstairs" to threaten him.

"I wouldn't mind extra sugar in my tea," Emm called out. "Maybe something a little more substantial than the strawberries to go with it." His stomach had been too jumpy to eat lunch before they left Darold's. Now he was ravenous to fill the emptiness inside.

"Sure, Father. I've got sesame crackers and Brie. Also, paté, although that might be a bit rich for your stomach. Just tell me what you're used to eating and I'll shop tomorrow." Garnish came back carrying a tray and put it on the coffee table. He opened a small folding table, inlaid with wood, and set it in front of Emm. It was too fancy to be called a television tray, and Emm, his right arm still shaky, was afraid of spilling something and staining it. He put a purple linen napkin in his lap and ate slowly with his good hand.

Garnish draped himself on the couch and twirled a mint sprig, the way a girl might twirl a daisy before tucking it in her hair. As his son bent over to pluck a strawberry from a glazed dish, Emm, feeling more stable now that he was seated, was finally ready to look at him. Garnish wore a shiny shirt with a pointed collar, beneath a cable-knit cotton vest that was belted in the middle. Was it like some ancient gladiator's tunic, Emm wondered, or closer to a woman's short skirt?

More jarring were the plaid pants and an oversized pinky ring, encasing what appeared to be a lock of hair. Emm wondered whether Garnish's own dark ringlets were still natural or if he dyed them to cover the gray. Had his son always had curls? Emm's memory was blank. Garnish cupped his hand and brushed the hair back from his forehead. The delicate gesture was similar to Izora's before she bobbed her hair. Men typically swept their hair away with their forearm, the same way they wiped the sweat off their brow.

Too uncomfortable to continue looking at Garnish, Emm switched back to the apartment. "You've got quite a place here. I guess you call this style modern?"

"A mix of modern and antique. I buy what I like. Or more accurately, only what I love. I've learned that as long as you buy things you really care for, they end up going together."

Emm's eyes did another tour around the room. It was then that he noticed, on a simple wooden table near the door to the hallway, what could only be called a shrine. Filled with baby things: a rattle, a bottle, and a teddy bear, plus a clear plastic cube filled with another lock of fine hair. It was creepy. He wondered who the hair belonged to, whether it was from a child who was still alive or had died. He'd read once that Victorians wore lockets with the hair of their beloved dead ones. Emm thought momentarily of Garnish's dead twin. He hadn't looked at her long enough to remember if she was bald, like many newborns, or had arrived with hair on her head.

He turned back to his son. "I'm glad your apartment is quiet." Erissa's housing complex had been filled with noisy neighbors, while Foy's group home buzzed with ever-present chatter. After living alone for so many years, Emm had found himself exhausted by the constant sound in those places. "I won't have trouble getting enough rest here," he told Garnish. "Since the stroke, I tire easily. Not that I'll be a burden. I'm quite self-sufficient as long as things are in reach."

"I'll make sure there's an assortment of dishes on the bottom shelf." Garnish looked at the wall unit. "You shouldn't have a problem using the stereo. Any books you want to read that are too high, I'll be glad to move to a lower shelf." Garnish stretched his legs across four sections of the sofa. "Fair warning, though. I do a lot of entertaining, often until the wee hours. Even though your bedroom is at the end of the hall, I'm afraid the noise will keep you awake at night."

That explained what Garnish did with all this space. Emm worried he'd have to set up a new routine to remember to take his medication before bed, which might now be at unpredictable hours. He didn't want to sound ungrateful, however, so he told Garnish that as long as he could sleep late the next morning, and nap in the afternoon, he'd be all right.

"In that case, you better rest before dinner because I'm having a party for the cast and crew of *Guys and Dolls*. Our final performance was last night, and every show was sold out. We're ready to celebrate." Garnish slid his legs to the floor and led Emm to the spare bedroom that would now be his. On the way Emm peeked in the bathroom—more hanging plants, a floral pastel shower curtain. The spicy-sweet aroma in his bedroom came from scented candles on top of the dresser. He'd have to open the windows to breathe and hoped he wouldn't need ear plugs to muffle the street noise. Tomorrow, he'd ask if Garnish wouldn't mind removing the candles.

Emm waited for Garnish to leave before examining the rest of the room. He pulled back the spread on the double bed, uncovering blue silk sheets. He wondered who else had slept there and what had gone on, then banished the thought. Darold had unpacked Emm's suitcase, using up only two drawers and a few hangers. Next to his pants were coats, presumably Garnish's, and a turquoise robe with a red and gold dragon embroidered on the back. Behind four pairs of slippers sat large pieces of electronic equipment with tangled wires. Emm had no idea what they were.

He was afraid his nerves would keep him up, but Emm slept soundly until the whirr of gadgets in the kitchen woke him up. After visiting the bathroom, and finding nothing unusual in the medicine cabinet, he sat at the big round table and watched Garnish cook. There was a bowl of cubed meat, shredded cheese piled beside a mountain of torn bread chunks, and dark chocolate slabs with cut-up fruit. Emm couldn't imagine how those ingredients would go together in a meal.

"It's a fondue party, Father." Garnish explained how the guests would use long-handled forks to dip the meat, bread, or fruit in hot oil, melted cheese, or melted chocolate, respectively. He asked if Emm would like to help mix the dipping sauces for the meat.

"I'm afraid of spoiling it," said Emm. "I'm not much of a cook. Heating is as far as I go."

"Then you'll like the fondue," said Garnish. Emm doubted it. His stomach craved Izora's simple but hearty casseroles. Even Bruna's fancy cakes were easier to get his mind around than chocolate fondue. He hoped Garnish wouldn't sneer at the plain foods Emm asked him to buy.

***

Emm sat in "his" chair as the guests arrived. He debated greeting them at the door with Garnish, but that implied this was his house too, which wasn't yet the case, if it ever would be. Besides, from his perch, Emm could see each person and prepare his face and a word or two before being introduced. He expected a parade of oddities. Instead, the men and women, some single, others in couples, were rather ordinary. Pretty much like Emm, in fact. A few dressed like Garnish, but most wore plain clothes. They were young and middle aged. Several were older, also like Emm.

At dinnertime, Garnish set the bubbling fondue pots in the middle of the table and handed out color-coded forks. Emm sat between the young red-haired woman who had played Adelaide in the show and a fifty-ish man who did the lighting. Emm's right arm shook as he speared pieces of meat or bread and aimed for the oil or cheese. He switched to his left hand but that was even clumsier. Stymied, he looked around at everyone else jabbing, thrusting, swirling, and talking.

"Let me get that for you." The redhead took his fondue fork, cooked several pieces of meat, dipped each in a different sauce, and put them on Emm's plate. "There you go."

Meanwhile, the lighting expert made him some cheese fondue. "Takes practice to get the hang of it. Wait a tad before you bite into a morsel. They tend to absorb a good deal of heat." Emm half expected the man to blow on the food to cool it off for him. He felt like a baby being served and coddled at the grown-up table. He had to concentrate so much on getting the meal to his mouth that he couldn't pay attention to the conversation flowing around him. Garnish looked over now and then, smiled encouragingly, and went back to chatting with his neighbors. When the meat and cheese were exhausted, he brought out the chocolate fondue and coffee, which he called espresso and served in tiny cups. Emm longed for a mug of Lipton tea. He remembered that by the time he drank his second cup at Bruna's, she already knew to give him lemon and extra sugar.

Several guests helped clear the dishes and then everyone moved to the living room. Emm returned to his chair while others took the remaining seats or sat cross-legged on the floor. "Hit it," said Garnish. "You first, Jeanine." Someone offered Adelaide a hand-kerchief. She pretended to blow her nose and belted out "A person can develop a cold." Several other numbers from *Guys and Dolls* followed, ending with Sky Masterson singing about "My time of day, a couple of deals before dawn" to Sister Sarah. To Emm, there was nothing magical about those early hours. That's when Izora crawled out of bed to feed the crying babies and he went back to sleep. Nevertheless, he hummed along with everybody at the party. Before long, he was enjoying himself.

After covering their recent musical, the group switched to numbers from their past shows—*Pajama Game*, *West Side Story*, *The King and I*, and *Cabaret*. Emm was both touched and a bit embarrassed when the man who dressed most like Garnish sang "Willkommen" directly to him. The others clapped and asked Emm if he had any musical favorites.

Emm remembered crooning to Izora. There was a time, way back, when she wasn't the only one who sang around the house. Her carols were for the children, but his serenades were for her. "When Garnish's mother and I were first married, we were partial to Cole Porter and Noel Coward." Emm cleared his throat and softly began "Let's Do It." The others joined in, and by the time they got to "People say in Boston even beans do it," his baritone came out loud and clear. He next suggested "Don't Put Your Daughter on the Stage, Mrs. Worthington," an old theatrical number that turned out to be a favorite of the group, especially the line "She's a bit of an ugly duckling, you must honestly confess, and the width of her seat would surely defeat her chances of success." Hearing the clever lyrics for the first time since he'd sung them to his wife, Emm wondered if they were behind the comfort he'd found making up rhymes after her death. Singing them tonight made him more comfortable with Garnish's friends; they also made him miss Izora.

As much fun as he was having, Emm was eager to get to bed. The party finally broke up at an hour when Sky Masterson would have been in his element. Women hugged him and men clapped him on the back, urging him to attend their next musical, *My Fair Lady*. Adelaide told him to audition for a part. "I bet the director would show you favoritism in the casting."

Emm said he'd think about it. He'd enjoy playing Eliza Doolittle's father, "getting married in the morning," and figure out a way to dance with his walker. He took his pills and slid between the silken sheets. Performing on stage was like being a car salesman, persuading people to go along for the ride. Of course, in the theater he'd be singing as well as talking, and he wouldn't be the only actor on the floor. He'd have to learn to become a member of the troupe, but it was never too late to try something new. Emm was confident he could do it, with Mr. Carnegie's encouragement. "The man who goes farthest is generally the one willing to do and dare."

Mrs. Cray would second that idea. The next time Emm called her, it might be to tell her he'd gotten a part. And to invite her to be his guest on opening night.

CHAPTER 26

The next morning, Emm stood at the window, hungry, anxiously awaiting Garnish's return. They had gone over Emm's shopping list before Garnish went to a grocery that he called a gourmet shop. The first item was soup. The store didn't carry Campbell's. A brand named Progresso made tomato soup, but it was chunky with the skin left on. Garnish asked if chewing was a problem. Emm had an image of his roommate's dentures soaking in a puddle of cloudy water during his overnight stay at Kingsbridge. "No. Thank goodness, I've still got my choppers."

Second on the list was bread. Garnish asked if Emm liked the sourdough he'd served with the fondue or if he'd like to try the Swedish rye that the bakery next to the grocery was famous for. "Whatever is simplest," Emm answered. Garnish assured him that buying either wasn't any trouble, but that wasn't what Emm meant. He meant that he wanted simple, honest food. A favorite expression of his mother's when he or his siblings clamored for a fancy food they'd eaten at a friend's house was that "Bread never lies." Emm didn't suppose his son would understand those words any better than he had back then, but they made a lot of sense to Emm now.

At last, a bright red convertible swooped to the curb and braked to a sudden stop. Garnish slid out and carried the bags inside. Emm's stomach gurgled in anticipation, and relief, when his son took from the waxed bakery bag a loaf that resembled one from the supermarket: white, rectangular, and sliced. They sat a few seats apart at the big round table. It felt strange with only two people, and Emm wondered how Garnish must feel eating there alone. Unless his son often had company in the mornings too. The thought simultaneously titillated and repulsed him.

Garnish made them an omelette. Emm declined yogurt and fruit but the Earl Gray tea wasn't bad. The orange marmalade was delicious, but he couldn't fully enjoy it for worrying about the cost of the food Garnish had purchased. In the places he'd lived so far, Emm had given each child the weekly amount he was used to spending at Dominion, but Garnish shopped at more expensive stores. Assuming Emm ended up staying here, he couldn't afford the gourmet food. Ditto toiletries and other necessities. Garnish's tastes ran to nice things. Like that convertible.

"Sporty little car you're driving, I see. Nothing like the big, beige or blue family models I used to sell." Emm spooned more marmalade on his toast.

"The red convertible was Helma's idea."

Emm's hand paused halfway to his mouth.

Garnish continued eating between sentences. "Red is Helma's favorite color. And she has a wild streak, hence the convertible. Lucky for her she never had to grow up and buy something more sensible." At last, Garnish wiped his mouth and leaned back. "You think I'm crazy, Father?"

"Well, I do wonder where you get such ... crazy ideas from. Your sister is in her grave."

"She's also in here." Garnish pointed to his chest. "I started talking to her when I was six. We had our own private language. The only other person who knew about it was Mother."

"Goodness," said Emm. "And she thought it was ... all right?"

"She never said otherwise, just listened when I told her what Helma and I talked about."

Bile rose in Emm's throat. How could Izora have let such madness go? If she'd stopped it, perhaps Garnish wouldn't have grown up to be what he was. Emm was no psychologist, but he didn't need a shrink to tell him that Garnish acted like a woman to compensate for the loss of his sister. Oddly, his next emotion was jealousy. He felt excluded from the special bond that Izora had with Garnish. Which he knew was absurd. If he resented his wife's attention to their children, he shouldn't have had so many. It was natural for a mother to put them first. Hadn't his?

"You and your mother were close," Emm said, deciding it was pointless, let alone unkind, to speak ill of Izora now. "You loved art. She used to clear a space for you at the table and shoo away the other kids so you could draw pictures in peace."

"Maybe that's why I like having such a big table now. There's always room to draw."

"Your pictures were taped on the refrigerator, but your mother framed her favorite to put on the dresser. It wasn't a picture *of* something, just odd shapes in different colors." Similar to what Garnish painted now, Emm realized.

"Do you still have it?" Garnish's fingers twitched.

Emm shook his head. Other than the furniture still filling his old house, nothing remained from the years when his children were growing up.

"Was Mother artistic? Do I take after her?"

Emm tried to remember. Garnish had been ten when Izora died, too young to be aware of his talent or question where it came from. "She liked art in high school, but she never did anything with it after she graduated. Women didn't in those days. The closest she came was her flair for clothes. Your mother had a knack for putting together outfits that looked like no one else's. Not expensive, just stylish."

Garnish smiled. "I take after her in that respect. Except for the not expensive part. I don't remember her dressing up, though."

"By the time you were born, her body had spent too many years carrying babies, not clothes." Emm pictured Izora's gaunt

181

face, sagging breasts, and thin frame. Only her stomach muscles pouched out like she was perpetually pregnant. "What *do* you remember?" he asked.

"I remember Mother's smell. Sweet maple and sour milk."

Strange, thought Emm, that a man who lived by sight and sound recalled smells. At least he called his parents Mother and Father, not pansy names like Mummy and Dada. Emm looked away from his son. He should be ashamed for thinking that way; it was as bad as labeling Foy a "retard." Hard as it would be at his age, he had to stop thinking harshly of Garnish. The rest of the world was mean enough to his kind. Worse than to Foy's. They made fun of people they called retarded, even locked them away out of sight, but some people actually wanted to kill homosexuals. Emm wasn't one of them, but he still considered them "those people." It surprised him that Garnish was so sure of himself, given the taunting or bullying he must have endured.

"Were you teased growing up?" The words came out before Emm realized how intrusive they sounded. They hardly knew each other. He amended the question. "About your name?"

"Garnish, to decorate." He plucked a parsley sprig off the omelette plate, then answered what was obviously Emm's real question. "I was teased all the time for being effeminate in the way I moved, dressed, and talked. But I couldn't help myself. That's simply who I was."

"And now?" Times were changing, but even Darold, who spoke so openly about Foy, had become tongue-tied and uncomfortable when Emm asked about Garnish.

"It's rarely a problem. On the contrary, it works to my advantage. People think gay men are artistic, which helps when you earn your living as a designer."

What Garnish said made sense, yet Emm found it hard to believe that being a homosexual was anything but a disadvantage. "Did Arvil pick on you for being ... girlish?" Emm hoped his son wouldn't take the word as an insult.

Garnish didn't seem bothered. "Arvil was eight and a half years older than me. Too big a difference for him to notice I existed. Cleon was the one who tortured me. I was his favorite target."

Emm was taken aback. "It's normal for brothers to fight, but why would he act so mean? Especially to you?"

"Because Cleon was obsessed with being a he-man. And I was his exact opposite."

"Did your mother know? Did I? Did we do anything to stop it?"

Garnish crushed the parsley in his hand. "I never told you. I assumed you'd be on Cleon's side. As for Mother, the worst happened after she was dead, when we were teenagers. Cleon made me punch him in the gut to show how strong his muscles were. When I didn't hit him hard enough, he'd 'demonstrate' by knocking the wind out of me. Leaving bruises where they didn't show. The name calling was even harder to take."

"The rare times your mother raised her voice was when you kids called each other, or one of your schoolmates, a bad name. She wouldn't have allowed it."

"Yes. I like to think she would have defended me. Helma says Mother would have beaten the you-know-what out of Cleon." Garnish relaxed his fist and brushed off the crumpled parsley with his napkin. He smiled. "Like I said, my sister has a wild streak and a naughty mouth. Helma would have been quite a handful for Mother. Maybe more of a troublemaker than Erissa."

Garnish's sister was dead, but if she'd lived, Emm didn't find it farfetched to imagine Izora passing on her own wild streak to Helma and the others. Izora had bobbed her hair before most women dared and tossed her head if anyone stared in disapproval. Back before the babies came, she would have liked riding in a red convertible. Emm might enjoy it now, provided he could fold himself into it and climb back out. As with acting, it was never too late to try something new.

Later that week, Emm was ready to test himself. He had an

appointment with Dr. Sawyer and, still thinking of Izora, asked if Garnish would drive him to the cemetery after his checkup.

"Yes, if you'll visit my sister's grave after Mother's. Helma says you've never been."

Emm stiffened. He could imagine Izora living long enough to pass down traits to their children, but it was impossible to acknowledge a child who'd never existed. He refused, saying it would be unwise to walk that far. "Who's more important, your live father or your dead sister?"

Garnish's answer was to order a taxi to drive Emm to and from the doctor. He said he'd go to Helma's grave alone. "I see her every week, Father, in case you ever change your mind.

"I wouldn't feel comfortable riding in that silly little car anyway." Emm pouted like Foy on one of his bad days. He was embarrassed but he couldn't help himself. That's simply who *he* was.

CHAPTER 27

For the next two days, Emm and Garnish ate at opposite ends of the big table. On the third day, Garnish moved their place settings closer together again and served Emm Campbell's soup and supermarket bread. He said he would take his father to the doctor after all. Then he would drop him off at Arvil's and Izora's graves while he went to Helma's on the other side of the cemetery. He'd return an hour later to pick Emm up.

Pleased that he'd gotten in and out of the car without much help, and eager to tell Izora about the latest turns in his life, Emm was impatient during the examination. He tapped his foot when Dr. Sawyer said he'd better exercise his right side, or the muscles would atrophy and told him he was taking up hoofing. It tickled him that the doctor didn't know what the word meant.

He grew more annoyed when the doctor asked about his memory. Because staying with his children had brought back so many, Emm answered that it was fine. Dr. Sawyer said he was referring to short-term memory. Was Emm remembering to take his medicine? Did he remember how ordinary things worked, like the toaster and coffee maker? Emm had no idea how to use the complicated coffee maker at Garnish's, but he said yes, he took his pills and made breakfast.

Next, Dr. Sawyer told him to state today's date, the name of the current Prime Minister, and how old he'd be on his next birthday. The questions were the sort you'd ask a schoolboy, but Emm answered. Anything to be done, fetch Garnish in the waiting room, and be on their way.

"What are the birth dates and ages of your children?"

Emm bristled. "Why on earth are you asking me that?"

"To test your sense of time."

"I know very well what time it is. And how much time I have left."

"Are you depressed thinking about death, Mr. Benbow?"

"No. I'm thinking about where I'm going to live until then." Emm got dressed and left the room before Dr. Sawyer had finished writing up his notes. He didn't wait for the doctor to say how much time it should be until their next appointment.

***

Five months had passed since Emm stood in front of Izora's grave. He had a lot to account for. "I'm not ready to ask your forgiveness yet, but I'm finally getting to know our children. I'll start at the beginning, shall I?" He sat on the bench. Child by child, it would be a long recitation.

"This may not surprise you, but it did me. Arvil was no saint. He was a typical big brother and occasionally even an awful kid." A chipmunk scampered across Izora's grave as if to say that yes, she already knew their son misbehaved. Emm chuckled. "The funny thing is, his brothers and sisters told me the bad things Arvil did to knock my first-born down in my estimation. They'd be unhappy to know it had the opposite effect. I like him all the better for being normal. For acting naughty. He'll forever be the child I love best." Emm bowed his head. "I'm ready to be forgiven, if that's not such a horrible sin." The chipmunk chattered. Izora had absolved him for playing favorites.

"Bruna is a devoted aunt and a good teacher. Also, an excellent cook. I don't mean to hurt your feelings, but in some ways she's better than you. Of course, she has more time to spend in the kitchen, not being a mother." Emm hesitated. "Maybe that's why I couldn't quite connect with her. I don't understand why a woman wouldn't want children. At least two or three." Emm looked for the chipmunk. It was gone.

"Cleon was next, going in alphabetical order. He's a wonderful husband. With the children grown up, he and Betty are happy just being together." Emm shuffled his feet. "To tell the truth, I didn't get along with her. She was outspoken, the opposite of you. Maybe if I'd been a better listener, you would have spoken up more too. I'm sorry." Emm didn't know how to interpret the silence. "In the end, I decided to let Cleon and Betty be. I didn't want to be a third wheel." Emm hoped Izora would credit him for the sacrifice, even though he knew he was looking after himself.

"Now Darold, sickly as he was—still is—has done well for himself. He inherited my business acumen if I do say so myself. On the other hand, his nature is more like yours. Kind and open-hearted. You'll also be happy to know that you don't have to worry about Foy. Darold takes good care of his brother. It was too much to ask him to take care of me as well. Darold felt bad, but I reassured him I'd be fine." More points for me, thought Emm. He wondered if Izora was keeping score. He wanted to win, although what and against whom he couldn't say.

"Both boys, Cleon and Darold, are conscientious family men. Model parents. They didn't get that from me, it's all from you. I think their kids take after them in turn." Emm told Izora that she'd started a chain reaction. "It may have been bigger than you wanted, but you planted enough seeds to start an orchard. I'm sure it's bigger than what Charles Vance Millar had in mind when he set up the Derby in his will. All he cared about was the total number of children. You cared about nurturing each one."

Emm wished he could claim to have been more like Izora than Mr. Millar. Instead, he'd been taken in by the man. After losing, when Emm wallowed in self-pity, he'd blamed Millar for starting the race that ended in his defeat. Now Emm was on the verge of confessing that he had no one to blame but himself. Mrs. Cray would be almost as happy as Izora to hear him admit that.

It was time to share the bad news, hopefully cushioned by the praise Emm had doled out. "Erissa is what's called 'a work in progress.' Face it, a girl needs her mother. I wasn't much of a father so after you died, I didn't even try to take on your role. Bruna and Darold have done their best to support her. She's back in rehab. I don't know how many times this makes. I hope she finds what she's looking for, and if I can help now, I will." Emm looked at the hazy summer sky. "Say a prayer for her. You know I don't believe in that stuff, but if Erissa does, it may work."

There were so many names and failures, both his and theirs, to report on. Emm moved down the alphabet and brightened. "Foy. Like I said, Darold looks after him and now I look in on him. Mostly at his group home, but I visited his sheltered workshop once. Foy's a good worker. Very proud of himself, but in a humble way, if that isn't a contradiction." A gentle breeze told Emm that Izora understood. "Foy never read Dale Carnegie, but he's figured out how to win friends and influence people on his own. He shows a genuine interest in them. I'm hoping his positive attitude rubs off on me. I'll pack it in my suitcase if I have to move to the old age home."

Almost at the end. "Garnish drove me here. I'm living with him now. He has a beautiful apartment. You'd appreciate his flair for decorating. If you were still alive, he'd decorate you." Emm sighed. "You were so beautiful when we were young. You'd have made a grand old dame." He wouldn't let his mind wander there. "I can't say I'm comfortable with Garnish's mannerisms, but I'm developing a taste for quiche Lorraine and rumaki. They're both made with bacon."

Suddenly Emm felt squeamish. "What I can't stomach is Garnish acting like his twin sister is alive. As if she has a personality. It's downright ghoulish the way he talks to her." He paused. "Although I suppose it's not so different from my talking to you, is it?" Or Eudora talking to Robert, Emm thought, and she was the least crazy person he knew. In fact, speaking with the dead could help the living stay sane.

Emm stood, wheeled closer to Izora's grave, and stared at the simple words on her headstone: Beloved Wife and Mother. He'd brought her up to date from "A" to "G" but "H" hung, unnamed, in the air. "The thing is, Garnish wants me to go with him to visit ... the grave."

A strong wind flattened the tall grasses in the field beyond Izora's headstone. In a clear voice, she demanded that her husband say their daughter's name. Startled, Emm looked around. No other living person was in sight, and he wondered: if we assume the dead listen when we talk to them, is it any odder when they speak to us?

"Should I visit ... Helma?" Emm choked out the last word. The wind ceased. He waited for his wife to say more, but the red convertible pulled into the parking area. They'd run out of time.

He was running out of time too. Emm told Izora it wouldn't be long before he joined her. Then he turned to meet Garnish on the path, halfway between the grave and the car.

***

If Emm hadn't listened to Izora in life, he was determined to do so in death. The following week, he accompanied Garnish to visit Helma in a far corner of the cemetery, where he sat on a folding director's chair that Garnish had carried from the car. The headstone was full size, unlike the small ones typically marking infants, and made of pink marble with carved cherubs. "Helma Oxana Benbow, Beloved Daughter, Born and Taken Home by God, July 13, 1935." Emm hadn't known her middle name, probably taken from Oxmoor. Izora's way to claim the child Emm refused to.

Garnish placed a single red rose on the well-tended grave. The trees were mature and full of birds, but Emm couldn't hear them. There was too much traffic nearby. Garnish told him that when Helma was buried here, that part of the cemetery was isolated and peaceful. Since then, the river had been built up and the nearby highway made it noisy. "It's harder to lose myself when I visit," he said, "and sometimes I can barely hear Helma speak."

"What do you talk about?"

"The job. I tell her about my projects, listening to myself figure out a design problem. She gives me offbeat ideas that somehow work. I also ask her advice about the latest musical I'm directing. We sing duets." Garnish looked sideways for Emm's reaction.

He didn't have one. The thought of the twins, one alive and one dead, singing together, no longer seemed strange to him. Besides, he was too tired to talk. Parking for this section of the cemetery was far from the grave sites. Emm's head began to droop.

"We also talk about our favorite places in Toronto. Politics. Food. Sex. There's practically nothing we *don't* talk about."

Emm's head jerked up, but Garnish didn't elaborate, leaving Emm to his imagination. Instead of having lurid thoughts, however, it suddenly occurred to him why Garnish would have started speaking to Helma in the first place. Who else could he talk to about his homosexuality when he was growing up? Certainly, no living member of his family. Whereas Helma, a girl, was as good as Garnish's identical twin. Garnish plucked a few yellowed leaves of grass. It was late August; things were beginning to lose their color. "Our favorite topic of conversation is the family. Helma recalls how Mother sang Christmas carols year-round and regrets that she stopped, overwhelmed by the sheer number of children. Bruna sometimes sang after Mother died, but it was all she could do to keep us clean and fed. Especially Foy, who used to soil himself. It was Helma who finally explained to me one day why my older brother was slower than I was. I tried to stay out of everyone's way, especially Cleon, and left it to Helma to tell people off whenever I felt picked on. She didn't mince words."

So, Garnish didn't just speak to Helma, he let her speak for him. Emm got up the nerve to ask if Helma ever talked about him, how her own father wouldn't even recognize her birth.

"No. That's the one topic she refuses to talk about."

Emm was relieved, yet disappointed. He assumed the conversation was over until Garnish resumed talking. "You barely paid attention to me, either, but I watched you closely and listened. Sometimes, you were very funny. When Polaroids were invented, you said people could no longer deny or pretend to forget their bad behavior. Then you joked that you would never be caught with one of those cameras in your house. I wanted to laugh, but I was afraid. I sounded too girlish."

"When Land invented Polaroid, he made sinners paranoid. Even the exhibitionist crossed cameras off his Christmas wish list."

Now Garnish did laugh, a musical, full-throated peal. "Odd, I don't remember you making up rhymes. I wonder if that's where I learned to appreciate the witty verses in musical comedies."

"I doubt it. I didn't start until after you children were grown and gone. Before then, I was like Bruna, too busy providing for the family to have time for such nonsense."

"You did work hard. I got my industriousness from you, although I never believed in your Dale Carnegie blather. It didn't apply to 'my kind' of man." Garnish smiled. "I didn't doubt your love for Mother, though. When you thought we weren't looking you nuzzled her neck and buried your face in her hair. Sometimes you massaged her lower back. That was so intimate. And kind."

Yes, thought Emm. He hadn't been totally oblivious to the strain that having so many children put on Izora's nerves and body. He was surprised that Garnish, of all his offspring, had noticed these good qualities in him. He thanked his son.

"I was an outsider," said Garnish, "so I had more sympathy for you."

Emm protested. "I wasn't an outsider. I was a normal man."

"In society, yes, but you were an outsider in your own family."

The truth stung, but it was the goad that made Emm realize what Izora was asking of him: to move Helma's grave next to hers and Arvil's, where Emm would one day be buried too. That part of the cemetery was still quiet and restful. Izora wanted them all together there, enjoying the peace they'd missed when they were alive. Emm promised he'd also save a spot for Garnish, so he could go on speaking to his sister. Perhaps Emm would at last address Helma too, by name.

CHAPTER 28

When Garnish said he was having another party, Emm confided he'd been brushing up on his Cole Porter and Noel Coward and was looking forward to it. Garnish winced. "Sorry. Different music, different guests this round. You'll have to practice disco dance moves with your walker."

Emm had read about disco in the newspaper, but he'd never actually heard it. Garnish put a record on the stereo and explained that the name came from discothèque, French for a library of phonograph records, like bibliothèque for books. The craze had started in Paris nightclubs and spread around the world. Garnish swayed and pivoted. "C'est la dernière chose, Papa."

"Huh?"

"The latest thing. A la mode. Pyjamas le chat. Très chic et très chaud. Hot stuff."

Emm was impressed. The only French-speaking Canadians he knew hailed from Montreal. He vowed to pick up a few foreign words along with the latest dance steps. "You're never too old to learn," he'd gotten in the habit of telling himself. A pep talk. Eudora Cray would approve.

The partygoers didn't arrive all at once, as they had with the theater group. They drifted in beginning at ten, an hour after Emm's usual bedtime, and continued showing up after midnight. Although Emm should have expected it, he was surprised that they were all men. His sense of not belonging returned. He considered going to bed, but curiosity got the better of his distaste and appre-hension. He stood in a corner, half hidden by a potted Ficus tree, to watch the show.

The clothes were more extravagant than the costumes in the Busby Berkeley musicals he and Izora used to adore. Most of the men wore shiny shirts with wide collars, open at the chest, some-times down to their navels. Gold or silver paint was smeared on their exposed torsos, while their sculpted buttocks wiggled beneath tights pants with form-fitted waists and flared bottoms. Their plat-form shoes and short boots, which Emm had only seen on women before, looked ungainly on their big feet. Ditto the chains and medallions draped around their necks. At the other extreme were a few men dressed in ultra-feminine drag, with elaborate piled-high hairdos and thick makeup. Emm had to sit down to take it all in. Fortunately, Garnish had moved Emm's chair to a corner to clear space on the dance floor.

Unfortunately, he'd also set up the sound system next to it. Now Emm knew what the tangle of gear in the closet was for. Garnish, acting as DJ, named each piece of equipment for him—mixer, crossfader—and explained how he combined strings and horns with electric piano and bass to create a lush background effect. He threw in terms like reverb and equalization, more incompre-hensible to Emm than the French words had been. Garnish varied the music to get the guests keyed up, then wound it down so they could recharge. He was a master puppeteer.

Emm's jaw dropped, and his anxiety rose, as the men gyrated to the deafening music, doing dances that Garnish told him were the Bump, Penguin, Boogaloo, and Robot. Nothing was as overtly sexual as The Hustle; however, while the song "Love to Love You Baby," which Garnish played over and over, reminded Emm of a woman having an orgasm. As much as he could remember what that sounded like. Decades had passed since he and Izora had made love, her excitement disappearing after their third child. By then, even Emm pursued sex more for profit than pleasure. He let the thumping music drive that thought from his head.

A couple emerged from his bedroom. The taller, leaner man, wearing a lavender shirt and tight purple pants, tapped Emm's walker. "Care for a spin on the floor?" His words were slurred. Emm pulled the walker closer and said he was sorry, but it was hard enough to walk let alone dance. He stared at those who were dancing, hoping that by breaking eye contact, the man would go away. Instead, he planted himself in Emm's line of vision and sneered. "Hey, old man. You can't come here just to ogle. You gotta get *in* on the action if you want to get some action *out* of us later." Then he tugged so hard on the walker that he nearly pulled Emm out of his chair.

"That's enough, Clive." Garnish loosened the man's grip and yanked him back. "Go cool off in the spare room until you come down from your raving high." Clive glared until Garnish gave him a shove. Then he boogalooed to Emm's bedroom and slammed the door.

Garnish quickly changed the music to something orchestral, turned off the blinking lights, and came back to make sure Emm was all right. "Sorry, Father. He's either on blow or poppers. Between music and drugs, people work themselves into a frenzy and things get out of control."

Emm grimaced. "Isn't that the point?"

"For some. It helps them forget what the rest of their lives are like. Others prefer disco biscuits. It slows them down and makes them feel like their arms and legs have turned to Jell-O."

Emm, remembering the helplessness following his stroke, couldn't imagine why anyone would voluntarily choose to lose control of their limbs. Garnish had sipped nothing stronger than white wine mixed with seltzer water all night. "No drugs for you, though?" he asked.

"After seeing what they did to Erissa, I swore not to get caught in that trap. Addiction seems to run in our family."

Emm wondered if Garnish was also referring to Cleon, and if he was aware of Foy's obsession with candy. Perhaps he was thinking of Emm's fixation on winning the Derby, but the party wasn't the time or place to ask. Besides, what Emm wanted now was not a discussion, but the oblivion of sleep. He stood up when Clive returned to the dance floor ten minutes later. The bathroom was free. Emm took his pills and escaped to his now empty room. But even with the door closed, and his fingers in his ears, he couldn't blot out the loud music. Nor could he bring himself to crawl between the rumpled silk sheets. He'd never be able to lie down in that bed again.

***

The next morning, after Emm awoke in the chair where he usually draped his clothes, he found that Garnish had already cleaned up and made him bacon and eggs for breakfast. Emm had no appetite. "This isn't going to work," he said, accepting a cup of Earl Gray. It was true that Emm no longer thought of Garnish as "one of them." His son was a truly nice person, with many nice friends and some questionable ones, who behaved decently regardless of the company he kept. All the same, Emm couldn't join that company. Unlike the level of comfort he'd finally achieved at Foy's group home, here he would always feel like an actor who'd been miscast.

"The parties don't usually run that late or get that wild," Garnish said, "but I can arrange for you to stay with Bruna or Darold the nights I have that crowd over."

"It's not simply a matter of getting enough rest." Emm blew on his tea. It was already cool enough to drink, but he needed a moment to choose his words. "You've gone out of your way to make me feel welcome, but there are some things I'm too old to learn after all. I can't change."

"Neither can I, Father. We're both who we are."

Regret hung in the air. "It's funny," Emm continued. "When I first moved in, I thought it would be your talking to Helma that drove me out. Now that seems normal, by comparison."

Garnish smiled. "I'll tell her."

"I'll tell her myself," said Emm. He laid out his plan to move Helma's grave next to where Izora and Arvil were buried. "I thought I'd buy a plot there for you too, seeing as how you can't have another family of your own. Would you be all right with that?"

"I'll be more comfortable living with you in the forever after than you'll ever be living with me here." Garnish motioned for Emm to eat. "So yes, Father. And thank you with all my heart."

While Emm finally ate, Garnish changed the sheets on his father's bed. Emm marveled at how easily they'd talked about death. It had brought them closer in life. A frank discussion might help him draw closer to his other children as well. Perhaps rotating whom he lived with wasn't such a bad idea after all. It would give him more than one chance to get to know each of them. The next time he talked to Mrs. Cray, he'd ask if that ever happened with her other clients.

***

Emm expected Bruna or Darold to call and tell him where he was headed next. Instead, Cleon phoned and said he'd be moving in with Zona. Emm asked if Bruna had once again used her powers of persuasion to convince another of her siblings to take him in.

On the contrary, Zona had volunteered, and was excited about it. Emm was surprised. He asked Cleon why, if Zona was so eager, she'd never volunteered before. "No one asked her," was the answer. "We never thought she'd want to." Emm again asked why. Cleon didn't answer.

Emm, at a loss to remember anything about this daughter, stopped asking.

PART NINE:
ZONA
OCTOBER–DECEMBER 1976

His hopes raised, then dashed, Emm pestered Izora to have one more child when Garnish turned two months old. After three failed tries at getting her pregnant, he accused his wife of turning her mind against her body. Izora retorted that she wished she'd done so after Bruna was born. Emm attributed her uncharacteristic harshness to fatigue and frustration, but he held his tongue after that. His mother was fond of saying that you could catch more flies with honey than with vinegar, so Emm went out of his way to be nice to his wife, slipping a hassock under her feet, massaging her shoulders, once even splurging on flowers. Izora conceived the following month.

The baby was expected late in October, days before Mr. Millar's ten-year deadline. As the due date came, and passed, Emm unashamedly asked his mother, sisters, women he scarcely knew, about ways to induce labor. He gave up a temporary carpentry job to spend an afternoon at the library researching how to speed up the process and presented Izora with a list.

First, he suggested intercourse. Several articles had said that an orgasm could bring on contractions. Izora rejected that idea outright. She was too uncomfortable and couldn't imagine her body climaxing when she could barely drag it from the bedroom to the nursery. Emm, still guilty about forcing himself on his wife the night Cleon was conceived, didn't push her this time. He moved to the second choice, nipple stimulation, which was less invasive. He read from his notes, "All you have to do is lie back and enjoy the pleasurable sensation." Izora agreed to give it a try. Emm worked on her as if he was coaxing forth a piece of bread stuck in one of the pop-up toasters he used to sell. Izora claimed to feel nothing. After half an hour, she fell asleep.

Next on the list were things his wife could eat or drink. Fresh pineapple wasn't available at this time of year. However, raspberry tea was. Mrs. Benbow used the dried berries from her summer garden to brew gallons of the stuff. Izora drank it, but with the baby pressing against her bladder, all she did was urinate more. With reluctance, she tried castor oil, whereupon the resulting diarrhea dehydrated her. Emm gave up on food and medicine. He also crossed off acupressure, which he had no idea how to do, but held out hope for vigorous exercise. Dragging his wife outside for a brisk walk, he told her, "The swaying motion of your hips is supposed to nudge the baby down the birth canal." Izora, weak from dehydration, nearly fainted on the porch, and Emm, panicked, called inside to his father to help carry her back into the house.

On the morning of October 31st, Emm reached the last method on his list—a bumpy car ride. Mr. Benbow drove at high speeds down deeply rutted roads; because of the Depression, the city hadn't repaired them in six years. Emm and Mrs. Benbow, on either side of Izora in the back seat, held her arms so she wouldn't pitch forward. They'd gone only a mile when the zigzagging made her nauseous and she threw up all over her enormous belly. "Enough," said Mrs. Benbow, wiping her daughter-in-law's mouth and brow. "Take the poor woman home and leave her be."

Izora's water broke at 4:30 in the morning on Sunday, November 1, 1936, after which her labor progressed quickly. They were leaving for the hospital when a powerful contraction stopped her halfway out the kitchen door. Dropping to the floor, she gave birth to a healthy girl at five o'clock. Emm grumbled that for a baby who took its time deciding to come out, it did so in a terrible rush when it finally made up its mind. Izora seemed grateful that Mrs. Benbow was there to take charge, ordering Mr. Benbow to boil towels that she used to wrap the mother and baby. Bruna, age eight and a half, took care of her alarmed younger siblings, reassuring them that, despite the bloody mess, mommy was okay. Emm was dispatched to fetch Dr. Marsh, who followed him back to the house in his own car. Emm ran into the kitchen just long enough to grab a bottle of whiskey from under the sink and did not return home until dinnertime.

"I'm naming her Zona," said Izora, her way of declaring that there would be no more.

"I don't give a damn what you call her," said Emm, staring at the stained linoleum floor and ignoring the newborn asleep in his wife's arms. "The child is of no use to me."

CHAPTER 29

Zona was the child Emm least wanted to live with, but she was the only one remaining between him and the old age home. Bruna drove him from Darold's to Zona's, not because Darold was busy with chores, but because he and Virginia were off for the day to see the fall colors. "Darold said it was thanks to you," Bruna said, backing slowly down the driveway. A neighbor looked askance at her big, rusty car. "I thought maybe you'd driven my brother into his wife's arms."

It seemed that Bruna's scorn was the price she'd make Emm pay for taking him to Zona's, but she continued, "I was wrong. Darold wasn't escaping you. On the contrary, he was taking your advice. You convinced him that a husband and wife need to spend time together, alone."

Emm was relieved but spoke cautiously, never sure when he might provoke a barrage of criticism from his oldest daughter. "I wish I'd done that with your mother. It's easy to lose sight of why you married each other. I didn't want Darold to make the same mistake."

Bruna sped up when they'd reached the main road. She nodded. "That makes sense."

In those three words, Emm heard grudging admiration. He didn't know if it was for him, or for Darold making amends with Virginia, but he was content to accept it without question.

"According to James," Bruna added, "his parents are a lot nicer to be around these days." Bruna's grin of approval was unmistakable. Emm smiled back with a hint of pride.

"I can't say the same for Zona and her relationships," she went on. "The men she brings to my house aren't worthy of the label. The latest is half again her age and she acts half her age around him. Her nieces and nephews don't know what to make of an aunt who never grew up."

Emm was already nervous about this last-chance move. Bruna's comments were not reassuring. In fact, they were rather thoughtless given his situation. He tried to buck up himself by defending Zona. "It's not her fault she acts that way. Her childhood wasn't normal. Zona was only nine when her mother died, and you and Darold babied her after that."

Bruna gripped the steering wheel. "It's not what *we* did, Father. It's what *you* didn't. Zona didn't miss Mother, she missed you. You ignored her from the moment she was born."

Now Emm defended himself. "I was no different from other fathers with a lot of mouths to feed." It sounded lame, even to his own ears, so he played for sympathy. "Later, after Arvil and your mother died, I was too grief-stricken to reach out." He couldn't explain that not only had he lost the two people he loved most, but he'd also lost his last remaining dream. In the face of every setback, Emm had continued to imagine what his oldest child would grow up to be. How could he care about his youngest, who would never replace his real son or the rosy future he pictured for him?

Bruna's tone softened, but her body remained rigid. "Even if being sad makes sense," she said, "it doesn't excuse your behavior. Or make Zona's any easier to take."

They drove in silence the rest of the way, far outside the city limits. Emm distracted and calmed himself by looking at the vibrant trees. Half an hour later, Bruna pulled her big car into a graveled driveway behind a small yellow car with butterfly decals on the doors and hood. Before them was a trim white cottage, with a reddening maple in the front yard and gold-leafed Hosta and russet sedum around a bright blue door. Emm remembered Izora planting the same perennials at the house he'd bought between the births of Arvil and Bruna. When they lost the house during the Depression, and had to move in with his parents, Izora had mourned the loss of her garden more than the house itself. Mrs. Benbow preferred vegetables and herbs, practical plants rather than pretty flowers, and hadn't ceded any yard space to Izora. Not that his wife had the time or energy to garden by then. It had been a long time since Emm noticed the few plants—chives, mint— that continued to come up at the house where he'd live all but a few years of his life. Until now.

While Bruna helped Emm stand up behind his walker, a large brown mutt came bounding out of the house, put its paws over Emm's hands, and barked. Emm instinctively drew back.

"Riley, get down." Zona, wearing a nurse's uniform and pigtails tied with red ribbons, ran down the walk after the dog. "Don't worry, Daddy. He's friendly. See, his tail is wagging." She pulled the dog back. Riley immediately crouched at Zona's feet.

"I'm not afraid he'll bite me. I'm afraid he'll knock me down."

"I'll train him not to jump on you anymore." Zona patted Riley's head. The dog slobbered on her white shoes. "He gets overexcited when I come home after a night shift, and I got back from the hospital later than usual this morning." Zona sighed. "Poor Mr. Timmy. Again."

Emm and Bruna looked at each other and then at Zona.

"Thomas Carson. My oldest patient on the gerontology ward. It was his second cardiac arrest this month. Dr. Sewell and our team brought him around."

It was Emm's turn to sigh, as if he, not Mr. Carson, had been saved.

Zona hugged Emm, leaning over Riley so she wouldn't dislodge him. "I'm not due back at work until tomorrow, so I can help you get settled. Except would you mind if I took a quick run into town this afternoon to check on Mr. Timmy?"

Emm said she was welcome to go while he napped, provided the dog was tied or locked up so it wouldn't bother him. Zona said Riley had a kennel and run in the back yard.

Bruna, her back pressed against her car, eyed the dog suspiciously. The look she gave Zona was equally unfavorable. "Shall I carry in Father's things? There's only one suitcase and a carryall with his medicine and toiletries."

Zona wrung her hands. "Just set them by the door. I'll bring them into the house." She turned back to Emm. "It's just a short step up. Same out the back. There aren't any stairs inside."

Another sigh of relief. Emm said he could navigate one step, although he'd feel safer if one of them stood next to him the first time. He looked back and forth between his daughters.

Bruna deposited Emm's bags next to Riley. "I'll leave you to Zona, then, Father." She touched his left hand, Emm's good side, bid him goodbye, and drove off.

Zona, looking less like a real nurse than a child dressed in a doll's outfit, laced her fingers in Emm's right hand. "It's just you and me, Daddy," she said. The dog whimpered. "And Riley."

CHAPTER 30

Although Zona hovered in case Emm stumbled, he climbed the short step up to the house easily. Zona put Riley in her room while she gave Emm a tour. The dog pawed at the door briefly but was soon quiet. Emm hoped it would be the same when Zona was at work, or he'd never get any rest despite the absence of street noise or neighbors. It was peaceful out here.

The cottage had two bedrooms, a sunny kitchen with a stenciled design above the counter and herbs growing in pots on the windowsill, and a living-dining room with an old oak sideboard. The floors were wood, scratched from the dog's nails, but otherwise the place was spotless. Emm thought it was cozy and charming, like a doll's house. He'd have no trouble getting around.

The only thing that worried him were the low shelves and tables filled with knickknacks, which he might bump into and break. On closer inspection, he saw that all the tiny figurines were ceramic dogs. Riley was a mixture of God-knows-what, probably adopted from the pound, but these miniatures were a collection of purebreds. Emm guessed there were a hundred, maybe more.

Zona saw him looking and blushed. "My one indulgence, Daddy." She proudly showed him a dachshund, a border collie, and a cute terrier with an eye patch. A few she named by what Emm took to be the manufacturer of the tiny replica: Goebel W. Germany schnauzer, Hagen Renaker white poodle. Shyly, she beckoned him to a glass-fronted corner cabinet, explaining that the dogs inside were rare and costly. Handling them with the care she might show a frail and elderly patient, Zona held up a Rosenthal miniature bulldog, a Staffordshire porcelain Beagle, and a Basset Hound whose long ears spilled onto the shelf. This last one she handed to Emm.

He cradled it with his good hand and looked into its sad brown eyes, expecting glass beads but instead staring at a pair of luminous dark jewels. "Smoky topaz," Zona told him, as she took the dog back, kissed its tiny nose, and returned it to the hutch. "I'd give anything to own a set of Royal Doulton China English sheep dogs, but on a nurse's salary it will be a score of Christmases before I can afford them."

"Do you think it's wise to spend your money this way?" Emm certainly didn't. Zona was unmarried, a condition not likely to change if Bruna was to be believed. She had to think seriously about her future. Children could live carefree in the present, not grown-ups. Even if Zona now figured on adding his pension to her household income, it wouldn't go far and neither would he.

His daughter's face fell. "You're right. I won't buy anymore. It's good to know when to stop." She forced a smile. "Let me show you the backyard." Emm shuffled behind her, worried he'd been too harsh. After all, she lived modestly otherwise, and what else did she have to give her pleasure?

A cool wind blew two dried leaves into the kitchen when Zona opened the back door. She draped a shawl around Emm's shoulders. He tried to shrug it off, but she tightened it and gently scolded him. "I won't have you catching a chill. Besides, there's no one out here to see you." She studied him, then nodded her approval. "You look like an old-fashioned gentleman." Emm let her lead him down the shallow step; Riley was led, without protest, to the kennel.

Most of the plants were done blooming, but Zona pointed to their foliage and named them all. They were like the flowers in the nursery rhymes his mother used to recite: here we go round the mulberry bush, ring-a-round of roses, and contrary Mary's silver bells. There was even a vine with two tiny pumpkins where Peter Peter kept his wife. Emm hadn't kept Izora in a pumpkin shell, but he thought about how trapped she must have felt with so many children to care for.

Zona plucked off the dead blossoms and pulled a couple of weeds. "Time for the garden to sleep," she said, "but spring will be here again. I can't wait for you to see what comes up."

"I'm sure I'll like it," Emm said. If I'm still here, he thought.

They went inside so Emm could nap while Zona went to the hospital to look in on Mr. Timmy. His room was small but neat, like the rest of the house. Zona had taped foam padding around the corners of the bed frame, dresser, and a small bookshelf with *Schiffer's Antique Dogs*, *Flea Market Fidos*, and *Collectors Monthly* magazines. There was a nightlight by the door so he could find his way to the bathroom without tripping. Of all the jobs his children had, Zona's work as a nurse, especially with elderly patients, made her the best person for Emm to live with after all. It was worth considering. In some ways she was more childish than Foy, yet, despite what Bruna had said, she seemed old enough to take care of him. Time would tell, or it would simply run out.

Dinner was waiting when Emm woke up. Like the safety precautions she'd taken with the furniture, Zona cooked the kind of healthy food a man who had high blood pressure and was recovering from a stroke should eat. Emm would live longer here, but without the dash he'd come to enjoy at Garnish's. He sighed. He didn't need Dale Carnegie to tell him he couldn't have it all.

Zona ate the same roasted chicken and steamed vegetables she'd prepared for Emm. He wondered if she'd secretly salted hers beforehand, but she seemed too guileless. He noticed she'd taken off her nurse's uniform and loosened her hair. "No red ribbons at dinner?" he teased.

She laughed. "I wear those to cheer up the patients. A different color every day. The old ones appreciate it the most. They're my favorite people to work with."

"I guess they like having young blood around." Emm couldn't remember seeing any cheerful young staff members at Kingsbridge. He'd been too busy looking at the old folks.

"You're right. Only I'm not so young anymore. I'll be forty the first of next month." She grimaced, then brightened. "It won't be so bad because you'll be here to help me celebrate."

Emm figured that he'd last until then.

Zona clapped. "I'm so happy you're living with me Daddy. Riley's good company, but it gets lonely. Of course, I have Arnold." Emm looked under the table for a hidden animal. Zona giggled. "Arnold Pembrooke, my boyfriend. I can't wait for you to meet him. I wanted to have today alone with you, but he's coming over for dinner tomorrow. I just know you'll like him."

Recalling Bruna's derogatory words, Emm was doubtful. He couldn't summon forth the same reassurance he'd given Zona about looking forward to seeing the spring flowers.

***

Emm was nearly asleep when the phone in Zona's room rang. He didn't want to eavesdrop but his door and hers were both open, so he couldn't help hearing her side of the conversation.

"But I already started to marinate the pot roast, with pepper and cloves, your favorite."

There was a long pause. Emm guessed it was filled with an explanation at the other end.

"Of course, Honey. I understand." Zona sounded like a child who'd just been told Santa wasn't coming. "Saturday lunch? Apple cobbler?" A short silence. "Good. I love you." Click.

Seconds later, Zona knocked on Emm's door frame. "Are you awake, Daddy?" She plucked a tissue from the box on the nightstand and perched on the bed. "Arnold can't come tomorrow. Something came up at work." To be polite, Emm asked what Arnold did. "He brokers deals between companies. It's too complicated for me to understand, but there are lots of last-minute negotiations." Emm took that to mean that Arnold frequently cancelled their plans.

"I hope you like pot roast. And red potatoes." Zona spoke bravely through her sniffles.

"I'll eat a double serving," he said, "and have the leftovers for lunch the next day."

"Thanks, Daddy. I'm so glad you're here."

Those words sounded needier than when she'd said them at dinner. They made the right side of Emm's body ache. He forced a yawn.

Zona stood. "I'm being selfish not letting you sleep after such a long day. I'll fix us a nice breakfast before I leave for my shift in the morning, and I'll get a bell for your bedside on my way home so you can ring me if you need anything during the night." She kissed his cheek and left.

Emm waited a few minutes before getting up and closing his door. Before returning to bed, he parted the curtains and stared at the clear October sky. There were more stars visible in the country than he'd ever seen in seventy-five years of living in town. He closed the curtains and slid under the down comforter. An hour later he was still awake. The night light beside the door shone in his eyes, as brightly as the stars outside, but that wasn't the reason he couldn't sleep.

CHAPTER 31

Zona worked the Friday night shift. Instead of going to bed when she got home, she fussed over the next day's lunch for Arnold. Just as he'd done at Garnish's, Emm sat and watched the preparations. Riley lay quietly at his feet. Emm was beginning to grow fond of the dog. While Zona was at the hospital, Riley sprawled beside Emm as he read, napped, or ate the healthy, homemade meals his daughter left for him. Zona was training the dog to bring Emm his slippers.

First, Zona made two pans each of lasagna and apple cobbler, along with tossed salad and garlic bread. Next, she spread Brie on crackers, then topped them off with slivers of salmon and halved cherry tomatoes. Emm noticed the age wrinkles beginning to form around her eyes as she painstakingly sliced and arranged the canapes on a platter. Finally, Zona set out vodka, Galliano, a pitcher of fresh-squeezed orange juice, one cocktail glass, and two tumblers on the sideboard. "Arnold loves his Harvey Wallbangers," she explained. "I don't drink, and you're under orders not to, but I bought us a bottle of sparkling cider to toast the meeting of my two favorite men."

Half an hour after he was expected, Arnold's key turned in the front lock. Zona raced to the door. Not Riley. He pawed at the back door, eager to be let out. Emm opened it, wishing he could flee too, then turned his walker around to study Arnold. Zona's beau was Emm's height, with graying hair combed over a sizable bald spot. He wore faded blue jeans, a peasant shirt, and painted beads. A paunch bulged beneath his woven poncho. Emm judged him to be in his mid-sixties, as Bruna had said, and despite his attire, clearly too old to have grown up in the hippie free-love era. Emm disdained people like him, but with today's reverence for youth, men who neither dressed nor acted their age were everywhere. He wondered where Zona had found him.

Arnold twirled Zona until her short skirt flared out. "Doesn't she look great?" he asked. "Not a day older than she looked in high school, I bet." Emm, who had no recollection of his daughter at that age, replied that Zona was indeed a lovely woman. "She's my girl," Arnold said.

Emm knew that older men often chose younger girlfriends to prove their virility. He'd never been tempted. With a house full of children, he had a lifetime's evidence of his manhood. He assumed Arnold was childless, although Zona hadn't said. It was none of his business.

Arnold collapsed in a chair. "I almost didn't make it," he said, tossing his poncho toward the couch. "My stomach was acting up again, but I didn't want to disappoint you." He gave Zona a small package of dog treats. "Liver flavored. I thought Riley would like them." She beamed as though he'd offered her a slice of the moon and emptied half a dozen treats in the dog's food dish.

Zona handed Arnold his drink and poured two tumblers of cider. "I want to propose a toast." Without waiting, Arnold took a big swallow and pulled the plate of canapes toward him. Zona froze, the tumbler raised in her hand. Emm clinked his glass against hers and drank. Zona smiled weakly, took a sip, and carried her cider into the kitchen. Hearing the water run, Emm wondered if she was masking the sound of crying. By the time Zona came out with the rest of the food, Arnold had eaten most of the salmon.

"Nice snacks." He turned to Emm. "The kid's as fine a cook as my mother." Zona put the last canape in Arnold's mouth and said it was sweet of him to say so. "Mom is near ninety," Arnold told Emm. "She's still in her own place, but it's not safe for her to cook anymore. I take good care of her. I'm a good son. Her only child. A daughter wouldn't have treated her better."

"I lost my oldest boy in the war," said Emm. "If he were alive, he'd look after me."

Zona's lips quivered. "That's my job now, Daddy." She looked with dismay at the empty hors d'oeuvres plate, as if suddenly aware that she'd just failed.

Arnold pulled the lasagna pan toward him. "You're taking care of me, Baby." He helped himself to a large piece and pointed to the bread. Zona tore off a hunk and handed it to him. For a man with an upset stomach, thought Emm, Arnold's appetite was as healthy as a horse's.

Zona nibbled at her salad. "How did your meeting go the other night, Honey?"

Arnold looked puzzled. Zona said she meant the last-minute meeting on the night he was supposed to come for dinner. "Oh, fine," Arnold muttered before stuffing his mouth.

Emm cut a square of lasagna as big as Arnold's although it was more than he could eat. "Zona tells me you're a businessman. You broker deals between companies."

"Something like that." Arnold mopped up tomato sauce with his bread.

"I was a salesman," said Emm, "and a pretty good deal-maker myself. Cars. New ones."

"Easier than selling used ones," said Arnold. "With old cars, customers want to look under the hood, even if they don't know the first thing about engines. That's why I never let my clients examine one another's affairs too closely. They don't know what they're looking for either. I'd rather they let me call all the shots." He took a second slice of lasagna and held out his glass.

Zona brought him another Harvey Wallbanger. She pushed

away her nearly full plate and hesitantly asked, "Honey, after lunch, could you look at the hose connecting the humidifier to the furnace? It clogged at the end of last winter and you promised to fix it before this winter began."

Arnold sighed loudly and chewed bread with his mouth open. "I'll do it next week when I'm feeling better. Besides, what's the rush? It's still October."

"I'll fix it," said Emm. "The weather's already cold enough for the heat to kick on." He was actually looking forward to making the small repairs that he'd long ago stopped doing in his own house. He'd ask Zona if it was okay for Darold to drop off Foy to act as his "assistant."

Arnold protested that he was going to fix the hose just like he'd promised, but Emm easily spotted a con man. Arnold had no intention of making good on his word. Only Zona, who hadn't looked under the hood, could believe that this old model would run as advertised.

As soon as Arnold had eaten dessert, he pushed back from the table and said he had to go. "Business beckons." Zona packed him a week's worth of meals—the second trays of lasagna and cobbler she'd made last night and frozen left-over pot roast from the dinner he'd cancelled. "As long as you're cooking old-folks food for your father, be a doll and make extra for me to take to my mother."

"Sure, Honey, no trouble. These will get you started." Zona added a few other containers from the refrigerator and put her arms around him. "Call me?" she asked in a plaintive voice.

Arnold pecked her on the cheek and mumbled, "Mmm." He gave Emm a firm handshake, put on his poncho, and headed toward the door. "Oh, Baby, you haven't forgotten about coming with me to the executive dinner on Tuesday? If the client thinks you're my wife, he'll trust me more."

Zona frowned. "I told you that I'd be coming off a double shift and would be too tired."

"And I told you to either cancel or trade the second shift. This meeting is important."

Arnold was a man who didn't take no for an answer, so Emm wasn't surprised when his daughter said yes, she'd change her schedule. While she walked him to his car, Emm hoped the relationship wouldn't last through the winter. "Arnold wears love beads but gives out no love. He makes the peace sign but isn't a dove. Arnold's a devil who is mean to sweet Zona. He sprouts horns; she an angel's corona." Clever as he found his own verse, Emm vowed to keep his opinion to himself. He'd learned with Erissa that it was dangerous to tell his kids how to improve their lives. It could have unintended consequences for them. Worse, the upshot could backfire on him.

***

Zona washed the dishes. Riley, having turned up his nose at the liver treats, stretched out beside her on the worn linoleum tiles. "I'm sorry Arnold wasn't feeling better, Daddy. And that he had to leave before the two of you got to talk more. I hope you still liked him."

Emm dried the lasagna pan three times before answering. "He's colorful. An interesting character." He waffled on the vow he'd taken minutes before, then added. "Maybe a mite pushy. Keep looking. You don't want to take the first car off the lot."

Zona stiffened. "He's hardly my first."

"I only meant ..."

"Arnold is good to me. He compliments my cooking. He says I'm pretty. He calls me his girl." Riley stood and positioned himself between Emm and Zona, as if to protect her.

Emm backed down. He'd been at Zona's place less than a week, and hers was the last set of wheels left on his lot. He searched for something nice to say, changing the topic at the same time. "Arnold works hard. I like that. A man needs to keep busy. You're too young to remember, but in the Depression so many were out of work. It wasn't their fault, but they felt like failures."

Zona patted Riley's head, and the dog, an eye still on Emm, lay down again. "I'm glad I don't remember that awful time, but I wish I had more memories of me and Mommy from then."

Relieved to have peace restored between them, Emm searched the scraps he'd retained from Zona's childhood. "You loved animals and begged to have a pet, but my mother said that our home was already a madhouse without one."

Zona heated two mugs of cider and they moved to the table. Riley followed, brushing against Zona with every step. "Was I very disappointed?"

"Your mother tried hard to make it up to you. She took you to Riverdale Zoo. It was like an old farm on the banks of the Don River, and they allowed children to pet the animals."

"Riverdale! I still like to go there. I'm the only person over twelve who pets the animals." Riley put his head on Zona's lap. She stroked his head. "Did you ever go to the zoo with us?"

Emm wrapped his hands around the warm mug. "No. I wish I had."

"Me too. Was it just me and Mommy or did the other kids come with us?"

"Your mother picked one special thing to do alone with each of you. It wasn't easy for her to find time, and I admit I wasn't much help, but your grandmother pitched in when she could."

"I don't recall much about Grammy either. Mostly, I remember Bruna and Darold taking care of the rest of us. Of course, that was probably after Mommy died."

"They still look after the family." Emm recalled Bruna's harsh criticism of Zona. "It must be hard for them to think of you as a grown-up. Do you still think of them as parents?"

"Not Darold. He's what he is, a nice big brother." Zona gulped her cider, then shuddered. "But Bruna is scary, like the wicked stepmother in a fairy tale." Her hands flew to her mouth.

Emm nodded to reassure her it was okay to go on.

"Every Sunday afternoon, I fight with myself about whether to go to her house, but half of the time, I'm too much of a puddle of pudding to drive into town."

Emm smiled at the alliteration. Foy would have liked it too. "How about your other brothers and sisters? Erissa is closer to you in age than Bruna." He couldn't remember their birth dates, but "E" came several years later in the alphabet than "B." Both Erissa and Zona had grown up without a mother's guidance during their teenage years. That might draw them together now.

Zona shook her head. "I have nothing to do with Erissa. When I was little, I watched from the sidelines as she got all the good attention. When I got older, all I heard was the bad gossip. Either way, she didn't seem part of my life, and she certainly had no room in hers for me."

"You know she's back in rehab?" Emm studied Zona's face. There was no sign of concern, but neither was there disgust. "When she gets out, you might try to offer her a hand."

"Why? She's got Bruna and Darold."

"They're too much like parents." A role Emm had bungled with Erissa, twice. "What she needs is a sister. You're a nurse. Taking care of others comes naturally. And even though you're younger, it would be the grown-up thing to do." It might even impress Bruna, Emm thought, but after looking at Riley's skeptical half-open eyelids, he vowed again to stop giving advice.

Zona scratched behind the dog's ears. "I've read that animals can help people in recovery. Maybe I'll ask Erissa if I can bring Riley over to visit her." She looked to Emm for approval.

He smiled. The dog closed his eyes and let Emm pat its head. "How did you come up with the name Riley?"

"I didn't. That's what he was called in the shelter where I found him. He's easygoing and lazy, like the character in that old television show, *The Life of Riley*. The name fits him. How did you come up with mine?"

"I didn't. It was your mother's idea." Emm thought it wisest not to say why. "We gave all of you odd monikers. I've been asking everyone what they thought of their names growing up."

Zona bit her lip. "I didn't like being at the end of the alphabet, like zebra. I was the last kid in class to get a turn. It was okay if we were being sent to the blackboard for arithmetic problems." She frowned. "But if it was for something good, like picking a cookie, all the big ones with the most chocolate chips had been taken by the time my name was called."

"Poor Zona." Emm hoped Izora was listening. This was one problem among their children that *he* was not responsible for.

Zona smiled slyly. "But some teachers felt sorry for me and let me take all the cookies that were left. So, in the end, I beat out everyone from Albert to Yvonne." She thought a minute. "The one thing I envied Erissa for, even when she was pregnant and strung out, was her name. It's as pretty as she used to be." She gazed into Riley's adoring eyes. "Maybe this time rehab will stick, and she'll be pretty again. If that makes her feel good about herself, it will help her stay clean."

"I knew you'd understand," said Emm, thinking what a good nurse Zona must be. "I'm sorry you were too young to get to know Arvil before he was killed." Just saying his son's name was painful. Sweet as Zona was, Emm wished it were a grown-up Arvil sitting opposite him now.

"I heard a lot about him. He was pretty much idolized by the adults. The kids too, at first." Zona squirmed.

"And later?" Emm knew by now not to be surprised unless Zona had a new revelation.

"The usual 'big brother was a bully' stuff. After Arvil was killed, everyone from Bruna on down watched the adults to know what was okay to say about him. As they got older, they felt freer to speak their minds, especially when it was just the kids talking among themselves. I didn't have much to add, so they probably forgot I was there and let it all out. I was a good listener."

"Did your brothers and sisters ever talk about the adults when they were alone?"

"They missed Mommy, but they never said anything bad about her." Zona grimaced. "I'm sorry, but they weren't always so nice about Grammy. She was bossy. Bruna takes after her."

Emm gripped his empty mug with both hands. "What about me?"

"Honestly, Daddy, I don't remember them saying much of anything about you."

That stung worse than criticism. It was as if Emm didn't exist for his children. It made sense, though, didn't it? All those years, they never really existed for him.

Zona wrapped her hands around his. "I'm off on Wednesday. Do you want to go to the zoo with me? Riverdale has golf carts so you wouldn't have to walk. You can ride around."

Emm hesitated. It would be nice to get out one more time before the snow came, and for something other than a doctor's appointment. On the other hand, he'd look like a doddering old man being taken for a spin in the fresh air by his hired caregiver. "Won't you be too tired for the zoo after a double shift the day before, not to mention dinner with Arnold that evening?"

"I've got all the energy in the world for you." Zona cleared the table. "I'll ask Arnold if he's free to join us too." Riley snorted. "On second thought, let's make it just the two us."

Hours later, in bed, Emm invited Izora to turn the date into a threesome. He'd become as strange as Garnish chatting with Helma, yet after lying awake that first night at Zona's, Emm had found that talking to his wife helped him fall asleep. They were spending time together, alone, after all and Emm didn't care whether their children approved of the bedtime whispering or not.

CHAPTER 32

For someone presumably stuck in childhood, Zona was excited about turning forty in two weeks and planned a special dinner. She bought French hens to stuff with apricots, ordered a butter creme cake from Delysees Bakery, and chose an expensive bottle of Dom Perignon champagne.

"I don't need a present," Emm heard her tell Arnold on the phone. "Just having you and Daddy here to celebrate with me is enough." Emm nevertheless hoped Arnold would buy Zona something nice and wanted to surprise her with a gift too. The problem was that he had no idea what to get or where or how to buy it. Bruna would resent taking him shopping for Zona, and he didn't want to impose on Darold, whose newfound domestic tranquility was still fragile.

Emm had resigned himself to giving Zona money to buy herself a present when he hit on a better idea. He was leafing through *Collectors Monthly*, Riley snoozing at his feet, when he saw the classified ad: Two Royal Doulton English Sheep Dogs, $200 or best offer. He slapped the magazine and shouted, "That's it!" Riley leapt to his feet. Emm would have, too, if he'd been able.

He dialed. The issue was three months old, and he was afraid the china dogs would be gone. The woman who answered said they were still available, but two buyers were in a bidding war, so the price had gone up to three hundred and fifty dollars. Emm gulped. He'd criticized Zona for wasting money, and now he was being asked to pay the most outrageous sum ever. On the other hand, he wanted to make his daughter believe she was worth it. He offered four hundred and told the seller to mail the dogs the minute she got his check. Fortunately, the package arrived when Zona was at work. He did his best to gift wrap the small box and hid it in his sock drawer.

November 1st brought the first light snowfall. Zona put the champagne in the refrigerator before leaving for work, picked up the cake on her way home, and was stuffing the birds ten minutes after she walked through the door late that afternoon. She chatted about the friends at work surprising her with birthday doughnuts from Tim Horton's and an oversized coffee mug that said "Forty is Feisty" in big red letters.

Emm admired the mug. "Zona is zesty," he said.

She smiled and said it was a nice present but repeated that all she needed to be happy was dinner with Arnold and her father. The dog whimpered. Zona patted his nose. "You too, Riley."

At six o'clock, the oven timer rang. Arnold was half an hour late. Zona said it must be slippery outside and that traffic was probably slowing him down. She turned down the oven and turned on the radio. The announcer said that the snow was actually lighter than predicted and that even the back roads had already been cleared. Zona put on her coat and Emm heard her shovel scraping the front walk, where the snow had barely dusted the pavement.

An hour later, Zona came back inside and took the shriveled hens out of the oven. The phone rang. "I see," she said and hung up. Then she knelt at Emm's knees and burst into tears.

"Did Arnold say why he wasn't coming?" Emm asked.

Zona sat up and shrugged. They both knew it didn't matter. Riley licked her tears, put his muzzle in her lap, and flicked his tail across Emm's shoes, which he'd polished for the dinner.

"Arnold Pembrooke isn't nice. Selfishness is his main vice. He doesn't do the things he oughter. And always disappoints my daughter." Emm watched Zona's frown turn into a sad smile. "Sit right there. You too, Riley." He went to his bedroom and came back with the small box.

Zona undid the clumsy wrapping and opened the lid. When she saw that the gift inside was covered in tissue paper, she lifted her still-wet eyes to Emm and slowly pulled out first one, then the other, china dog. She gasped. Her lips turned up in a genuine smile. On shaky legs, she carried her tiny treasures to the cabinet and cleared space for them in the center of the middle shelf. "It's the best present I ever got in my whole life," she breathed. "Except for the day you moved in."

Emm felt his own tears welling up. "You deserve it," he said. "You deserve better."

Zona picked the salvageable meat off the hens' carcasses and dumped it into Riley's bowl. She poured champagne for herself and Emm and cut them each a large slice of cake.

Emm stood. "A wise man said that 'happiness does not depend on external conditions but is instead governed by our mental attitude.' To happiness." For the second time since moving in, he alone clinked Zona's glass.

CHAPTER 33

The next day, a dozen long-stemmed red roses arrived with a card signed simply "Arnold." Zona crammed them into a vase and set them at the back of the kitchen counter, behind the flour and sugar canisters; they were already wilted by the time Arnold picked her up to go to the movies that weekend. For the rest of that month, he continued to come for meals, leaving with packages for himself and his mother, but Zona no longer talked to Emm about him with such adoration.

One day she came home from work and without even removing her coat and boots, took the ribbons out of her hair. "Mr. Timmy is gone," she said.

Emm made tea and sat with her silently while she sipped and sniffled. He tried to exude calm for her sake, but his muscles seized with fear. An old man had just died. On the gerontology ward, and at Kingsbridge, it happened all the time. He wondered what it would be like to walk into the dining room at the nursing home and find that the seat at your table where someone usually sat was suddenly empty. Or to pass an open door in the hallway and see that the smiling pictures of grandchildren on the dresser had been replaced overnight by unfamiliar faces.

"How old was Mr. Carson?"

"Nearly ninety. Fifteen years older than you, Daddy."

Emm relaxed, but only a little. His mother had lived into her eighties, but his father had died when he was only a couple of years older than Emm was now. Eight months ago, when Emm had fallen and couldn't get up, living hadn't mattered that much. He had little to get up for, other than reading the newspaper and watching the old house crumble around him. Now he had to make amends and keep his promise to Izora before joining her in the cemetery. So far, Foy was his only unqualified success. He'd done okay with two more, Darold and Garnish, three if he counted Helma. But he had to slot Bruna, Cleon, and especially Erissa in the failure column. Zona was his last chance to break even or come out ahead. Until now, Emm had worried that time was running out to find a place to live. Now he fretted that time would run out before death came to find him.

***

Zona wasn't the only one moping around the hospital after Mr. Timmy died. He'd been a favorite with everyone on staff. To boost morale, a coworker decided to throw a Roaring Twenties party, complete with costumes. Zona's eyes sparkled as she told Emm about it. He hadn't seen her this excited since she'd planned her own birthday celebration. Arnold promised to pick her up on time.

Emm barely recognized the woman who emerged from his daughter's bedroom the night of the party. Her dress was short, held up by thin shoulder straps, and covered in silver spangles that made even the lazy Riley snap to attention when they caught the light. "That's an adult-rated dress if I ever saw one," Emm told Zona as she twirled before him.

"Well, I *am* forty now." She pursed her lipsticked mouth and fluttered her blue-shadowed eyelids, before pecking Emm on the cheek. "And I am really glad to be going out tonight."

"You look beautiful," Emm told her. "Just like your mother in a flapper dress." He waited to feel sad about missing his wife, but all he felt was happiness for his daughter.

The phone rang. Zona didn't pick it up right away. When she finally did, Emm didn't need to listen to her end of the conversation to know what the call was about. Rivulets of mascara ran down her rouged cheeks when she emerged from her room. She unpinned the glittery rhinestone tiara from her hair and tossed it on the couch.

Emm picked it up. "Go to the party anyway," he urged. "It's a shame to waste that pretty dress." Or to waste tears on Awful Atrocious Arnold, he thought. The Pushy Mr. Pembrooke. A man who cared only about himself and bulldozed any resistance. Why did Zona stay with him? An article that Emm had read years ago suddenly flooded his memory. It said that people chose mates with their parents' flaws in an attempt to get the relationship "right." Were he and Arnold alike?

If so, it wasn't right that Zona ended up suffering. Emm gazed through the window at the clear night sky and asked Izora, "Isn't it my responsibility, not hers, to correct the errors of the past? To free Zona so she can do better from now on?" A star twinkled. Emm, feeling vindicated, was ready to applaud himself for getting this one right. Then he recalled something else he'd read long ago. Dale Carnegie had written that "applause is a receipt, not a bill." Emm hadn't earned the right to congratulate himself yet.

He replaced the tiara on Zona, who transferred it to Riley. "I'd rather stay home with you," she said. She changed into pajamas and bunny slippers, washed her face, and made popcorn and hot chocolate. They watched television, an old movie, *Scarface*, starring Paul Muni as Al Capone. "It's our own Roaring Twenties party," Zona told Riley, whose fur sparkled with glitter.

Emm remembered when the film came out, the year Erissa was born. Money was tight, but he'd scrounged enough for tickets and persuaded Izora to go. They hadn't stepped out, just the two of them, in years. His mother had agreed to watch the children, and Emm was as excited as a high school kid anticipating his first date. Then, at the last minute, Izora had said she was too tired. As long as Mrs. Benbow was babysitting, she'd just as soon use the free time to sleep.

Emm had eventually seen the movie with his friends, but they were a poor substitute for a night on the town with his wife. And here he was tonight serving as a substitute for his daughter's ruined plans. He was glad he was there to make her feel better, but if Zona was counting on him to make her happy, she was bound to be disappointed. Being a father was exhausting. Forty-four years after Izora had disappointed him, Emm finally forgave her for being too tired.

***

Emm was still in bed the next morning when he overheard Zona on the phone. She did most of the talking. "No, I've made up my mind." "One time too many." "I deserve better." "You can eat dog food for all I care." Ten seconds later, she plunked down on Emm's quilt, wearing red overalls and pigtails with blue ribbons. "You were right. I broke up with Arnold. I'm your girl, not his."

She went to make breakfast. The house smelled of yesterday's stale popcorn and today's fresh coffee, a child's snack and a grown-up's drink. Emm huddled under the covers, pleased that Zona had taken his advice, yet terrified of the pressure she was putting on him. Could he do what rehab programs promised, provide a safe space for Zona to recover and then set off on her own? Once more, Emm questioned his energy for taking on the belated task of fatherhood. Suppose Zona got stuck? Would he have the strength to push her out of the nest? Would he want to?

He went into the kitchen. Zona's face lit up. "Daddy, you got here without your walker." Emm looked down, surprised. He'd been so preoccupied, he'd forgotten to use it. He gripped the table before lowering himself into a chair.

"You see," said Zona, setting out plates. "You're growing stronger here. I'm helping you and you can help me. We don't need anyone else."

Emm put his hand over hers. The silver nail polish she'd put on for the party was already chipped. "It's been a long time since my children counted on me, and that was to put food on the table, not to help them be ... happy. I'm touched in a way I never thought possible, but in all honesty, I'm uneasy about your depending on me. I'm not going to be around forever."

"I intend to keep you alive as long as possible. We don't have to live out here. I'll move us to the city so you'll be closer to doctors and hospitals." Zona looked at the dog. "If I have to, I'll even give up Riley to rent an apartment. No more crutches for me, and no more walkers for you."

Emm was aware of his heart, but he couldn't tell if it was bursting with joy or collapsing under a huge weight. "We don't have to decide right away," he said, listening to the clock ticking.

***

It was a week later. Zona was due home in an hour. Three times that day, Emm had picked up the phone to call Eudora Cray, torn over his decision. Fifty years ago, he'd needed children to win the Derby. Once he'd lost, he didn't care that they needed him. Now, he needed them again, but he also appreciated what it meant to be needed by them. Mrs. Cray would ask once more what Emm had learned these past nine months. This time he had an answer: fatherhood was not measured in big prizes, but in small gifts of love. Mr. Carnegie himself couldn't have said it better.

Knowing this, however, wasn't enough to help Emm figure out what to do. He lifted the receiver a fourth time and heard Mrs. Cray's cheery yet firm voice. He told her things with Zona were going better than expected. "The child I least wanted to live with might work out the best."

Mrs. Cray was glad to hear it. "Have you found the right quote to capture your feelings?"

"'We are all dreaming of a magical rose garden over the horizon instead of enjoying the roses blooming outside our windows today,'" said Emm. He looked outside at the winter landscape. He was pretty certain he'd still be around in the spring, but he needed to make a decision before then.

The sun was setting. Emm walked to the window and addressed a golden cloud hovering on the horizon. "I'm ready to make amends, Izora, but Zona's needs are so great. I'm afraid of losing another contest, a more important one. Help me decide. The deadline is one month away."

PART TEN:
EMM
DECEMBER 25, 1976

As of midnight on Halloween, 1936, more than two dozen Toronto families claimed to have had at least eight children during the preceding decade. A distant next-of-kin surfaced to have the will invalidated, while lawyers and public policy experts argued that the bequest had encouraged women to have children out of wedlock and could not be allowed to stand. Judge Middleton dismissed the next-of-kin claim and rejected the challengers' logic, saying it was obvious that by "children," Mr. Millar meant "legitimate children." That legal opinion ruled out women like Pauline Clarke, who had five children with her husband and five more with the man she lived with after leaving him. Another woman with ten children was deemed to live outside Toronto's city limits, while one who had given birth to eleven was disqualified because four were born dead. It didn't help that one of the surviving children died of a rat bite before her first birthday.

In the end, after two years of court battles that enriched the pockets of thirty lawyers and countless bookies, a total of four women, each having borne eight children in the designated ten-year period, split the prize, now worth a half-million dollars. In a May 1938 editorial titled "The Last of the Stork Derby," the Ottawa Citizen *claimed the dispute, which took on "bedlamistic proportions" was "finis," but cautioned that if relatives of the deceased carried through on their threat to pursue further legal action, the mad race was not over yet.*

For the Benbows, however, it was. Izora summoned what strength she had left to raise her living children and, together with little Garnish, placed flowers every month on the grave of his twin sister Helma. She told Emm that she understood why he'd pursued Mr. Millar's reward, that the Depression had driven many men temporarily insane. But Emm knew her words were an after-the-fact excuse. He'd pushed her to enter the Derby three years before hard times hit. True, it acquired greater urgency at that point, but he couldn't pretend he'd stayed in the competition for the money alone. Maybe it was because the Depression had depleted his sense of manhood as much as his bank account. He'd never know for sure what continued to drive him.

Izora was less understanding toward Emm's mother and henceforth ignored her advice about how to bring up the children. Mrs. Benbow declared the entire brood unruly and told Izora that from now on, she was on her own. Mr. Benbow, tired of the chaos at home, bought a cottage outside of town for himself and his wife and gave the old house to Emm and his family. His siblings contested the action, but when the claim was rejected, they declined to waste money on an appeal.

The Depression finally ended with the onset of war. Emm found work at a munitions factory and earned enough to support his wife and children. Meanwhile, the contest's winners spent the prize money to house and educate their children. After the Depression's devastation, everyone was cautious and played it safe. The Derby passed into history and was soon forgotten by a press and public consumed with more serious battles, fought on a worldwide stage.

Only for Emm did the fight rage on, especially when he'd had too much to drink. He was consumed by "ifs." "If" that last child had been born just five hours earlier, they'd have split the prize with the other four winners. "If" his dead daughter had been born alive, they'd have won the whole pot outright. And "if" Mr. Millar hadn't been a manipulative rich man whose crazy scheme Emm had fallen for, he and Izora would be living happily in the house he'd bought after Arvil was born, adding a bedroom or two until they stopped after three or four children. When Emm and Izora died, their small inheritance would have been equally divided among them—no race, no contested will, no news coverage. No regrets. Just an ordinary life.

CHAPTER 34

"Merry Christmas, Mr. Benbow." Mrs. Cray's cheery voice greeted Emm when he answered the telephone. He was feeling more melancholy than merry. Arvil would have turned fifty today.

Mrs. Cray clucked sympathetically before nattering on. "I'm heading to my sister's later, but beforehand I'll fortify myself with mulled wine." From her chatty tone, Emm guessed she'd already started. "Given Jorgie's penchant for flaunting tradition, I always prepare myself for the unexpected. Last year she served hot dogs with toasted marshmallows for dinner, then made us fish for our presents in a tub filled with caramel corn. What that silliness had to do with Christmas is beyond me." Mrs. Cray laughed and asked about Emm's holiday plans.

"The family is getting together at Bruna's. It's been an annual tradition since the year after the last Benbow child left home, but this will be my first time joining them."

Mrs. Cray caught her breath. Or maybe she hiccupped. "Goodness. Why haven't you gone before today? What did you do instead?"

"Told them I wasn't up to it, down with a cold or stomach virus. Something like that. After a couple of years, the children didn't ask me again. They'd come by one at a time to see me over the next few days, bring a tin of cookies, a new pair of socks, a muffler. At some point, they even stopped doing that." Emm had been truthful when he said he wasn't up to seeing them all, but not because he'd caught a bug. It was easier to be alone than to try to make conversation or remember the names of their growing families. He was ready for company now, but still nervous about spending a whole day, not only with his children, but also their children and grandchildren. According to Darold's family tree, there were twenty-eight of them, not counting Erissa's daughter. "We'd be more than thirty with Arvil, Helma, and the children they'd have had."

In a sober tone, Mrs. Cray advised Emm to stop counting. "Even the ambitious Mr. Carnegie said to be grateful for what you have instead of regretting what you don't."

"You're absolutely right," Emm said. "I have seven living children and that makes me a lucky man." He hesitated. "But aren't I allowed to wish that Izora was there to see them all?"

"Of course, you are. Holidays can't help being tinged with sadness for those who are no longer with us. I miss Robert terribly at this time of year. Maybe because we didn't have children, we created our own grown-up rituals." She sighed, and sniffled. "Listening to Handel's *Messiah* and taking a twilight walk in the snow."

"It's too bad you and your sister didn't create a special ritual to follow every year."

Mrs. Cray laughed. "That's not Jorgie's style. She isn't the sentimental type." Emm heard her take a sip of wine. "On the other hand, if you can begin a new tradition by spending Christmas with your family, I see no reason my sister and I can't start one too. A game of charades to guess what presents we bought for each other? That would be right up her alley."

"It's never too late to change. Or begin," said Emm.

"Dale Carnegie couldn't have said it better."

Emm accepted the compliment, but he wasn't starting a new tradition. He was joining an established one. Alas, one that Izora would never be part of. If only she'd lived to see her children grow up and become parents themselves. Even his mother, imperfect as he'd come to realize she was, had genuinely enjoyed and been proud of the grandchildren he and his siblings had given her.

"Would you like me to take you to the cemetery tomorrow so you can wish Izora a Merry Christmas?" asked Mrs. Cray. "Arvil too?"

"Yes, thank you. And Helma."

"Who?"

"I'll explain tomorrow. It's been a while since we've talked."

"We also need to talk about what happens come the first of January, whether you'll live with your children or move into Kingsbridge. They're down to one opening. You only have six days to decide before they give it to the person at the top of the waiting list." They arranged for her to pick up Emm the next morning at Darold's house, where he planned to spend the night. That way, she wouldn't have to drive out to Zona's. Mrs. Cray told him to dress warmly.

"You sound like my daughter. Are you sure I can't live with you?" Living with a social worker who helped elderly clients might be just as good as a nurse who took care of old people.

"Didn't you just agree to appreciate the children you have instead of wishing for another?"

Emm despaired of ever being able to do so. Then he reminded himself, it was never too late. "Someday I'll be content with my piece of cake and stop making the same greedy mistake."

***

Zona dropped Emm off at Bruna's and said she'd come back later. Like Mrs. Cray, she intended to fortify herself before facing her sister. Unlike Mrs. Cray, she wouldn't sip wine. Instead, she would snuggle with Riley. Zona drove to Bruna's grim-faced, knocked on the door, and left as soon as Emm crossed the threshold. Bruna stared at her retreating back. Emm's eyes swiveled from one to the other. The sisters hadn't even wished each other a Merry Christmas.

The apartment was hot and already felt crowded, even though Emm was the first to arrive. Looking at the extra chairs and presents, his stomach clenched picturing the upcoming crush when the seats were filled with grown-ups and children, keyed up, were running around. Waves of heat, bearing the aromas of gingerbread and turkey, wafted in from the kitchen. One end of the living room was dominated by a huge tree filled with handmade ornaments: a lumpy Santa with a cotton-ball beard, a dozen tin foil stars, a baby Jesus swaddled in a pale blue doll blanket. If any of these trinkets dated to when his own children were growing up, Emm didn't recognize them. Presumably, most were made by the next two generations of Benbow offspring.

Bruna cleared a space for Emm in the armchair where he used to sit and offered him tea or hot cider. Her easy movements and calm voice led him to conclude she was more relaxed about the upcoming party than he was, and possibly less nervous around him than vice versa. Either her anger had dissipated in the nine months since he'd moved out or holiday spirits had brightened her mood. He gladly accepted the hospitality without trying to decipher how she really felt.

As Emm sipped his cider, Bruna carried food to the portable trays she'd set up around the living room, then knelt at a coffee table to wrap presents. She explained that the adults had long ago stopped giving gifts to one another, there were simply too many of them, but no one stinted on toys for the children. Emm estimated that Bruna had bought two dozen presents for her eight great nieces and nephews. She was halfway finished wrapping them when a timer jangled in the kitchen. Exasperated, she threw down the paper and tape and struggled to her feet.

Emm reached out. "Hand them to me. I'll wrap them."

"Really, Father, I can take care if it myself." Bruna tucked in the gray hairs escaping from her bun. Her calm demeanor was frayed, and the old edge had returned to her voice.

"Please, let me help. My hands are nimble even if my legs aren't." He flexed his fingers.

"Well, all right. But be careful when you put the presents under the tree." She looked at the extra tables and chairs scattered about the room. "It's a bit of a minefield in here."

"I can take care of myself, too," said Emm. He carefully measured and cut the wrapping paper, feeling as competent as the old days when he did home repairs, then carefully labeled each gift in large block letters. He checked his copy of the family tree so he could connect each child's name to his or her parents, and their parents in turn back to his own children. To his surprise, he knew who most of them were before he looked. Did that prove his memory was still sharp or, as he'd once read in the paper, did people remember the things that were important to them? If the latter, at what point in the past year had this new interest in the Benbow family emerged?

Emm steered his walker to the tree with one hand while carrying the smaller presents with the other. The biggest box, however, he'd have to hold with both hands. Recalling his unassisted trip down the hallway at Zona's, Emm left his walker behind and moved slowly across the room, carrying the present in front of him. He tripped over something he didn't see—a table leg, a throw rug— just as Bruna raced in and caught his elbow. He waited for an irritated "I-told-you-so" look, but her eyes mirrored only concern. She steadied him, put the package under the tree, and led him back to his chair.

Emm was still shaking when he sat down. His mind returned to the day last spring when he'd fallen and there was no one around to help, or even to find him, for two days. He'd lain in his own excrement, betrayed by his body, as helpless as a newborn. Despite his fantasies of someday returning to the old place, he knew beyond a doubt that he'd never be able to live there alone again. As he watched his daughter navigate easily around the room, filling plates and hanging decorations, Emm made a painful decision. "Bruna, I'm going to leave the house to you."

Bruna stood still, a plate of cookies in one hand and a sprig of mistletoe in the other. Her eyes narrowed. "Why?"

"So, you'll have enough space for everyone, not just on the holidays, but for the weekly family gatherings and the children's playtimes and sleepovers."

"You'd really let me do what I wanted with the house? Sign over all the papers? Not keep holding onto the strings?" Emm nodded. Bruna scowled. "You should have done something with the place years ago. It needs a lot of fixing up. I don't have the money to pay for repairs."

Emm said she didn't have to do it all at once. The house was structurally sound. He'd give her a check each month, from his pension, while the work was being done. If he continued to feel better, he might even try some of the easier repair jobs himself. Maybe get some of her siblings, or their adult children, to lend a hand. A sort of family project.

"Suppose the others see your giving the house to me as playing favorites? Won't they be resentful?" The memory of Arvil hung in the cinnamon-scented air.

"I don't think so," said Emm. "You've taken care of them your whole life. I should think they'd be happy for you and, in a way, for themselves. This way, they can still get together at the old place, and from now on, the rest of their families can too."

"That would be nice." Bruna took a deep breath. "Of course, you're welcome to come too, Father. As often as you like."

Emm liked that idea, although getting there would be complicated if he lived with Zona.

Bruna sat on the arm of his chair and enfolded Emm in an awkward hug. "It's a grand gift, more than I'd ever dream of asking Santa for. Thank you." The words sounded sincere, yet Emm couldn't swear to his daughter's gratitude. The truth was that she would never trust him, and he would never be able to read her. All the same, he'd made the right decision. The house would stay in the Benbow family for a third generation, and possibly one or two to follow. The inheritance wasn't as big as Mr. Millar's, but it would keep Emm's family together, not tear them apart.

***

Half an hour later, Cleon's family arrived in a caravan. Emm thought his son had lost more hair and gained more weight since last spring, but he was wearing a bulky reindeer sweater, probably a present from his wife Betty, so it was hard to tell. While they stowed their coats, Emm glanced at the family tree. Cleon's two sons had each had a son and a daughter. One of the grandchildren was Jonah, the boy who'd bombarded Emm with questions the night he'd slept over at Bruna's.

The child now presented himself to Emm and studied him. "You're Great Gramps. I had a birthday. I'm six." He held up the correct number of fingers; Emm congratulated him. "I can read J-O-N-A-H." He pointed to the gifts with his name on them. Then, finished with his declarations, the child returned to asking questions. Today he wanted to know what was inside the boxes.

"I don't know," said Emm, "and if I did, I wouldn't tell. It's supposed to be a surprise." Jonah's face fell. "Why don't you guess?" suggested Emm. Jonah perked up immediately. "Did I get a bicycle?" Emm asked if any of the packages were the right size. Jonah admitted they weren't big enough. "Try shaking one, gently," Emm offered. Jonah picked up the smallest box and held it to his ear as he slowly moved it back and forth. "Hot wheels!" he shouted. "I bet it's hot wheels."

Jonah put the present back under the tree, grabbed a handful of gingerbread cookies and candy canes, and ran off to play with his cousins. Emm hoped the child was right, or that there was at least something inside the box that he really wanted. He remembered the excitement of Christmas morning when he was a child, tiptoeing down to the living room of the house where Bruna would soon live and the whole family would gather a year from now. He closed his eyes and wished that he would be there with them too. That was the present he really wanted.

Bruna brought him more cider and asked if he needed anything else. Emm was content to just sit and watch. Cleon and his sons, Mark and Paul, talked hockey. The Montreal Canadiens were favored to win their twentieth Stanley Cup, but Cleon was rooting for Toronto. Mark and Paul said he should resign himself to losing, as usual, at which point Cleon popped a second beer.

Emm remembered the days when not getting what he'd set his heart on made him turn to alcohol too. His drinking was sporadic, though, and dwindled as the Derby was left farther behind. Cleon's drinking was steady, seemed to be increasing, and was spurred by anger at something being taken away—the glory of an athlete, the respect due a father—rather than something he'd never gotten in the first place. Emm hoped his son would make peace with his demons. It was too bad that Betty put up with it; she was the only one who could get Cleon to stop. On the other hand, he loved her for accepting him as he was, and her disapproval might destroy him for good.

Just then Bruna emerged from the kitchen, frowning, with Betty on her heels. Betty kissed the top of Cleon's head and carried his empty bottle to the kitchen. She soon came back out and straightened the presents under the tree. Then she walked around the small tables laden with food, squared the edges of the napkins, and scooped crumbs into her palm.

"Leave it be," Bruna snapped at Betty. "It's only going to get messier when everyone else gets here. I want people to relax and have a good time. I'll clean up tomorrow."

Cleon put down his beer and stood behind Betty, who held the fistful of crumbs to her chest. The room grew quiet. Suddenly,

Emm felt like the only grown-up in the room. He coughed. "The way my mother did it was to clean up right after a party so she wouldn't have to face a mess the next morning. I'm sure Betty would be happy to stay after the others leave and help out then."

Betty nodded and lowered her fist to her side.

Emm jabbed his walker. "I would stay and help if I could, but I'd probably trip and make a bigger mess than all the children combined. Right, Bruna?"

His daughter nodded too, although her back remained rigid.

Emm faced Jonah, his sister, and their cousins. "Great Gramps would help BUT he'd land right on his BUTT. Oops!" He covered his mouth. The children looked toward their parents for permission to giggle. They nodded and laughed as well. Then everyone resumed what they'd been doing.

Betty, blinking back tears, balled up the crumbs in a napkin and brought Emm a plate of cookies. She slipped a coaster under his mug. Then, avoiding the kitchen, she sat by the tree and read to her granddaughters. Emm wasn't sure why he'd defended her. Her constant cleaning drove him crazy too. Perhaps, he was sympathetic because he still felt the sting of Bruna's anger.

Just as Bruna had never gotten over the sting of his anger when she was a little girl.

Cleon finished his third beer and raised it to his father in thanks. Then he rose and clapped his hands. "Jonah, Melissa, Eric, Kelly. Time to go outside and build a snow fort." Kelly and Melissa said they wanted to stay inside and keep reading with Betty. Jonah whined that it was too cold. Only Eric went to the bedroom to get his coat.

"Bring Jonah's too," Cleon called after him, before turning to Jonah. "Don't be a crybaby. You're a big boy now and big boys aren't afraid of a little cold." He threw the coat at his grandson.

Jonah let it fall and walked over to Emm, his eyes silently imploring Great Gramps to stand up for him too. It seemed as though Emm was going to play referee the entire day. For a minute, he envied Zona, resting at home with Riley. Dogs were easier than children.

In a voice as calm and neutral as he could muster, Emm told Cleon, "Even big boys like me would rather stay inside sometimes. Maybe Jonah will go out later when the rest of his cousins get here." He looked at Jonah, who stared at the floor, ungiving. "Meanwhile, Jonah's learning his letters. I asked him to read me a book. Shall we do that now?" The child went to get one.

Cleon spluttered. "I only meant that he needed fresh air and exercise. It's ..."

"Healthy," Emm finished the thought. His son looked lost. Disrespected by his children; disobeyed by his grandchildren. He didn't need further punishment. Emm spoke gently, "You're right, though, about taking care of ourselves. Frankly, I could use more fresh air and exercise too." He'd said the words to help Cleon save face, but they really were true. Emm had an idea that could help them both. "Suppose you made up an exercise plan for your old man and took me out every week? You'd be doing me a big favor."

"You mean drive all the way out to Zona's house?"

Emm hadn't thought this through. "Well, wherever I decide to live."

Cleon looked skeptical. "That old age home might not even allow me to do it."

"I'm sure they're happy whenever family members take the residents out." Emm certainly hoped so. "Although you might have to sign a waiver saying you'd be responsible if anything happened to me while I was in your care."

Now Cleon looked alarmed. "Let's see where you end up, Dad. Then we'll talk about it."

Jonah came back with *Hop on Pop*. It wasn't clear whether he'd chosen the book because he could "read" it by heart or remembered Emm making up rhymes at Bruna's last spring. Those verses had gone over the children's heads. By contrast, Dr. Seuss's vocabulary was simple at the same time that his stories were delightfully convoluted. Fun for every generation. Emm vowed to copy him and do a better job next time. Give more thought to what the little ones needed. Maybe Cleon would copy Emm and do a better job with his grandchildren in the future too.

The irony of setting an example for Cleon wasn't lost on Emm, but today, to his chagrin, he'd seen how much of himself was in his son. Hearing no for an answer could turn them both into bullies. Emm had second thoughts about his exercise plan. Someday Cleon might bully Emm if he could no longer do what his son thought was good for him. In fact, the less Cleon took care of his own health, the more he might impose an unreasonable regimen on Emm. Like the childless Mr. Millar, urging others to have big families when he'd failed to marry and have even one child himself. Emm's bile rose as he thought of the misery that miserable man had caused him.

"You look tired, Father. Would you like to take a nap before the others get here?" Bruna hugged Jonah and sent him off for another candy cane. She helped Emm to the bedroom where he used to sleep and removed the coats from the lower bunk. "I'll put these in my room. Have a good rest. You'll need it."

Emm was glad to take a break from his family, knowing that sixteen more would arrive that afternoon. When Bruna moved into the old house, she'd have enough space to give him a bedroom of his own there. But did he want that? Emm looked at the upper bunk where Jonah had slept last spring and knew the answer immediately. No. It wouldn't provide enough of a retreat, and besides, running away in your own home wasn't a solution. Wherever he ended up, it would have to be a place that Emm wanted to live in, not one he was anxious to escape from.

CHAPTER 35

The light flicked on and off twice, then back on. Emm opened one eye, ready to scold Jonah.

"Popsy!" Foy bounced on the bed, banging his head on the underside of the upper bunk. Emm, still groggy, opened the other eye and grinned. "Darold and Virginia brought me. They only fought once in the car, when Darold skidded and Virginia yelled at him to slow down and he told her to be quiet and let him drive." He lowered his voice. "Erissa came with us too. She didn't say anything the whole way here. Is she angry at me?"

"How could anyone be angry at you, Foy? She didn't feel like talking, that's all." Foy asked why. In an effort to explain, Emm thought of the rare times that Foy was silent. "You know how you get quiet when you concentrate on something, like fixing a broken clock?" Foy said yes but couldn't figure out what Erissa was concentrating on. "Um. Fixing herself," answered Emm. Foy nodded as if he understood. Emm wasn't sure if he did but was glad when Foy let it go.

"Garnish is here, too," said Foy, "and James and Cynthia and Barbara and Fred ..." He reeled off the names of everyone else in the family—his siblings and their spouses, and their children and grandchildren. Everyone except Zona. Emm wondered when, or if, she would arrive.

"Let's go play." Foy helped Emm get out of bed and scampered ahead, like an excited puppy, to the living room. He was soon on the floor playing Candy Land with the children. "Turn on the television," he said to no one in particular. "I want to watch *Charlie Brown Christmas*."

"No television today," Bruna told him. "We're just going to visit and talk to each other."

Foy pouted, then looked at the game board. "But since it's Christmas I can have all the candy and cookies I want, right?" Bruna shook her head. "Not even to bring to my friends?"

"I'll wrap up a package for them before I take you home," Darold said. "Meanwhile, let's fix you a big plate with one of everything." Foy counted the types of cookies, candy canes, and other treats. "Two of everything," he insisted. Darold laughed. "Okay, since it's Christmas."

Bruna's frown reversed to a smile. "I'm outvoted. When you finish everything on your plate, it's time to play hide the mistletoe. Foy can go first." Izora had invented the hiding game years ago to keep their restless children busy; Emm was pleased it had survived. Meanwhile, Foy lit up like a holiday light. Bruna's smile meant she was his friend again. Treats and fun lay ahead.

That was Foy, thought Emm. Easily contented, good natured, occasionally pushing the rules but never too far. No wonder he was thriving in a group home. Emm assessed himself. He'd become nicer in the past year, but compared to his sixth child, he was still more irascible, less forgiving, and more demanding. The kind of person who might be threatened with "upstairs."

"Hi, Dad." Darold stood beside Emm and surveyed the room. "Where's Zona? Didn't she bring you?" Emm said she'd dropped him off and gone to run some errands. Darold snorted. "On Christmas Day?" Emm reassured him Zona would arrive soon; Darold said seeing was believing. He perched on the arm of Emm's chair. "Have you figured out who everyone is?"

Emm admitted he'd depended on the family tree at first but was pleased to discover that he could now attach faces to most of the names without it. Not merely a function of memory, he repeated to himself, but a sign of caring about them.

"Now that you've mastered our immediate family, you're ready to tackle the next chart." Darold opened a diagram showing Emm's five brothers and sisters, their spouses, and three succeeding generations. There were a lot of names. "I'll be visiting all of them this week before I go back to work in January. I do it every year, an annual rite. I call it making the rounds."

"That's quite a few people to see during your week off. Doesn't Virginia resent it?"

"Less than she used to, probably because the two of us are spending more time alone these days." Darold looked toward Virginia, haphazardly stacking presents on top of the teetering pile. "She even promised to join me on a couple of visits this year. Want to tag along with us?"

Emm studied this second family tree. For a while after their parents had died, he and his siblings exchanged Christmas cards, but that ended decades ago. Emm hadn't seen the point once he could no longer keep track of his nieces' and nephews' families. According to Darold's tree, his three brothers each had three or four children, while his two sisters had stopped at one apiece. Maybe the girls didn't want to become like their mother. He pulled out the first chart and held the two side by side. Save for Erissa's three failed marriages and out-of-wedlock baby, his other daughters had neither married nor borne children. They didn't relish a life like Izora's.

The pattern was repeated in succeeding generations. Overall, family size was shrinking, no more than two children apiece now. True, large families had gone out of style, but something else was at work. Growing up in a home overflowing with children wasn't as much fun as Emm had painted it to be. He and his siblings had been short-changed. His and Izora's children had it worse.

Darold was waiting for an answer. Would his father make the

rounds with him? Emm shifted in his seat. "Maybe I'll join you next year, when I'm feeling stronger," he said.

"Are you sure it's wise to wait? Uncle Willis turned eighty-two in March and Uncle Cam was eighty this fall. Even Aunt Leona, the baby of your family, turns seventy-one in February. I hope every one of you lasts a long time, but you're all getting up there. No telling when ..."

"We'll be called upstairs." Emm handed both charts to Darold. "I'll take my chances. Besides, in the extra time it would take to pick me up and drop me off, you can be with Virginia."

His son looked at his wife again and she beckoned him over. Emm waved him towards her. He'd been right to leave Darold and Virginia to themselves. It had been a sacrifice. Well, not completely. Virginia hadn't exactly welcomed him, but he did give up being with Darold. Emm had behaved selflessly to ease the strain on their marriage, but he was admittedly in search of a more hospitable place for himself too. So, his action wasn't purely generous, but it did result in a good outcome for others. Emm pleaded with Izora to let him take a little credit for his good deed.

***

He settled back and marveled at how comfortable he felt with his family compared to last spring. As he congratulated himself, he noticed Erissa sitting alone in a corner, nearly invisible behind the tree. Was she hiding from her siblings or trying to hide something from them? They glanced her way now and then, but no one approached her. Emm hoisted himself up and navigated around the tables and children until he was standing in front of her. Erissa stood, motioned for him to take her chair, and sat cross-legged on the floor at his feet. They eyed each other warily.

"You've gained a little weight. It looks good on you," Emm said.

Erissa looked at her stomach which poufed out from a pretty embroidered shirt, a sign she was taking care of her appearance again too. "Amazing, considering how awful the food is in rehab. But Bruna puts on a good spread, and as long as I've been let out for the day, I plan to eat and drink my fill." Emm raised an eyebrow. "For goodness' sakes, Papa, non-alcoholic. I'm clean, and this time I intend to stay that way." She looked at him, unblinking.

Emm couldn't return her stare. "I hope so. I know it's hard." Actually, he didn't know. Giving up alcohol hadn't been a big deal for him; he'd never been a regular drinker. Giving up his dream of winning the Derby had been harder. He'd depended on it every day for a decade and continued to dwell on it for years afterward. "The cider is good. I haven't tried the punch yet."

"Too sweet for my taste. Bruna mixes it that way to make the kids happy." Erissa glanced over her shoulder at the children playing in front of the tree. "Where are you living now?"

Emm said he was at Zona's house, trying to make up his mind where to finally settle. Just as Darold had moments earlier, Erissa looked around and asked where Zona was. This time Emm answered that she'd been called to the hospital for an emergency but would come as soon as she could. "Zona's got a small house in the country, with a big garden out back. You'd like it. Visit her when you get out for good. I'm sure she'd love your ideas on what to do with all that land."

Erissa shrugged. "I doubt it. We've never had much to do with each other." She studied her fingernails, which were bitten to the nub. "I'm thinking of enrolling at the community college in the spring. Centennial. My counselor says she'll help me fill out the application."

"Will you take courses in landscaping?" asked Emm.

Erissa nodded. Her voice became animated. "I have a part-time job at a florist this month, but the owner likes my work so much she wants me to stay on when the holiday season ends."

"That's wonderful." Emm squeezed Erissa's hands. "Let me know if you need help with tuition or books. Where will you live? Will rehab help you find a place when you're released?"

Erissa searched Emm's face. "I was thinking maybe we could try again? Another small garden apartment where I could grow a few things and you could sit outside in the summer?"

Emm hadn't considered that as an option, not trusting Erissa to recover once and for all, although Bruna and Darold seemed to think it was possible. Why else would they keep bailing her out? Or had they resigned themselves to rescuing her as often and for as long as she needed? At his age, Emm didn't know if he could handle the uncertainty, but he didn't want Erissa to think he doubted her. "I have to decide before you get out," he told her, "but things could change later on. First get better, then we'll see what comes next. Meanwhile, I'll visit you. Darold will take me."

Erissa smiled. "When you decide where to live, I'll send you a flower arrangement as a welcome home present."

That smile. As he had before Erissa's relapse, Emm again saw the pretty little girl who had beguiled their whole family. Was there a chance Emm would live with that Erissa again? Unlikely. While he doubted her less than he had an hour ago, she'd still need all her reserves to stay clean. At some point, Emm would become a burden, and he didn't want to be responsible for tipping her back into addiction. Nor, if she did have a setback, did he want her to become a burden to him. Better to help Erissa move forward with her life while he eased through what was left of his.

***

"Christmas cheers, Father." Garnish came over to Emm, now back in his armchair, and embraced him. "You're looking snazzy. More dressed up than usual." Emm smiled.

"You look good too, son. More dressed down than usual." In fact, their clothes were similar but with a few telling differences. Both had on light blue shirts, gray pants, and knit vests, Emm's a beige tweed and Garnish's a red and green argyle. On Emm a red tie, on Garnish a gold ascot. Emm's socks were plain black, while Garnish's sported a snowflake pattern with tiny bells at the ankle.

Emm jingled one of the bells. "Did Helma choose the socks?" he asked.

Garnish laughed. "She picked them off Santa's sleigh. Who chose your wardrobe?"

"Zona. At the hospital." His son looked around but thankfully said nothing about his sister's absence. Emm explained that at first he thought Zona was bringing home clothes from patients who had died and he'd refused to wear them. Garnish agreed it sounded creepy. Instead, they belonged to men who were well enough to be discharged, but were too thin, and would remain so, to ever wear the clothes again. Family members, grateful for how kind Zona had been to their relatives while she was their nurse, had given them to her.

"What did they think she was going to do with old men's clothes?"

"Exactly what she did. Give them to me. Apparently, Zona has been bragging to staff and patients alike that I'm living with her now."

Garnish grinned. "She's obviously pleased. I'm glad it's working out for you."

"Mmm," said Emm. Frankly, Zona's public announcement made him uncomfortable, as if, by telling everyone, she was committing him to stay. It was like reciting marriage vows before the entire community so you'd be less likely to get divorced afterwards. Suppose Emm decided not to live there after all? Zona would not only be privately hurt by him, but she'd also be ashamed in front of her coworkers and the people who looked up to her.

Garnish excused himself and said he'd be right back. Emm watched his son put artfully wrapped toys under the tree and then, with a flourish, hand Bruna a platter of dried fruits, nuts, and cheeses that radiated out in a circle of stars. Bruna looked at the simple plates and bowls that she'd set out earlier, now picked over and in disarray. She pursed her lips. "Really, Garnish. There was no need. I always make plenty of food."

"My apologies, big sister. Next year I'll check beforehand." Garnish bowed slightly.

Bruna said a curt thank you and set the platter on a corner table farthest from the tree.

"Bah, humbug," Garnish whispered in Emm's ear when he returned. Then he reached inside his pocket and pulled out a glass globe with red and green swirls under glittering white dots and streaks. Emm recognized Garnish's brushwork from the canvases hung in his apartment.

Cleon snorted. "What on earth is that supposed to be?" Garnish, who'd remained jaunty in the face of Bruna's snappishness, now held out the shiny ornament with a trembling hand.

Foy skipped over and twirled it. His eyes shone. "It's a Christmas snowstorm! Right?"

"It's beautiful," breathed Betty. "The design is so delicate."

Others murmured in agreement. Emm's eight great-grandchildren fought over who should put it on the tree until James said that since Garnish had made it, he should. The children groused but cleared the way for him. After the globe was hung, everyone clapped. Except Cleon.

When Garnish again returned to his side, Emm said he was sorry that Bruna and Cleon had been unkind to him. Apparently, Emm could patch things up between himself and his children, but he was powerless to make them get along better with one another.

"'No space of regret can make amends for one life's opportunity misused,'" recited Garnish.

"Huh?"

"It's a line from *A Christmas Carol*, the show my theater group puts on every year. I'm Bob Cratchit. A cast member's child plays Tiny Tim. Would you like to come see it?"

Emm said he would, maybe take along one or two of his great-grandchildren.

"You're also welcome to come to my New Year's Eve party," Garnish continued.

"With your theater group?" Emm smiled, imagining another night of singing show tunes.

"No," said Garnish. "My other group of friends." Emm declined. They both laughed.

"Toast time," announced Bruna. People raised cider mugs, punch cups, wineglasses, and beer bottles. Erissa's hands hung at her side. "To another Benbow Christmas," Bruna said. Darold nodded at Emm and added, "To everyone in the family." Foy ploddingly recited the names of the twenty-seven people there, including himself. No one mentioned Zona.

"Here's to those who are no longer with us," said Emm. "My dear wife, Izora, the mother, grandmother, and great grandmother who created you all, and my son Arvil, your brother, uncle, and great uncle." Everyone said, "Cheers." Emm nodded toward Garnish. "And one more."

Garnish's ascot rose and fell. "Here's to my twin sister, Helma. Wherever I am, she is." He lifted a glass and drank, his gulp loud in the silence. Emm drank too. Five seconds passed before more glassware clinked, and the sounds of talking, eating, and playing again filled the room.

Emm made his way to the platter of food Garnish had brought and heaped his plate. He loaded a second and, leaving his walker behind, slowly balanced his way back to where Garnish stood. He handed one plate to his son and patted him on the arm. "My social worker is taking me to the cemetery in the morning. Is there a message you'd like me to deliver to Helma in person?"

"Tell her I'm being nice today, but tomorrow, after Santa has returned to the North Pole, I plan to be naughty." Garnish emptied his wineglass and ate a handful of candied nuts. "Say that I give her permission to be naughty too."

Emm lowered himself into the armchair, relieved to be sitting again. As he ate a dried apricot, it brought to mind his mother overruling the Oxmoors to make a traditional Benbow fruitcake for his and Izora's wedding. It was one of the rare times his wife had wanted to splurge, and her wish had been ignored. "I'll give Izora permission to be naughty tomorrow too," he said. "She deserves to have the fun in heaven that she missed in life." He pictured his late wife bobbing the wings of the angels as short as her hair and dancing the Black Bottom with them until not a trace of white remained on their wiggling posteriors. Garnish refilled Emm's punch cup and they drank a toast "to the two wild women in our family."

Father and son remained side by side, observing the others, until Betty beckoned Garnish to tell the children how he'd made the snowstorm globe. He was soon making up a story about paint-laden witches' brooms and sparkling fairy dust. The little ones were rapt. As Garnish acted out the roles, his body moved with fluid grace and his face glowed with an impish grin. He then assigned parts to the children and encouraged them to add their own plot twists.

Emm watched the tale unfold. He could never live with the high drama in Garnish's life, but he was satisfied that his son had surrounded himself with a cast of characters that made him happy. The next time he and Garnish visited the cemetery together, they could put on a musical for Izora, Arvil, and Helma. Garnish could concoct the plot, and they'd sing familiar tunes, with Emm writing new rhymes to replace the old words. He was humming Cole Porter to himself when his reverie was broken by the sound of shattering glass.

"You broke it," Foy cried. "It was my turn to hold it," said Kelly. "No, mine," shouted her cousin Jennifer. Betty, looking stunned, knelt silently beside the scattered pieces of the globe.

Cleon's son Paul, who was Kelly's father, and Darold's daughter Brenda, the mother of Jennifer, faced off in front of the tree. Paul said that Jennifer was a spoiled only child who never shared. Brenda retorted that Paul and his wife pampered Kelly because she was the baby of their family. Each accused the other of raising an unruly child. "Kelly's the one who is spoiled," said Cleon, joining the fight. "It's always the youngest who goes unpunished, just like Zona." Heads swiveled. "Watch. She'll be a no-show, as usual, because she can get away with it."

Emm felt as though he was back in his own household, listening to his mother criticize Izora for letting the children run wild. He should have defended her then, but he couldn't defend anyone now. He didn't know these parents and children well enough. Meanwhile, Kelly and Jennifer cowered together, while Foy, upset by the raised voices, wailed louder and began to rock. Darold tried to soothe him with a cookie, but Foy was beside himself with grief and anxiety. Garnish, downcast, stood alone, until Betty moved next to him. The others kept their distance.

Finally, Bruna stepped forward. "For goodness' sakes, it's not that big a deal. We have plenty of other ornaments, and the children can make new ones. Out of *plastic*. The only thing that matters is that no one gets cut." She got a broom and dustpan. Betty stayed where she was.

Everyone else retreated, married people to sit with their families, single ones to sit alone. Emm wondered whether they wanted to avoid stepping on the shards of glass or on each other.

CHAPTER 36

It would soon be dark. The children were bored and restless, impatient to unwrap their gifts. "We can't wait for Zona any longer," announced Bruna. "Time to open the presents."

Garnish spread his arms. "'For tis good to be children sometimes, and never better than at Christmas, when its mighty Founder was a child Himself.'" His voice shook. Emm guessed that he recited those lines with more conviction during a performance than at this moment. Alas, real children weren't as angelic as Tiny Tim, nor were their parents as even-tempered as Bob Cratchit.

In a few seconds, eight pairs of sticky hands had ripped off all the wrapping paper. There were dolls and dress-up clothes for the girls, G.I. Joes and hockey and baseball equipment for the boys. Emm felt like Scrooge, ashamed that he hadn't gotten them anything, until Jonah swooped a model airplane past his nose, pointed at Emm's chest, and grinned. Darold winked at his father. Apparently, he'd bought a gift on Emm's behalf for each of his great-grandchildren.

Emm spluttered thank you.

Virginia crushed a piece of wrapping paper under her heel. "He spent too much on them."

Darold looked annoyed. "We can afford it. Besides, how many children are lucky enough to have a great grandfather to get presents from?"

"Technically, they're not from him. They're from you."

"Would you like me to reimburse you?" asked Emm, worried how much it would cost.

Virginia answered, "Nah. It was fun wrapping them. I helped him." She rested her head on Darold's shoulder. "We polished off a quart of spiked eggnog by the time we finished."

Emm shrugged. He couldn't figure Virginia out. Thankfully, she was Darold's problem.

The children, meanwhile, didn't care who the packages were from, only what lay inside the ones for them. They grew more excited as they tore through the mountain of gifts, barely stopping to exclaim over one before opening the next. Betty hovered, picking up wrapping paper, smoothing it flat, and folding it into a neat pile. Bruna sighed but otherwise held her tongue. Emm was relieved that another fight had been averted, for Foy's sake as much as his own.

Not that Foy might have cared this time. He was busy with his own present, the only adult to get one. It was a transistor radio, which he hugged to his chest. "It's not broken," he marveled. "It's brand new." Darold showed him how to use the headphones so the music wouldn't bother his housemates. Emm thought about buying one for himself if he moved to the old age home after all. He could listen to the news without disturbing his roommate. Even better, he could blot out the bodily noises and chatter of the other residents.

"Can I listen after lights out?" Foy asked Darold, who said he'd have to check with Martha and Joe first. "I'll brush my teeth before bed," Foy promised, "if they let me." Emm wondered about the rules at Kingsbridge, and to whom and what he'd have to promise if he wanted special permission to play his radio or do anything else outside of regulations.

One enormous package remained. Thomas caught his breath when he opened his Air Hockey game. The side of the box said "Fast action surface, 46 x 22 inches, wood with sturdy steel legs, built-in score keeper. Assembly required." His father James set to work, joined by his father Darold and Uncle Cleon, who were soon assisted by Mark and Paul, Cleon's sons, and Fred and Larry, Darold's sons-in-law. Half an hour later, when a frustrated Thomas ripped a page from his sister Melissa's new coloring book, James left to calm his children. The other men continued to study the instructions amid a stack of miscellaneous parts, screwdrivers, and wrenches.

Foy removed his headphones, turned off the radio, and wandered over. Without looking at the instruction sheet, only at the picture on the box, he methodically began to assemble the pieces. Ten minutes later, it was finished. "Foy fixed it," yelled Thomas, racing over to his new toy.

Erissa had been staring intently at Foy the whole time. He waved a screwdriver at her, as if to say, "Me too!" Emm wondered whether Foy had in fact understood his comment about his sister fixing herself or was simply reaching out to include her, as he did with his friends. She clapped and the others joined in. Foy smiled shyly. Emm wished her siblings could clap for Erissa as well. Too bad she couldn't put herself together as easily as Foy had the hockey game. If only she kept working at it, though, Erissa had a chance to be more successful than all those dads.

***

By now it really was dark. Bruna closed the blinds and actually thanked Betty when she helped clear away the dirty plates and crumpled napkins. The children, filled with sweets and sugary punch, had barely eaten dinner. They were tired and cranky. So was Emm. He was dozing when there was a quiet knock at the door and Zona slipped in. Cleon's slow, exaggerated clapping broke the stillness in the room. Virginia muttered, "About time." Erissa smiled. Not at Zona, but to herself, as if to say, "Thank goodness someone else will be under the microscope for a while."

Bruna, lips pursed, pointed to the bedroom, where Zona retreated. Ten minutes later she emerged, minus her coat, with red-rimmed eyes. She handed gifts to the children, but by then they were as sated with toys as with candy and cookies. Only Emm revived at the sight of his youngest child. Her hair was braided with red ribbons, appropriate for Christmas Day. Ditto her sequined snowman sweater.

Zona perched on a folding chair beside him. "The tree is lovely." She didn't make up an excuse for being late. Emm regretted that he'd tried to invent one for her earlier. Darold brought her a plate of food, which she ate dutifully, head bowed. Not until she'd finished did Zona look up and around the living room. Children sprawled across their parents, who sat with heads thrown back and legs outstretched, like soldiers dazed after a winless battle.

Only Erissa, no longer behind the tree, sat upright, eyes wide open. Emm's first thought was that she'd snuck off for a stimulant, but he was pretty sure she hadn't ventured from her spot. Being with the family was its own kind of drug. It made you high and depressed at the same time.

Zona followed Emm's gaze, touched his wrist, and moved next to her sister. Erissa shrank back, as if heeding the standard rehab warning to avoid people who, by association, could get you into trouble. Her eyes narrowed when Zona took out her wallet. Emm was puzzled too. Was she giving Erissa money? A business card? Zona flipped to the plastic picture holders at the back and handed the wallet to Erissa. "This is Riley."

Erissa cautiously examined the first photo and asked what kind of dog he was.

"A mix of mutt and monkeyshines."

Erissa smiled. Her smile broadened as she looked at the rest of the pictures. When Zona described the circumstances of one photograph—Riley had tangled with a skunk in the garden last summer and was shaking off after a tomato-juice bath—Erissa laughed outright. The Benbow children snapped to attention. They hadn't heard that sound in decades.

Emm felt a laugh bubble up inside him too. Maybe he wasn't totally powerless to improve relationships among his offspring after all. He vowed to ask Zona to drive him to visit Erissa so he could bring them together more often. As he continued to watch them, two more thoughts came to him. One was to accept Darold's invitation to visit his own siblings. Once again, Emm decided to wait a year. He needed time to work things out with his children first. The other was to carry pictures in his wallet too. Who would want to see them? Not Mrs. Cray; childless people usually weren't interested in those of others. He thought of his roommate's photos at Kingsbridge. If Emm lived there, shots of his great-grandchildren would be an icebreaker for meeting people. Plus, whenever he felt lonely, he could look at them himself. And share them with Izora.

From the kitchen doorway, Bruna watched Zona and Erissa talk. Emm tried to gauge her expression. Curiosity? Jealousy? Bruna had probably never gotten Erissa to laugh so loudly and spontaneously. Maybe there was also a touch of gratitude for Zona's kindness. He didn't think Bruna was ready to soften toward Zona, but maybe her armor had melted a chink or two.

Silently, Emm addressed Izora. "Wouldn't it be something if Erissa was the reason that our three daughters—the living ones—connected?" His wife slipped into the empty chair beside him and answered, "Sometimes it's the least likely person who ends up being the peacemaker."

***

Bruna dimmed the lights and placed candles on the taller pieces of furniture, beyond the reach of small hands. She nodded at Garnish to lead the singing. Emm would have taken the gesture as her making amends, but the expectant looks on everyone's faces suggested that he did this every year. Perhaps singing, unlike feeding, was not an activity where Bruna's role as the family hub was threatened. They sang the usual songs, "Hark the Herald Angels" and "Away in a Manger." Emm's baritone was unwavering, yet melancholy. He remembered the staff and patients at the hospital singing "O Holy Night" when Arvil was born, and Izora singing carols at the house year-round.

Only the last one they sang, "The Huron Carol," was unusual. Canada's oldest Christmas hymn, it was written by a Jesuit missionary in the native Huron/Wendat language. An English version came out in 1926, the year of Arvil's birth, and Izora had taught it to the family. It celebrates Jesus, born in a lodge of broken bark and wrapped in a rabbit skin, surrounded by hunters, and given fox and beaver pelts by tribal chiefs. Emm had never known why Izora liked it so much, but listening to the words again after all these years, he understood. It was her way of saying that riches, such as those promised by Mr. Millar, were not what mattered. A simple, but natural life, was enough.

When they were growing up, the Benbow children would get on their knees at the last line and warble, "Come kneel before the radiant Boy, who brings you beauty, peace and joy." Tonight, they, with their children and grandchildren repeated the ritual. Emm, unable to kneel, bowed his head. Only Zona did not join in. By the time she'd been born, Izora had stopped singing.

***

The lights were turned back on. Emm wondered if the party was over, but no one got up to leave. He looked at the baby Jesus, a singular child, nestled in the branches of the tree. It had taken half a century, but in the past nine months, Emm had begun to learn about each of his children. Would he lose touch now that this year was coming to an end? Perhaps he could rotate among them after all, an idea he'd opposed after his stroke. There were five who could take him in, six with Erissa. That meant two months a year with each, plus visits with Foy. He, and they, could manage. Zona wouldn't like sharing him, but if she were more connected to the rest of the family, she'd be okay.

Emm's children stood and formed a circle. Their spouses and the two younger generations sat on the floor inside the ring. Bruna motioned for Emm to join those standing and they all joined hands. She explained, "We started doing this six years ago, on the twenty-fifth anniversary of Mother's death." Going around the circle, in order of age, each person bestowed a wish upon the others. Bruna told everyone to enjoy the love of family and friends, Cleon wished them all success in school and work, Darold said a blessing for good health, and Erissa dittoed him. Foy said he hoped everyone made a new best friend and smiled at Emm. Garnish said their days should be filled with creativity, Zona with the satisfaction of caring for others. Then it was Emm's turn.

He didn't want to bestow a general wish upon all his children, not after he'd finally come to know each of them as individuals. Slowly, he made his way around the circle.

Bruna, my daughter, both generous and fair/You are your mother's truest heir.

If ever Benbows should stray or roam/Welcome them back to your new old home.

Cleon, I hope that you stay vital/And your beloved Toronto teams win every title.

May your sons grant the respect you're due/And model themselves on Betty and you.

Darold, your kindness needs nary a tweak/May angels clean your house each week.

Should life stomp on or rudely spin ya/Find comfort in the arms of feisty Virginia.

Worried he'd gone too far, Emm looked to see how Darold's wife had taken this verse. He saw the corners of her mouth twitch into a smile and, reassured, moved on.

Erissa, may you no longer feel numb/And flower like plants under your green thumb.
Thrive in school and also in work/And find an unmarried boyfriend who isn't a jerk.

Dimples appeared in Erissa's cheeks, which seemed to have filled out even more in the last couple of hours. Emm squeezed her hand.

Foy, you're the child who was heaven-sent/You taught me how to be content.
May your sweet disposition persist/And may you have no cavities at the dentist.

Garnish, your creativity is a gold mine/I hope your talent continues to shine.
Relish the flair that makes you clever and arty/And have a blast at every party.

Zona, infused with light from above/May you be embraced by kinfolk with love.
Frolic and cuddle with your dear Riley/Whatever happens, stay hopeful and smiley.

Emm considered making up verses for Izora, Arvil, and Helma but decided that this round robin belonged to the living. He returned to his place between Bruna and Zona. One at a time, his delighted children thanked him. The poetry wasn't his best, but he'd do better next year. The important thing was that he'd started a new holiday tradition. Emm hadn't been sure he believed himself when he told Mrs. Cray it was never too late, but he'd just proven his words were true.

Spouses and families stood up and side by side, four generations of Benbows made a chain that hugged the walls of Bruna's living room. Twenty-eight voices sang "Silent Night." After the last "Sleep in heavenly peace" had faded, Garnish quoted Tiny Tim, "'God bless us, everyone!'"

CHAPTER 37

Darold and Virginia dropped Foy off before taking Emm home with them for the night. Clutching his bag of goodies, Foy couldn't wait to share them with his pals—and to watch television. "I'm home," he called as he ran up the walk and banged on the door. Joe and Martha let him in, waving and calling out holiday greetings as Darold backed the car down the driveway. Through winking lights around the uncurtained windows, Emm saw his son surrounded by housemates, doling out treats and looking as pleased with himself as Santa.

Virginia rested her head on the seat back and her hand on Darold's shoulder. He patted it, smiled at her briefly, and drove on in silence. Despite their spats, they fit together like Foy fit with his friends. Emm wondered if it might be kindest of him to try fitting into Kingsbridge after all, sparing his children the burden of his day-to-day care. Perhaps the old age home deserved another chance, like Erissa. Residents quaked and murmured about upstairs, but how many of them had actually seen it? Perhaps, like him, they'd come upon someone in the corridor having a bad day, but didn't everyone? Bad days didn't last forever; even the Depression had ended.

Only death lasted forever. What if their fear of upstairs was really a fear of death? Could Emm peek at death before going there for good? Maybe it wasn't the bugaboo that everyone feared. The past nine months had been hellish in many ways, but there were heavenly moments too. Like today. Emm decided he was brave enough to take a look. Tomorrow, when he saw Mrs. Cray, he'd ask her to arrange another visit to Kingsbridge. Including a tour of upstairs.

An hour later, grateful to be in bed in the old maid's room— which, he was pleased to see, Virginia hadn't refilled with junk— Emm's mind was nevertheless too jumpy to sleep. He skimmed a small pile of newspapers until his eye was caught by an article on the fourth-place contestants in last summer's Olympics. A reporter had contacted them, five months later, to see how they'd handled coming so close, only to narrowly miss winning a medal. Most said they'd turned the loss into a gain, either vowing to work harder and win in four years or abandoning sports entirely in favor of school, work, or community service. With a few exceptions, they seemed happy.

Unlike these Olympians, when Emm lost the Derby, he'd compounded his loss. Frustration and rage pushed him to drink, which only made him angrier. He'd been so bitter that he failed to enjoy the children he had. He'd short-changed Izora, then she was gone. Emm thought, as he had that day in the cemetery, how his desire to bring so many lives into the world had ended hers too soon. And now, after nine months of getting to know his children, he realized the price they'd also paid for his obsession. He had taken away their mother's love and deprived them of a father's.

Could he turn that long-ago loss into a belated gain? What if, like creating a new tradition, it was never too late? If so, the first step was figuring out where Emm would call home. If only he had the same confidence about this decision as he had when entering Millar's contest, but with the wisdom to make a better choice this time. Suppose he set out on another bad course of action that he was powerless to reverse before his final race ended?

Mrs. Cray was coming at nine. In five hours, Emm would have to answer her question about where he wanted to live. At the cemetery last March, after saying that people overcame their fears by facing them, she'd asked Emm if he ever wrote serious poetry. He'd laughed off the idea at the time, but now he understood the advice implied by her question. Before he could decide what to do going forward, Emm had to reconcile with his past. Seriously.

He went to the small desk in the den he'd cleared out six months ago and wrote a poem to his late wife. The words came from his heart, not merely his wits.

For Izora

My thoughts harken back to 1926
When, determined our future to fix
Chomping at the bit
Cocksure I was fit
I entered a race you gently tried to nix

I said the money would set us all free
Our children would grow up wealthy
You'd sing a happy tune
I would buy you the moon
But I was really just thinking of me

I was too busy counting every child's head
Not cherishing precious moments instead
A first step, a first word
The first robin a baby heard
Minus joy, our home was filled with dread

My single-minded race down Derby Lane
Was a major cause of our children's pain
I saw life as win-lose
And overlooked their virtues
I regret I can't raise them over again

Perhaps worse is the grief I caused you
Saddling you with an unwieldy crew
Your voice so fair
Your artistic flair
I silenced them, another thing that I blew

After my hopes for the Derby were lost
I made everyone pay a high cost
I was depressed and angry
So you gave up on me
After that, our paths rarely crossed

But I've learned the futility of berating
A second chance is what I'm awaiting
If you could see me today
You'd know I'm on my way
I'm not there yet, but I'm still gestating

Our sons and daughters are educating me
About patience and generosity
Joy and acceptance
Forgiveness and repentance
I'm earning my branch on our family tree

I miss you with a full heart and I long
To eternally hear your sweet song
But please undertaker
Before I meet my Maker
Give me time to right my grave wrong

Dearest, I can't rush to join you above
To lie beside you, our hearts interwove

For until my life ends
I must first make amends
To be worthy of your undying love

From Emm
December 1976

Emm reread the poem. He worried some lines were too flip, the opposite of his intention. But since irreverence was part of who he was, he let them stand. More rhymes popped into his head: humble and bumble; laugh and gaffe; ambition and demolition. He nearly added more verses, then stopped himself; why exhaust all his ideas now? Emm would save—savor— them until next year. In fact, he'd start another tradition, writing Izora a poem every Christmas. And, like the verses he'd made up for his children, he'd get better at it with time. "Do the little jobs well, and the big ones will take care of themselves," Mr. Carnegie had counseled. Pen a collection of little poems, and Emm would create a whole book to match the family photo album.

It was eight o'clock, a full hour before Mrs. Cray was due. But finishing early didn't make Emm a winner. His only race now was against death, and Emm was the only contestant. He'd gotten past the starting line; the ending and the prize were unknown. Emm would take this derby one leisurely lap at a time, stopping along the way.

ACKNOWLEDGEMENTS

Writers labor to polish the beginning of a manuscript and to nail the ending. Deciding where to begin and end a book's acknowledgements likewise requires care and craft. Without the encouragement, feedback, skill, and influence of many people, that book would not exist. From conception to delivery, *The Great Stork Derby* had many nurturing midwives.

During a gestation period longer than an elephant's, my two critique groups offered invaluable help. The "Saturday Writers Group" workshopped the short story that eventually grew into this novel. Although our numbers have changed over more than two decades, I'd like to acknowledge long-term members Amy Gustine, Marni Hochman, Keith Hood, Danielle Lavaque-Manty, Paul Many, Cathy Mellett, Polly Rosenweig, and Sonja Srinivasan. My "Sunday Writers Group" provided ongoing commentary and support as I projected the story fifty years forward to create the novel. Thanks for advancing the manuscript, and sustaining me, belong to Marty Calvert, Janet Gilsdorf, Cynthia Jalynski, Danielle Lavaque-Monty, and the late Jane Johnson.

The team at Vine Leaves Press has now honored me by publishing three novels. I owe thanks to Peter Snell who gave the green light to all of them; Melissa Slayton for her astute feedback as the development editor; Amie McCracken for designing the interior and shepherding the book through production; and especially Jessica Bell for her creative energy in founding this amazing press as well as designing the evocative cover. I also extend a worldwide embrace to the VLP community of staff and writers who celebrate one another's accomplishments, commiserate over setbacks, and form an international network of colleagues and friends. Your collective talent and spirit are impressive and I'm so fortunate to be a member of our remarkable group.

The Great Stork Derby is about family and mine is a grounding and renewable source of care, inspiration, laughter, and strength. My daughter and booster Rebecca Epstein, endlessly curious son-in-law Milton Dixon, and exuberant grandsons Oscar and Emmett sustain me with love and play, two of life's necessities. Unlike my protagonist Emm, I have no fear of ending up alone in a dreaded old age home or being banished "upstairs."

Finally, I send a belated thank you to my late father, David Savishinsky. Like a complex character, he continues to surprise me as I realize how much I am like him and how "Silent Cal's" often unrecognized gifts enrich my work and my being.